Letters of Hope
Tania Roberts

Red Rose Publishing

First published in New Zealand in November 2025 by Red Rose Publishing, New Plymouth

This novel is a work of fiction. The persons and events in this book may have representations in history, but this work is entirely the author's creation and should not be construed as historical fact.

A catalogue record for the book is available from the National Library of New Zealand.

Format: Print ISBN   978-1-0670288-4-8

Format: Print on Demand ISBN   978-1-0670288-5-5

Format: EPUB ISBN   978-1-0670288-3-1

Cover Design: Kura Carpenter Design, thebookcarpenter.co.nz

Letters of Hope

Chapter 1

24 August 1914

Dominique heard the clip clop of hooves on the cobble stone road before she saw a laden wagon emerge through the morning mist ambling its way towards Porte Fauroeulx, the southern gate into Le Quesnoy.

She opened her bedroom window, pushed the wooden shutters back against the ancient building's concrete walls, and leaned out to get a better view, filling her lungs with the morning scent wafting up from her mother's rose garden.

It was too early, and the wrong day, for the local farmers to be bringing their wares to market. Changes in routine weren't normal for this quiet town. Something was amiss. As slowly as the clod of the hooves, images from the last few weeks pieced together to paint a picture that made Dominique's insides quiver. She braced herself against the window frame as a new reality began to dawn. Things had been askew since the beginning of August when Germany declared war on France.

As the summer sun warmed the air and dispersed the mist, Dominique noticed the wagon wasn't heading into town but out. Its load was a precarious mish mash: the legs of an upturned table pointed skyward like church spires, topped and tailed chairs reminded her of her twin brothers sharing a bed, and cooking pots and pans dangled and jangled. Trunks, suitcases, and carpet bags bulging with more than enough for a holiday were haphazardly stuffed in between everything else and tied down with rope. At the back of the wagon, several children sat on a pile of mattresses, their legs bouncing in midair and their excited giggles hinting at an adventure. Dominique knew better. This wasn't a family going on holiday but another group of Quercitains escaping.

"Good luck," she murmured, stepping away from the window.

Was leaving Le Quesnoy an option for her family? Her pere had retired from the military, giving up a long career as a surgeon, hoping to live a peaceful life in the small town in the north of France but medicine was in his blood, and he would never abandon someone in need. The residents found the brass plaque that announced Dr Henri Favier lived behind the large arched wooden doors on Rue Brancion. When their ailments didn't justify a visit to the hospital, they knocked on the door and pleaded for his help. He kept a room on the ground floor. He told Mere it was his office, necessary for looking after the accounts for such a large property but Dominique had seen the people that entered the room. They weren't bankers or lawyers but common people from the side of the town where the houses weren't as grand as theirs.

It was a rap at the door that had stirred Dominique this morning, even before the rooster made his morning call, rousing the menagerie of animals that made the yard their home: chickens in the pen at the back corner, rabbits in a row of hutches and their dog Remy tied up at his kennel. She heard voices echo up the stairwell.

"Bonjour. What brings you at this early hour?" her father asked.

"Doctor Flament needs your help at the hospital, monsieur. There's been an influx of wounded soldiers."

"I'll just grab my bag and be right behind you," Henri replied.

He'd mentioned at dinner last night that the hospital was full to overflowing with British and French soldiers injured in the Battle of Charleroi. His calm voice as he relayed the day's events indicated there was no cause for alarm, even though some of Le Quesnoy's own regiment were among the wounded, but things must be getting bad for Pere to be called to the hospital. Doctor Flament usually handled everything there. If Pere was downplaying the situation to ease her mother's nerves, then Dominique would have to catch up with Alice or Clemence. Her half-sisters worked at the hospital and would know what was going on.

Dominique had overheard the whispered discussion of Pere's daughters from his first marriage; Alice and Clemence complained he put his second wife, Lucie on a pedestal that would surely topple if he wasn't there to support it. They might just be upset that he'd remarried after their mother died. Whether they were right or wrong didn't matter, if Pere wouldn't leave Le Quesnoy, then neither would the family. Besides Charleroi was across the border in Belgium, miles away from Le Quesnoy, so there was no need to heed her mother's worried state. She was always fretting about something.

Even if the war reached Le Quesnoy, the town's fortifications would keep it safe. The house they lived in had been standing for several hundred years, surviving battles through the centuries as opposing countries fought for control over the town. Tucked in behind the ramparts next to Porte Fauroeulx, their house was surrounded by high brick walls and had a secret tunnel that adjoined the ramparts. Normally a favoured place in games of hide and seek it could provide an escape route, if needed.

Dominique shook herself. "Stop worrying about things that might never happen."

She quickly removed her nightgown and dressed ready for the picnic she had planned with her best friend, Nathalie.

"I didn't hear the train arrive. Where did all these people come from?" Dominique scanned the crowd. They weren't Quercitains, she knew all the townsfolk of Le Quesnoy.

"There's too many for the train, Dominique. Even you can count that high," Nathalie teased.

"It's the school holidays, Nathalie," Dominique pretended to be offended. "And Mademoiselle Forestier is not here to make me do arithmetic."

"Perhaps they've come to join our picnic."

The best friends were ready to depart the town, heading to Foret du Mormal to escape the summer heat, lying in the shade of the oaks and gorging themselves on wild blackberries, but were diverted by strangers converging on the town square.

"We can't go on a picnic now." Dominique stood on her tip toes, like she was back in ballet class and studied the crowd, searching for clues as to their origins.

She knew they couldn't have travelled from the south; she would have seen that many people come through the Porte Fauroleux and surely the guards at Jolimetz would have stopped them. That was their job, to control the traffic. She listened to the murmurings rippling through the crowd, barely audible conversations in French but not in a dialect she readily recognised.

There were mothers with babies swaddled to their chests, bags, bulging with all their worldly possessions, in both hands. Others looked like they'd barely had time to dress, barefoot, slumped shoulders and weary downcast faces conveyed their desperate plight. Some pushed wheelbarrows piled high with clothes and utensils or acting as a stretcher for the sick. Packs and boxes were lowered to the ground, relieving the heads and backs of those who'd carried them, becoming makeshift seats for the weary travellers. Cows, tethered behind carts mooed in protest, stretching to nibble from the bales of straw stowed on the carts behind which they'd ambled into town.

"Look, they're filthy, covered in dust from head to toe!" The only people Dominique had seen so dirty were her brothers when they'd been having a dirt fight. "Where have they been?"

Nathalie had no answer; she looked as perplexed as Dominique felt.

There was no sparkle in the eyes of children cuddling bedraggled teddy bears and rag dolls. They weren't running about, playing hopscotch or even knuckle bones. It was as if they'd spent all their energy walking a hundred miles. Old men and women rested on walking sticks and each other for support.

The crowd was bereft of fit and able-bodied men but then so was Le Quesnoy. When Germany declared war on France, across the country all young men, except those too frail to fight, were conscripted, armed with rifles, ammunition and bayonets and equipped with uniform and supplies. In Le Quesnoy they formed three regiments, living in the military barracks, and training dawn to dusk until they were mobilised.

The last time there'd been a gathering in the town square, all the townsfolk had turned out to bid their fathers, sons and brothers an emotional farewell as they marched in time, packs on their backs, rifles over their shoulders, pride in their posture and anticipation on their faces.

On that occasion, there had been pomp and ceremony, the town band playing, streamers and confetti flying, townsfolk waving flags of support. The only similarity between the gatherings was Mayor Carlier and his deputies overlooking the crowd from a makeshift stage.

"Look Nathalie, your Pere is going to speak."

Dominique pointed at the mayor, who despite the summer heat still wore suit and tie. He adjusted the starched collar of his shirt as if it were too tight to enable him to talk and cleared his throat. Much like her own father, Mayor Carlier always looked serious, as if he carried the weight of the world on his shoulders. Perhaps that was the expectation imposed on the head of the household. If it was, Dominique was glad she'd been born a female.

Today, the frown furrowing Mayor Carlier's forehead appeared even more forlorn than usual.

"He's not looking very well, Nathalie, is your Pere alright?"

"There have been lots of meetings at home, the deputies, the councillors, the gendarmerie, a constant stream of people coming and going. I think Maman is worried about him, with his weak heart."

"We'd better listen." Dominique lifted her index finger to her lips to hush both herself and Nathalie.

Mayor Carlier raised his hand to garner the attention of the crowd and gradually the murmurings abated.

"I'd like to begin by expressing our sympathies for your plight, having to abandon your homes, being subjected to the brutalities of Germans at war is not what we wish for our Belgian neighbours."

"They're Belgians, Nathalie." No wonder Dominique couldn't discern their dialect; she'd never been to Belgium nor met a Belgian before.

The roll of Nathalie's eyes told Dominique her revelations weren't at all startling.

"We have talked long and hard to reach a solution to the situation we find ourselves in." Mayor Carlier removed a neatly pressed handkerchief from his pocket and wiped his brow. "Our decision was not an easy one, but the needs of our townsfolk must take precedence. If the Germans have chased you from your homeland, it is likely they will try and do the same to the Quercitains and we cannot allow that. Therefore, I regret to advise that we can accommodate you for one night and one night only."

Screams of anguish filled the town square. One woman fainted, dropping to the hard cobblestones. Mothers, eyes wide with terror, clutched their children, as if to let them go meant they would be lost forever.

"Non! Sacrebleu! You can't condemn us!"

"The Boche will torture us!"

"We'll be killed, like the others!"

"They've destroyed our homes. Ransacked our supplies."

"We cannot go back."

"There must be something we can do." Dominique gripped Nathalie's hand as if united the pair could save everyone.

Nathalie squeezed Dominique's fingers but remained silent, focusing on her father's next words.

"We suggest you head south," he continued.

"We can't go any further. We're exhausted," a woman with a tear-stained face protested.

"We will ensure you are rested and fed but must ask you to leave at first light." Mayor Carlier's eyes remained downcast, he shifted awkwardly on the stage, as if guilt denied him the ability to meet the gaze of the refugees directly. "We will accommodate as many of you as possible in the military barracks so you may rest up for the night."

The Cernay barracks sat just off the town square; a brick double-storey building last occupied by the Regiment d'Infantes. It had been home to the enlisted young men, some who still looked and acted like teenage boys, that had only been a year ahead of Dominique at school. They must have had their eighteenth birthdays, or they'd faked their age to be able to join the adventure.

Dominique had never been inside the building, girls weren't allowed, but she knew Gabriel slept in the bunk next to the third window from the left on the top storey. Whenever she walked past, which she found excuses to do daily, she gazed up at the window hoping to see Nathalie's nineteen-year-old brother, her insides pirouetting in anticipation.

She looked over to the window, but her wishful thinking remained unfulfilled as she remembered the day she'd had to cast aside self-pity and smile at Gabriel as he marched out of town. She was certain the glance he cast her way conveyed a special farewell.

"I have issued a plea for the townsfolk to offer a bed to the remainder of you," Mayor Carlier continued. "The patisseries have been requested to do a special bake to ensure you have food to take on your journey."

The crowd held back, casting suspicious looks at the mayor and his councillors.

"How can we trust you?"

"Looks more like a prison than a hotel."

Gabriel had complained the iron framed bunks with thin lumpy mattresses were readying them for sleeping on the ground and in trenches. If Dominique could do one thing for these poor people, it would be to provide them with a good sleep on a soft mattress.

"Are you siding with the Boche?" An elderly man raised his walking stick and pointed it accusingly at the mayor.

Mayor Carlier's head jerked up and he clutched at his chest as if pained by the insult.

"The Germans are our mutual enemy." His steely tone allowed no doubt. He stepped down off the stage and headed towards the barracks. "We wish only for peace and good health for all. We will send you onward with our prayers for a safe journey."

Gradually the crowd shuffled after the mayor, small steps, stooped postures and blank faces signalling there was nothing left to lose, they were bereft of choices.

"I'll take some home." Dominique raised her hand to volunteer. "You've got a huge house, you could take a dozen home, Nathalie."

"Maybe," Nathalie hesitated. "I'll ask Pere."

There was no time for Dominique to check with her parents, but she knew her pere would never abandon anyone in need. She was certain her father would approve of her helping the refugees, or more precisely, he would appreciate that someone was providing aid. Whether that someone should be Dominique was a question best left unasked for the time being.

Not all the townsfolk would welcome the Belgians into their homes. Everything was happening so fast, but it didn't take long for the Quercitains to reveal their allegiances. Some, like those Dominique had seen this morning, feared the worst, packed their bags, closed their houses as if they were going on an extended holiday and left to stay with relatives further south. Others were firm in their belief that France was too powerful to be taken over by the Germans and had no intention of going anywhere, prepared to fight with a passion for the freedom of their homeland. Somewhere in between were people who seemed happy to comply with any German demands for the sake of harmony. Dominique knew of all this, not because she'd been considered mature enough to have an opinion but through Nathalie, who listened behind the closed doors of her father's many meetings.

It was a young mother, with two barefoot children huddled into her sides, that caught Dominique's attention. The trio were on the far side of the square, slumped against a building, their wrinkled, dishevelled clothes as dirty as their faces. She imagined the woman's green eyes would have been dazzling under any other circumstances. Now it looked like the light behind them had been extinguished. Dominique wished to do all she could to reignite a spark or at least infuse some hope. She gave Nathalie a hug and the pair agreed to meet again later.

"Bonjour, I'm Dominique. Can I carry your bag?" Dominique reached to take the refugee's luggage, never entertaining the thought of a refusal but the woman stepped away, her tight grip on the bag whitening her knuckles. "It's alright. Don't be afraid." Dominique couldn't imagine what the mother had experienced but understood her wish to remain independent.

She knelt so she was face to face with the children. Round cherub faces with eyes as green as their mother's looked petrified.

What had they seen? Far more than eyes so young should ever have to bear witness to.

"Are you hungry?" Dominique asked. "Would you like an apple? A peach?"

They nodded enthusiastically, smiles almost forming until they glanced at their mother and froze.

"It's alright." Dominique stood and smiled at the woman. "We have an orchard full; you can have as many as you like. Follow me. My home isn't far."

Chapter 2

"Where have you been, child! You're going to be the death of me." Lucie called from the sitting room as Dominique ushered the refugees into the house.

Dominique would be seventeen next March. She wasn't a child, but she knew it was better to placate her mere all the same.

"Wait here," she whispered to the refugees. The wooden staircase wasn't the most comfortable spot for weary travellers, but it would have to do for now. "I'll be back soon."

Dominique slowed her step and smoothed the folds of her skirt before she entered the sitting room, knowing it was better to act like the lady her mere expected her to be.

"I've been helping ..."

"Who is making all that noise? Is someone here? Another visitor for your pere? Do I have a caller?"

Dominique paused. Should she reveal the Belgian's presence and seek her mother's approval or was it better to wait for her father to return home? She wavered.

"I think it's just Victor and Louis having a make-believe war in the back garden." Dominique's brothers were always pretending to be something older than their ten years would allow.

"Oh, boys will be boys," Lucie Favier sighed wearily. The constant concern Lucie had for her daughter, never seemed to extend to her sons who were allowed to create havoc wherever they went.

"The Belgians need ..." There was nothing to be lost from at least attempting to rally her mother's support for the cause.

"Fetch me a glass of water will you, dear. That's a good girl. I feel a headache coming on."

"Oui, Maman."

"I won't be long," Dominique whispered to the young mother and her children. She'd considered taking them to the kitchen, but its window overlooked the back garden, and she couldn't rely on Victor and Louis not to startle the frightened trio just as she was gaining their trust.

The kitchen was as Marie, their servant, always left it, everything tidied away and not a speck of dust to be seen. The fruit basket was piled high with apples and peaches picked from the laden trees Louis and Victor looked set to destroy. Dominique resisted the urge to open the back door and growl at them. She didn't want her brothers to come running back inside.

She stashed two apples and three peaches into her skirt pockets and carried one shiny red apple so she could pretend she'd taken it to eat herself. She rearranged the remaining fruit to look like nothing was amiss and poured a glass of water.

Grateful her mother's headache meant she didn't demand Dominique sit with her, partake in idle chatter or force her to do some inane activity like embroidery to pass the time, Dominique hurried from the sitting room. She checked her brothers were still outside and rushed back to the stairwell.

The young mother gasped and pulled her children tighter into her sides. She sent Dominique a defiant look, but her trembling chin gave away her inner fear.

"It's alright," Dominique tried to sound calm as she considered the options.

If the Germans were figuratively 'on their doorstep' the best place for the refugees might be in the cellar, but it was dark and cold, great for keeping food and wine cool and dry but not for young children who were already shivering. She could drag mattresses, blankets, food and candles down the narrow steps that burrowed under the house. It would make it bearable, but she couldn't bring herself to inflict any more suffering on the refugees, not when there were soft beds upstairs.

Dominique glanced over her shoulder again, put a finger to her lips and whispered.

"Follow me."

They tiptoed as quietly as the wooden boards of the old spiral staircase would allow. Dominique knew which boards to avoid but the refugees were unaware. Each time the aged boards groaned in protest Dominique froze as if she was playing a game of statues and the first one to move was out. She listened for a second, waited for her mere's call, before continuing.

They paused at the first-floor landing where the hallway led to her parents' rooms. On rainy days, Dominique spent many an hour in her mere's armchair. It was perfectly placed beside a window at the front of the house affording her a bird's eye view of the comings and goings on the cobble stoned Rue Brancion.

She ushered the trio ahead as they climbed to the second storey and made their way to her bedroom. Describing the room, decorated in floral wallpaper and delicate pink furnishings, as her bedroom, was still a novelty Dominique was getting used to. Until a few months ago she'd shared the room with her older sister Eugenie.

Eugenie was fortunate enough to be nineteen and enjoying a Parisian summer, wearing the latest fashions, attending the horse races at Longchamp, picnicking at the Jardin de Plantes and dancing the nights away at grand balls. Dominique got to do it all vicariously through her evocative letters. At least now Dominique would have something exciting to write back.

The children, a boy and a girl, looked from their mother to Dominique and back again. They stood, frozen in the middle of the room, too afraid to speak, move or touch anything.

"They're tired." The mother looked just as weary; her shoulders slumped with exhaustion.

"Here," Dominique handed over the fruit. "Please, eat, rest."

"Merci Beaucoup. You are very kind."

One-to-one, Dominique found it easier to understand the woman's Belgian dialect.

"I am Simone, this is Emily and Paul. Say hello children."

They nodded and smiled but with mouths full of crunchy apple were unable to speak.

"Sorry," Simone apologised.

"No need for an apology. It's better they stay quiet. It's best we don't draw too much attention."

Alert to and apprehensive of any danger, Simone looked ready to run.

"It's alright. You're safe here." Dominique placed a reassuring hand on Simone's arm. "My pere would never turn out someone in need. If anyone's in trouble, it'll be me, not you."

The children went to climb onto a bed.

"Children! You'll dirty the bedcovers," Simone growled. "Sorry."

"Please stop apologizing, Simone. It is I that am sorry you are having to flee your home, and I can do so little to help."

Dominique lifted a pitcher of water and a bowl from the dresser, placed them on the floor, and filled the bowl with water.

"It's cold but it's clean." She handed Simone her facecloth and towel and a bar of soap.

"They'll get dirty." Simone offered the white linen back. "We can't."

"You can." It was like a game of pass the parcel going backwards and forwards. "Please. Marie will wash them."

"Whose Marie?" Simone's eyes darted to the door.

Her obvious distrust of everyone saddened Dominique. What had the Germans done? Would they do the same if they reached Le Quesnoy? She swallowed the lump that formed in her throat.

She needed to focus on doing all she could now, not worry about what ifs and maybes.

"She's our servant. She is probably out gathering flowers for her soaps." Dominique pointed to the bar of soap she'd given Simone. "Smell it. Marie is as kind and gentle as the soap she makes."

"I hope she's safe." Simone inhaled the soap's lavender scent, and a calmness seemed to envelope her.

"You have a wash," Dominique said. "I'm going to find some footwear for your children."

Louis and Victor had no use for boots they'd outgrown and would be none the wiser if they disappeared from the back of their wardrobe. How far were these poor children going to have to walk to stay safe? They may enjoy being barefoot in the heat of summer but what about the cold nights and if they were still walking when the seasons turned?

By the time she'd rummaged through her brothers' wardrobe, found some discarded boots and returned to the bedroom, the children were fast asleep, tucked up in Eugenie's bed. They looked so innocent. Paul clasped a much-loved teddy bear, whose fur coat was threadbare in places and stitched with cotton to prevent the stuffing escaping where a glass eye used to be. Emily's ragdoll was even more bedraggled.

"Here, these are for the children." Dominique handed the boots to Simone.

"We couldn't ..." Simone's face coloured. "You've been too kind already."

"You can and you will," Dominique was adamant. "Do you know how far you have to walk?"

Simone's eyes glassed over, her chin trembled, and she silently shook her head.

"You rest." Dominique offered her bed to Simone. "I'll go and see what I can find out."

"I'm just going to visit Nathalie," Dominique popped her head around the sitting room door.

"Don't be late for supper again."

"Non, Maman." It wasn't Dominique's fault she didn't always make it back in time for the evening meal her mother insisted be served as the grandfather clock chimed six o'clock. Sometimes there were much more important things to do and places to be than sitting politely at the table, trying to remember all the etiquette her mother insisted she needed to learn.

Taking her normal route to Nathalie's house, Dominique passed a patisserie whose ovens had been rekindled on the mayor's request. The aroma of fresh croissants and baguettes, baked especially for the refugees, wafted through the open door. Dominique's stomach rumbled.

"Bonjour, Francois," she called out to the baker as he withdrew another batch from the oven.

"Bonjour, Dominique," Francois nodded, his white hat bobbing on his head. He moved the steaming croissants to a cooling rack and beckoned Dominique inside. "You need?"

She closed her eyes and inhaled. There was nothing better than warm flaky pastry melting in your mouth, but the baking was meant for the refugees. She should show some restraint; save the croissants for those whose need was greatest.

"Go on. One won't be missed." Francois winked. He must have read her thoughts. "I've another batch to go in the oven."

"Merci beaucoup, Francois." Dominique snatched a croissant before he could change his mind, tossing it between her fingers so they didn't get burnt. She wanted to ask for more, a stash for Simone and her children. Perhaps she'd call in the way back, so she wasn't tempted to eat them.

Mayor Carlier's motor car, a shiny Brouhout, was parked outside the chateau that became the Carlier's family home for the duration of his mayoralty. It was flanked by several other vehicles signalling there was another meeting of the town's officials in progress.

Nathalie must have seen Dominique arrive and opened the front door without her having to knock.

"Quick, come in." Nathalie grabbed Dominique's wrist and pulled her inside. "They're in the meeting room," she whispered. "I've been listening at the door but it's too risky, there are too many people coming and going. We'll go in here and hopefully be able to hear through the wall."

A wedge of light through a tiny window high on the wall revealed the storeroom's contents, shelves of minute books and ledgers, recording the history of the town's affairs.

"Have you heard anything?" Dominique hoped her quest for information wouldn't be fruitless.

"Only that the Germans are expected any day now."

Dominique gasped. "What are they going to do?"

"The Germans? The reports from other towns aren't good. We're to prepare for the worst."

Dominique sucked in a breath. Surely Le Quesnoy's fortified walls could survive another battle.

"What are your pere and the councillors going to do?"

"I don't think they can agree. There have been lots of raised voices. Nobody expected the Germans to get to France via Belgium. They've broken international law coming through a neutral country."

Nathalie sounded much more knowledgeable than her sixteen years. Even if she was merely repeating what she'd overheard, Dominique imagined her friend as the future mayoress of Le Quesnoy. If the town survived the Germans.

"We could just close the roads into the city, open the sluice gates and flood the moats," Dominique suggested.

"But they could blast their way through the gates," Nathalie wrung her hands as if the burden to find a solution was hers and hers alone. "We don't have any soldiers around to defend us, not since the regiments left."

"I saw a family leaving this morning, their wagon loaded up. They've abandoned their home and the rest of us. We can't leave but perhaps we should pack some supplies and hide in the Foret de Mormal."

The friends had enjoyed lots of walks and picnics in the shade of the ancient oak, beech and ash trees but despite her suggestion, Dominique wasn't eager to be sleeping there overnight.

"One of the deputies suggested we declare the city open; announce we're not going to fight and let the Germans march through."

"That sounds like a good idea." Dominique's relief was short-lived, trampled by an image of Simone and her innocent children. "But what if they catch the refugees? Or what if they do to us what they did to the Belgians?"

"The French troops or even the British might come to our rescue," Nathalie added another option. "Word has been sent. They're retreating from Charleroi. They could come here next."

"Oui, they can fight them off. Two countries against one; surely, we must win."

"But they might not arrive in time."

Dominique felt like the yoyo she'd been given last Christmas, up and down, high and low at the mercy of whomever held the string.

"Let's listen some more," she suggested, desperate for good news she could relay to Simone.

They sat with their ears against the wall. All Dominique could hear was her heartbeat thundering like an approaching tempest.

It was easy for Dominique to save some food for Simone and her children; after listening to the council's discussions, she had no appetite. Her unsettled insides churned with a nervousness she couldn't dispel as she pushed her serving of meat and vegetables around the plate with her fork.

"I do wish your pere would make it home in time for dinner." Lucie gazed at the empty seat at the opposite head of the table.

"They must be busy at the hospital." Full of wounded soldiers Dominique thought but didn't say.

"He's meant to be retired." Lucie sighed. "I do hope Eugenie finds a husband that isn't tied to his career."

Their mere's intention in sending Eugenie to stay with family in the city was to find her a suitable husband but Dominique knew her sister had already promised her heart to Andre. She'd stopped protesting about the trip when Andre enlisted and was sent to Paris for Officer's training. Dominique smiled. Any day now another letter would surely arrive, detailing how Eugenie managed to escape her chaperone and spend precious time with her beau.

"What are you smiling at, Dominique? Finding a husband is a very serious matter you will soon be having to turn your attention to. I suggest you start using some of the manners I've endeavoured to instil in you."

Suddenly, Dominique was grateful she was only sixteen. What if her mere sent her away too, before Gabriel returned from fighting? She wanted to marry for love, not some silly arrangement that she had to be content with, because a man could provide for her.

Besides there were much more urgent problems to deal with.

"Sorry, Maman. I was just thinking about all the fun Eugenie must be having in Paris. Have you ever been there?" Getting Lucie to reminisce about her glamourous youth was a ploy Dominique often used to distract her mere.

This time it also allowed Dominique to daydream about Gabriel. A sudden realisation that he might be one of the injured soldiers in the hospital was like a punch to her already upset stomach. She wrapped her arms around her midriff, a futile attempt to ease the pain the image conjured. Surely her father would have said. What if there were so many wounded soldiers he didn't know? What if Gabriel was so badly wounded her pere couldn't tell it was him?

Alice or Clemence would know. They would have contact with all the patients. Alice was unlikely to divulge information; she'd been a nurse for as long as Dominique could remember. She'd never married and was very serious about her chosen career, as rigid about the rules as the stiff white cap she wore when on duty. It seemed that a woman had to choose a career or a man; there didn't seem to be a way to have both. Clemence was the total opposite; she'd married Alphonse, one of the local brewers and was working part-time at the hospital for a few extra francs. Clemence was Dominique's best opportunity to find out what she needed to know.

Louis and Victor, having finished their dinner, started needling each other at the table.

"Boys! Table manners!" Lucie growled. "If you've finished eating, ask to be excused."

"Can we pleased be excused, Maman?" they chimed in unison.

Dominique took it as her chance to escape as well. "Can I please be excused too, Maman?"

"But you haven't finished." Lucie sighed and shook her head as if defeated. "Very well. Please ask Marie to clear the table and bring me a cup of coffee in the sitting room."

"I'll take the plates," Dominique offered.

"Dominique!" Lucie admonished. "That's what we have Marie for. You treat her more like a friend than a servant."

That's because she is. Seventeen-year-old Marie might have come from a family not as well off as theirs, but she was still a young woman, just like Dominique. She kept her thoughts to herself as she headed to the kitchen with the stack of plates and cutlery.

"Merci, Dominique, you shouldn't have." Marie blushed. "Your mere will growl."

"She already did." Dominique rolled her eyes. "Never mind. I need your help."

"With the refugees?"

Dominique raised a finger to her lips and lowered her voice. "You know?"

"Oui, I saw you bring them home from the square."

"Oh, hopefully you were the only one. I didn't want to worry Maman who, by the way, would like a cup of coffee in the sitting room."

Marie busied herself filling the coffee pot and gathering a cup and saucer. "What can I do for you?"

"They've got to leave in the morning. The patisseries are doing some baking, but I thought if you could make some sandwiches and spare some fruit too."

"I baked a lemon cake today," Marie smiled proudly. "Nobody will notice if a chunk of that goes to a good cause. I'll make a basket up."

"Merci, Marie." Dominique squeezed her hand in gratitude. "I thought I might give them a bar of your soap as well, if you don't mind. They were covered in dust when they arrived. It would be nice if they were able to wash when they get to wherever they're going."

"That's a lovely gesture." Marie eyed the plate full of food. "Are you unwell? It's unlike you to not eat your dinner."

Dominique hesitated. Should she reveal all she'd learned at Nathalie's? What purpose would it serve? There were no firm decisions, only speculation that might frighten Marie unnecessarily.

"I'm fine," Dominique replied.

"Did you not like your dinner or are you planning to give the refugees that too?"

"Oui, I'll take it up now." Dominique headed for the staircase before Marie could ask any more questions.

Chapter 3

25 August 1914

Morning came around too fast. Dominique never heard her pere come in last night but recognised his footsteps leaving again at first light and assumed he went back to the hospital. After the refugees had gone, she would have to visit to see for herself.

She dressed quickly, in the same long skirt and simple blouse from yesterday. She hadn't wanted to disturb Simone, and the children so slept in Clemence's old room, ignoring the musty odour that had accumulated since she'd left home to live with Alphonse in a little cottage close to the brewery.

Marie reached the top of the stairs just as Dominique went to rouse Simone and her children.

"I've filled the basket with as much as I can," she murmured as she passed a wicker basket to Dominique.

"Merci, Marie." Unable to resist lifting the checker napkin draped over the top, Dominique wished for a moment the basket was hers when she spied the cake, fruit and sandwiches stowed inside.

The bedroom door opened. Simone, Paul and Emily stood, already dressed and packed ready to go. The beds had been made.

The room looked as if they wished to wipe away any trace of their presence.

"We're as ready as we'll ever be." Simone's smile appeared forced, her children stood, tucked into the folds of her skirt, wide eyed and fearful.

"Marie made this for you." Dominique went to hand over the basket but pulled it back when she realised Simone was already laden with bags and would be unable to carry the basket as well. She knelt, lay the checker napkin on the floor, piled half of the food on top, drew the four corners of the napkin around the food and tied them into a knot. She removed a second napkin lining the basket and repeated the exercise with the remainder of the food. The parcels were now light enough for Paul and Emily to carry one each. "You can carry these for your mere, can't you? Make sure teddy and dolly don't eat it all."

The children looked at their bedraggled toys and back at Dominique but remained quiet. If only she knew what they were thinking, perhaps then she could say the right words to comfort them. She sighed. Could anyone feel reassured in these uncertain times?

She stood, smoothed down her skirt and headed for the stairs. Just as Simone had said, they were as ready as they'd ever be, for whatever lay ahead.

Simone hesitated at the open front door. The murmur of people already on the streets was punctuated by booming sounds that echoed through the streets.

"I think they're demolishing an old warehouse building on the other side of town," Dominique offered a reason for the noise she hoped was true, but one the lump forming in the pit of her stomach told her was far from reality.

Simone shook her head. "Cannons, Dominique, cannons."

"French and English cannons, chasing the Germans away," Dominique suggested.

"Or Germans coming to destroy your town too." Simone's eyes glassed over. "You should pack and leave."

"I can't." Dominique looked up at the only home she'd ever known. "We can't. My pere is a doctor. He's helping with the injured soldiers."

Simone leaned in and kissed Dominique's cheeks, one side then the other as was the custom. "Stay safe, Dominique," she whispered. "Merci beaucoup for everything. Come on children, let's go."

Dominique's heart filled with admiration for Simone's strength and determination. She reached out and squeezed her hand.

"Stay strong, Simone."

The trio walked the short distance to the end of the street and joined the steady flow of refugees heading towards Port Fauroeulx. Those barefoot stepped gingerly on the cobblestones, untouched by the morning sun and still carrying the night chill. Dominique's chest swelled with pride watching Paul and Emily in their boots; Paul's a perfect fit and Emily's with two pairs of socks and some screwed up newspaper stuffed in the toes, to hopefully avoid getting blisters. That she'd been able to do something to make their journey easier made Dominique want to smile but the sadness of their having to leave at all held the smile at bay.

Francois stood at the door of his patisserie handing out gratefully received croissants and baguettes. An old man ripped a chunk of bread off the end of his baguette with his teeth before stuffing the remainder into the pocket of his baggy trousers. He wandered off, cheeks bulging, a look of resignation and weariness furrowing his brow. Emily and Paul eagerly took the croissants they were offered. Simone allowed them one each for breakfast and insisted the others be stowed for later.

Dominique waved one final time as Simone, Paul and Emily disappeared out of view. What would become of them? She sighed. What would become of everyone if the cannons got any closer? Which side of the war did the artillery fire belong to? Were they friend or foe?

The thick walls of her home felt like a welcome haven, and she turned to head back inside but came face to face with the head of a horse. Her wandering thoughts had stopped her from hearing the clip clop of its hooves as it towed a wagon full of refugees from the barracks. She stepped back, stood in the door frame and watched the exodus continue. The only remnant left behind was a steaming heap of horse manure in the middle of the road.

Dominique studied the next group of people as they stepped around the excrement. They weren't Belgians but a family from across the road: Madam Severin, her two sons and her daughter, Madeleine who'd been a year behind Dominique at school. This family could have been the Favier family except Dominique never pictured her mother having the strength to lead her children into the unknown. She opened her mouth to speak but unsure whether to wish them well or castigate them for deserting, she remained silent. Madeleine kept her eyes averted. Perhaps, she too, was confused.

A need to see Nathalie, to learn the latest developments had Dominique walking across town rather than to the hospital. The stream of people, both French and Belgian, heading in the opposite direction continued, not in a quiet organised way but in a hurried panic. The slower walkers were pushed aside by those desperate to leave. Mothers growled at their children not to dally. Horses towing laden carts snorted and neighed in protest, unsettled and sensing their owner's fear. Dominique recognised more Quercitains among them, every other family was now someone she knew. People who would normally have stopped for a chat, brushed past Dominique with barely a hint of recognition. She passed the houses they'd abandoned, not even bothering to close their front doors. Peering into the darkness added to the sense of foreboding.

The closer she got to Nathalie's the louder the booms of cannon fire became. In the distance, grey clouds of smoke streaked the skyline as if every farmer in the district had chosen this day to have a burn off. The acrid smell of smoke drifted into town. Dominique held onto hope, crossing her fingers and wishing it was the cannon fire of the French and British holding the Germans at bay, fighting them back.

She could only manage short sharp breaths by the time she reached the mayor's house. The sight that greeted her halted everything: her movement, her thoughts, her breath. She froze, hanging tight to the wrought iron fence for support, fearful that her knees would give out beneath her.

The very soldiers she desperately wanted to believe were halting the Germans in their tracks were scattered across the front yard. Their distinctive blue and red uniforms, no longer new and clean, had lost the sharp crispness that made them look invincible. Ingrained with dust they looked as faded as the soldiers wearing them. They'd only been gone three weeks. What happened beyond the ramparts to sap them of their energy and determination?

Dominique scanned the faces. Was Gabriel among them? Had he finished fighting already and arrived home for good? The boom of a cannon, louder, closer, sent a shiver down her spine. Did it shake the ground she stood on, or was her imagination running rampant? Either way, she knew the fighting was far from over. Men mulling about, smoking, drinking from their tin cups, eating direct from cans or sleeping wherever they could get comfortable were of no help. She skirted around them and headed to the back of the house expecting to see more soldiers, erecting tents and setting up camp but the only men this side of the house were picking fruit from the trees, munching on juicy apples, grinning like they'd found paradise. She hurried through the back door into the kitchen.

"Dominique! What are you doing out and about?" The Carlier's servant, Madam Cacheux always fussed over Nathalie and her friend, worrying about them as if they were her own children. "It is too dangerous! You should be home with your family."

"Bonjour, Madam Cacheux." Dominique tried to sound bright, cheery and unaffected by what she'd seen. "I need to see Nathalie. Where is she?"

The servant sighed. With her hands covered in flour, kneading dough, she could only nod her head to indicate Nathalie was upstairs. Dominique pinched a scone from the batch already cooling on a rack and scurried away, devouring the warm baking as she went upstairs.

Nathalie was perched on her bed, staring out the window with views to the north.

"I thought you'd be downstairs listening in." Disappointed, Dominique slumped down on the bed.

"I was," Nathalie replied matter-of-factly. "But there's more to be learned from up here."

"What do you mean?"

Nathalie pointed out the window. "Look, Dominique. Look at the cloud of dust. That's them. They're coming."

Dominique swallowed. She stood and peered out the window. Nathalie was right. Beneath the clouds of smoke was a billowing haze, more sepia than grey as if a stampede of animals was stirring up the dust.

"More French soldiers? Or British?" The hopeful tone in Dominique's query was soon quashed by Nathalie's reply.

"Not according to the officer downstairs." Nathalie glanced wide eyed at Dominique and shook her head.

"The French soldiers outside will protect us." Dominique paced backwards and forwards on the rug beside Nathalie's bed, searching for solutions, clinging to anything positive. "They could man the gate. Stop the Germans from coming through."

"They're leaving."

"They're leaving!" Dominique's voice echoed her disbelief. "How can they do that?"

"They've received orders to retreat. To reinforce with more troops and set up a new line further south."

"What are we supposed to do?" Dominique silently prayed her friend had the answer.

"Leave too?" Tears welled in Nathalie's eyes.

"We can't do that," the pair murmured in unison, their eyes fixed on the burgeoning dust cloud.

"You need to leave here." Nathalie's solemn look reinforced the seriousness of the situation. "You need to go home and be with your family."

The best friends hugged, grabbing hold of one another as if this might be the last time.

Yelling from the front of the house drew them apart. They rushed through to Gabriel's room to the window that looked down over the soldiers. They were no longer mulling about but busy preparing to leave.

"Fall in, troops," commanded the officer with stripes on his shoulders.

The men followed his orders, formed organised lines and marched through the gates, eyes forward as if what or who they left behind was of no concern.

"You should follow them," Nathalie suggested. "You'll be protected then."

The soldiers weren't prepared to protect the town; why would they worry about Dominique? She'd best not rely on anyone but herself.

"I could go through the rampart tunnels. Skirt around the town under cover."

"That'll take you much longer." Nathalie gripped Dominique's hands. "I need to know you'll be safe."

"What about you?"

"When Pere gives the word, we're to head to the cellar."

Dominique was torn. She didn't want to leave her friend, but she knew Nathalie was right. She needed to be with her family. If her pere hadn't come home yet, her Mere would be beside herself.

"How long have I got?" Dominique asked, hurrying back to Nathalie's room to check the advance of the Germans.

Boom! Boom!

They dropped to the floor, covered their heads with their hands and cowered near the bed. It felt like time stopped, but Dominique's pounding heart told her she was very much alive.

"Are you alright?" she whispered to Nathalie.

"Oui … oui, I think so." Nathalie's voice was sapped of its confidence. "It seems to have stopped."

They lifted their heads to peek out the window. *Boom!* Another blast. Louder. Closer. There was no time to duck. They watched in disbelief. The ramparts had been hit. Grass, turf and fragments of shattered bricks were flung into the sky. The Germans were attacking the town's only form of protection. Dominique stared wide eyed at her friend, unable to find words to voice the fear that made her lips and chin tremble, and her hands clammy while a cold sweat prickled her spine. She blinked back tears, unsure whether to flee or hide.

"Nathalie! The cellar. Now!" Mayor Carlier's yelled command made them both jerk backwards.

It wasn't to be disobeyed. The situation demanded action.

"You should come to the cellar with us," Nathalie pleaded.

"I can't. Mere will be frantic if I don't make it home."

Dominique wiped the sleeve of her blouse across her forehead, gripped hold of the windowsill and pushed herself up. She felt her leg muscles tighten. She was ready to run for her life.

The girls hurried down the stairs. They hugged each other tightly again before going their separate ways. Dominique rushed through the kitchen, ignoring Madam Cacheux, and out the back door. She hung close to the walls of the building, skirting along the side, peeking around the front corner before darting across the yard. She couldn't be certain the Germans weren't already in the town. She chose not to follow the retreating French troops, turning left at the gate, knowing there was another way into the rampart tunnels if she needed it.

Unable to discern if the thrumming in her ears was the sound of artillery or the pounding of her heart, she ran as fast as her legs would carry her; her thigh muscles strained but she wouldn't let them give in. Dominique skirted across town, hugging close to the buildings, alert to any movement around her. She paused to catch her breath by the Lowendaal barracks.

"Why couldn't you still be there to protect us!" she growled at the empty building.

Boom! Boom!

Dominique clapped her hands over her ears, dropped to the ground and squeezed her eyes shut. Was she too late? Were the Germans here? Was she about to be tortured like the Belgians? She gasped for air, waited for the next blast, afraid to move, afraid to stay put. Seconds, or minutes, passed, she wasn't sure. Gingerly, she opened her eyes.

The barracks. Gone. Half of the second storey of the building was open to the air, bricks smashed, windows shattered, roofing iron twisted and flung to the ground.

"Non!" she screamed. What if French soldiers had still been there? What if the Germans had arrived earlier, when the Belgians were resting in the barracks? What if the next shell hit her home? What if the Germans killed her?

"Non, you bloody won't," she cursed, jumping back up, her eyes darting in all directions. "I'm too young to die."

She knew she wasn't safe. She took off, running as fast as her trembling legs would carry her. She reached the deserted town square. It was hard to imagine only twenty-four hours ago the place had been a throng of refugees or that Dominique and Nathalie had been planning a picnic. Would they ever get to enjoy a picnic again?

Dominique paused to catch her breath, looking across the square she took in the damage. A brick wall by the town hall had been hit but luckily the belfry looked to be intact. Perhaps she should make her way there. It was the perfect vantage point to watch all that was going on. Deciding she'd rather not see; she inhaled deeply and ran.

Chapter 4

"Is Pere here? Is Pere here?" Dominique followed the stretcher bearers delivering the ashen-faced body of Mayor Carlier to the hospital's first available cot. "Mayor Carlier needs his help."

Madam Carlier and Nathalie flanked either side of the stretcher, worry draining all colour from their faces.

Henri must have heard his daughter's plea for help and hurried into the ward, wiping his hands as if he'd just finished surgery.

Dominique saw her half-sisters; Clemence and Alice looked in unison at one another, at their father and then back at her. She knew what they were wondering - what trouble had she gotten into now?

Henri rolled his eyes before focusing his attention on Mayor Carlier. Beads of sweat peppered the mayor's top lip; he clutched at his chest and took short gasping breaths as if he couldn't get the oxygen he needed.

"I suspect Mayor Carlier may have had a heart attack," Henri replied.

Clemence and Alice stepped back out of the way, allowing Henri to administer the care required. They pulled Dominique aside.

"What happened?" Alice's tempered tone may have been free of accusation but combined with her hands-on-hips stance and knowing glare, she managed to rile Dominique.

It seemed to always be this way between the two. Often Alice's frustration was justified but sometimes she seemed to pick at Dominique for the sake of it. Not everyone could be as serious and rule abiding as Alice and certainly not Dominique who was often told she'd had a mischievous streak since she could crawl.

"Don't look at me like that, Alice." Dominique crossed her arms and frowned at her half-sister. "I had nothing to do with it. I was heading home after the first blast hit the ramparts. I got as far as the square. Another blast hit the barracks then I saw the mayor's car heading here so I decided to follow. To make sure everything was alright. Mayor Carlier has a lot to deal with. If you don't know, the Germans are on our doorstep."

"We know, Dominique, we know. The barracks are next door."

"Was the hospital hit too?" Dominique glanced around the ward and then back at Clemence. "Are you alright? Was anyone injured?"

"I'll check the patients." Clemence scanned the men whose beds lined either side of the hospital ward. "I heard some of the patients call out. They may have thought they were back on the battlefield."

"One of the patients?" Dominique scanned the beds again, wide eyed, as if she was searching for someone. "Gab ..."

"Who are you looking for?" Alice eyed Dominique suspiciously. "They're all soldiers. You shouldn't know any of them."

Clemence's knowing smile suggested she thought Dominique was about to say 'Gabriel,' but she didn't reveal the secret Dominique had entrusted her with.

"No-one." Dominique's cheeks coloured rosy red. "It's wonderful to see they are all getting better under your expert care, Alice."

Alice sighed and turned her attention to the new patient. "Can I help you with anything, Pere?"

"I've given him aspirin which appears to be having the desired effect," Henri replied. "It will be best if we leave him to rest now."

"Will he be alright?" Madam Carlier's finely shaped eyebrows drew together in a worried frown.

Henri pulled her aside. "With rest I believe he will improve. This isn't the first time his weakened heart has brought him here. He must take things easy. I cannot guarantee the outcome if he doesn't heed my advice."

"But, Pere," Dominique interrupted. "He needs to save the town from the Germans."

"Dominique!" Henri stopped, inhaled and exhaled long and slow as if gathering his patience. He pulled his watch from his pocket and read the time. "You are to get home to your mere. She will be worried about you."

"But ..." Dominique's protest was stifled by the look her father gave her.

"It might not be safe on the streets yet, Pere. Dominique could stay and help me check the other patients," Clemence came to her rescue. "Until you're ready to leave."

Henri glanced from Clemence to Dominique and sighed. "Very well then."

"Come on, Dominique." Clemence beckoned her to follow as she headed to the far end of the ward. "This patient is British; he doesn't understand a word we say so just smile and help reassure him."

"Rest up." Clemence placed a comforting hand on his shoulder and dabbed a damp flannel to his forehead. "The attack is over now."

Dominique gulped. It wasn't like he could do anything other than rest. Beneath the blanket his legs stopped just below the knee.

"How do you get used to their injuries?"

"Sorry, I should have realised, I've been so busy I forgot." Clemence straightened the blanket and readied to move on. "You and I, we're not nurses like Alice. Just keep your eyes on his face and pretend nothing is wrong. I've found it's the only way to cope."

Dominique hoped he couldn't tell her smile was forced.

Alice had suggested Clemence become a medic when the hospital ward, which normally would have half a dozen patients at most, was full to overflowing. While Alice went about her duties, remaining serene and focussed despite the chaos they now found themselves in, Clemence struggled, helping with the jobs the nurses were too busy for. She'd been forced to take on the extra work when the Germans fired the first bullets in this bloody battle. Her husband Alphonse's brewery could no longer provide for them, not with all the beer drinking men marching out of town to fight.

Clemence emptied the bowl of water, rinsed her cloth and refilled her basin before moving onto the next patient.

There was no point smiling at this patient. His head and eyes were heavily bandaged. A small triangle left a space for him to breathe, and another wedge showed his burned lips. Dominique felt bile rising. She had to swallow to stop herself gagging and imagining his concealed wounds.

She stepped back, willingly gave Clemence the space she needed to check he was sleeping and not dead. What if Gabriel was injured? How would she feel if he came home disfigured? How would she cope if he never came home?

"Bonjour, Jacques. How are you feeling?" Clemence had moved onto the next patient and Dominique quickly followed, leaving her terrible thoughts behind.

Clemence put a hand to the young French soldier's forehead to check his temperature. Jacques barely looked old enough to have donned a uniform in the first place. He had to be someone's son or brother. Thank goodness, Victor and Louis were much too young to be involved in the fighting.

Jacques grinned and opened his pyjama top to reveal the bandage that covered his chest wound. "Très bien, sister, très bien."

"Good." Doctor Flament must have overheard Jacques as he came up beside Clemence. "Prepare him to be moved please," he ordered.

"Moved?" Jacques's grin disappeared. He looked more like the frightened boy he was. "Where? Where am I going? I can't go back fighting. I'm not that much better." He slumped down in the bed as if appearing more infirm would change the outcome.

"We need the beds for patients worse than you." Doctor Flament's tone indicated there wouldn't be any reprieve in the influx of injured. He looked towards the window and listened. "There's bound to be an influx now the battle is on our doorstep."

Jacques squeezed his eyes shut and pulled the bedding up under his chin.

"Are we safe, Doctor?" Clemence's voice quivered.

Dominique stood back, waiting nervously for the doctor's reassurance.

"They're unlikely to destroy a hospital. Not when they might need our help themselves."

Clemence appeared to relax as she turned her attention to the patient. "Come on, Jacques, let's get you dressed. You don't want to leave in your pyjamas."

She had to unfold his fingers, one by one, to release the sheet he clung to. Jacques stared into the distance, his lips formed a thin unbreakable line, never to reveal what he saw. She clicked her fingers in front of his eyes. The attempt to break him out of the trance was futile.

"Come on, Jacques," Dominique came to assist. "You're not being much help to Clemence."

It was like dressing a baby. Lifting his arm, removing one sleeve at a time, poking it back through a shirt sleeve. Together the pair finished dressing Jacques and sat him on the edge of the bed. The young man who'd said he was very good was somewhere inside, like a turtle that had retreated into its protective shell, but they couldn't lure him out.

"Take him out to the courtyard, Clemence" Alice suggested. "Let him sit in the sunshine until the drivers are able to take him to Lille."

"Fetch a wheelchair, please, Dominique." Clemence pointed to a chair stowed beside the door to the surgery.

Jacques was like a dead weight as Dominique helped Clemence lift him into the wheelchair.

"It's like he's already dead." Dominique spoke quietly; her comment intended for Clemence only.

"I might as well be." A tear escaped the corner of Jacques's eye.

"We'll get you out into the fresh air." Clemence assumed her cheeriest of voices, all while raising a finger to her lips to hush Dominique. "You'll feel much better then."

Dominique blushed. If only she'd kept her thoughts to herself. She'd remember to stay quiet in the future. She pushed the wheelchair from the ward, it was the least she could do to assist Clemence, and it meant she couldn't see Jacques's downcast face.

Sunlight streamed into the enclosed courtyard, the walls of the hospital providing shelter on two sides, the annexed chapel occupying the third and a brick wall with a single gate providing privacy where the courtyard bordered the street.

"I'd like to sit and have a rest here myself, take the weight off my feet." The fresh air made Clemence yawn. "It feels like it has been an extra-long shift."

"Why don't you?" Dominique asked. "You and Pere have been working long hours."

"But others have been working longer."

Dominique sat on the stone bench next to Jacques's wheelchair. "A moment won't hurt."

Clemence sighed and gave into the fatigue. She sat, eased her feet from her shoes and wriggled her stockinged toes. Together, they leaned back against the brick wall and closed their eyes, letting the sun's warmth bathe their faces.

Boom! Boom! Boom!

The trio cried out in terror. Dominique cowered down beside the wheelchair, shielding her head with her arms. The blasts had been close, so close her ears rung with the reverberations. She was too frightened to open her eyes. What if there were more to follow? Doctor Flament said they wouldn't attack the hospital. Should they run inside?

She couldn't abandon Clemence and Jacques. Gingerly she lifted her arms and edged her eyes open. There was fresh blood oozing from a gash on Jacques's forehead. His face was coated in dust, not the colour of dirt but a reddish brown, the same hue as the hospital bricks.

Reality landed like a direct hit. The hospital wasn't safe. Doctor Flament was wrong.

The silence that followed the blasts was deafening. Were the German's preparing for another attack? Jacques whimpered softly. Dominique couldn't tell what was going on beyond the walls of the hospital, but in front of her was a distraught man whose urine seeped into the cracks of the courtyard cobbles.

"Clemence! Clemence!" Alice cried out as she burst through the door into the courtyard. "Are you unharmed? Oh, non, look at you, you're bleeding."

"I am?" Clemence shook her head but stopped. "Oh, my head hurts." She looked down at her uniform, no longer a hygienic white but coated in dust. She scanned her body for the source of bleeding. "Where?"

"Your ear." Dominique pointed then looked herself over in case she too had been hit.

Alice inspected Clemence's wound as a drip of blood landed on her shoulder. "We'd best get you all inside. In case there are more blasts."

Clemence's eyes darted around the courtyard. "What did they hit?"

Doctor Flament arrived to inspect the damage and answered her question. "The chapel. The courtyard. The barracks again."

The Lowendaal barracks sat to the north of the hospital, on the other side of Rue Juhel, closer to the Bastion Cesar.

"I assume they were aiming for the barracks again, hoping to kill any soldiers based there," Doctor Flament said. "Unfortunately, they got us too."

"What about the refugees?" Alice's worried look showed her concern for the Belgians. "They were staying there last night. Did they all leave this morning?"

"Oui, we watched them leave through Porte Fauroeulx," Dominique replied.

"Très bien." Doctor Flament rubbed his chin. "We'd have to prepare ourselves for more patients if they didn't."

The creaking of the chapel door drew their attention to the opposite side of the courtyard.

"Sister, are you alright?" Doctor Flament asked.

"Oui, just a little shaken." Sister Jeanne brushed down her tunic and mantle. "With God's blessing I am still here."

"God? Why didn't he stop the war in the first place?" Dominique's wish to keep her thoughts to herself was short-lived. "How can God inflict such pain and suffering on the poor soldiers?"

"It isn't God's work that caused the war, my dear." Sister Jeanne's demeanour and tone were calming. "Man did that without any help. It is God's gift to the doctors, nurses and medics, to spare these men from death so that we can nurse them back to health."

Dominique had no basis from which to argue. She silently resolved to again keep her thoughts to herself.

None of the townsfolk arrived at the hospital, which meant there were no injuries to warrant medical treatment, or they were too afraid to leave their houses. The ward eventually quietened, everyone breathing a sigh of relief that the attack was over.

Clemence, Dominique and Alice took a moment to enjoy a hot drink. Their rest was interrupted when the doors burst open again. Clemence, her nerves still shattered, jumped up, spilling drops of coffee down the front of her already dirty apron.

"More patients?" Alice stood and readied herself for the onslaught. "Locals or more injured soldiers? Perhaps the message to send them elsewhere hasn't got through."

Two elegantly suited men barged into the room, saw Mayor Carlier and headed straight for him, anxious looks on their ruddy faces.

"Monsieur Croix and Monsieur Deleporte," Henri stepped between the deputy mayors and his patient. "Mayor Carlier is in no condition to speak to you now."

"We need to confirm our plan of action," Monsieur Deleporte wasn't easily discouraged and tried to sidestep Henri.

Alice and Clemence moved to stand behind their father, adding another barrier of protection.

"We need to be prepared and if Mayor Carlier is unable to perform his role, he needs to delegate authority to one of us." Monsieur Deleporte puffed out his chest.

"Well, right now, he needs to rest," Henri calmly maintained his ground. "The Germans appear to have ceased their attack on the town. Mayor Carlier should be in a better position tomorrow to let you know his thoughts on the matter."

The deputy majors huffed in unison.

"Now, gentlemen, I suggest you be on your way and give the nurses the room to do their job."

The men left in the same manner they'd arrived, stomping across the ward and barging through the doors.

"Hopefully there will be no further visitors today." Henri listened to the patient's heart one more time then packed away his stethoscope. "Keep an eye on him, Alice."

"Oui, Pere."

"I will be here too." Sister Jeanne appeared to glide across the room, her face calm despite the calamity.

"I know you will keep him comfortable. but send for me if there is any deterioration in his condition." Henri ushered Dominique towards the door. "Right, Dominique, I think we can leave now too."

"I'll come see you tomorrow, Nathalie," Dominique waved to her friend as she trudged after her father.

"I suggest you go along too." Henri addressed Mayor Carlier's family. "Try to get some rest. Your husband will be in good hands here at the hospital. You will both need to stay strong for when he returns home and needs your help."

"Oui, Doctor. We will try." Reluctantly, Madam Carlier released the tight grip she had of her husband's hand and gently laid it across his chest. She leaned down and murmured in his ear. "J'taime ma cherie."

The mayor appeared to perk up at the words of endearment, but it was only momentary.

"Doctor Favier." Doctor Flament readied himself for more surgery. "Are you able to assist me?"

"I'll be right with you, Doctor," Henri straightened as if the opportunity to operate erased any fatigue he'd been feeling. "Dominique, go straight home, I will follow as soon as I can."

Chapter 5

There were no more blasts but the booms that echoed across the sky were replaced with an unfamiliar cacophony. Gunshots, glass shattering, wood splintering. High pitched screams of terrified women and children. Triumphant yells of marauding soldiers. Dominique didn't speak German. She didn't need to. She knew their intentions weren't good.

Banished from the hospital, she hurried home, not stopping until she shut the front door behind her.

"Quick, Dominique." Lucie was ushering Louis and Victor down the steps into the cellar. "Hurry, child. We need to hide. The Germans won't find us down here."

Dominique hesitated. She needed to stay safe, but waiting in the darkness of the cellar, not knowing what was going on above ground, would exasperate her.

"Where's Marie?" she asked, searching for an excuse to go upstairs rather than down. "Is she with you?"

"I don't know." Lucie glanced from the front door to the concrete stairs that curved down under the house as if the Germans were about to burst in and she didn't have time to worry about anyone other than herself, certainly not the servant. "Hurry! Before it's too late."

"Where's Remy? Have the boys got him?" Dominique knew her mere would care more about the family's pet dog than she would Marie.

"Non!" A look of panic crossed Lucie's face.

"I'll just go find Remy."

"Dominique! Dominique, come here right this minute!"

Dominique ignored the parenting tone of Lucie's command. She lifted her skirt and took the stairs two at a time.

"Remy!" The dog barked and ran to her when she reached the first-floor landing. "Marie!"

"I'm up here," Marie replied.

Dominique hurried up the second flight of stairs and found Marie in the bedroom at the end of the passage, perched on the seat built into the window casement that jutted out from the pitched roof. She climbed in beside her and clasped Marie's hands in hers while she caught her breath. Remy jumped up between them.

"I couldn't bear to be stuck in the cellar where I couldn't see."

"Me neither," Marie replied before they both turned to peer through the lace curtains that allowed a view of the street but hopefully kept them hidden from sight.

The first of the soldiers came into view, not marching in orderly rows but swaying about the street, swigging from bottles of wine as they slammed the butts of their rifles through windows. Dominique cringed when several of them stopped outside Francois's patisserie.

"Oh, non, Francois."

"Du hungrig bist?" a soldier yelled, rubbing his belly.

The others laughed and barged past him to kick the door in with such force that Francois's doorbell, which usually rung with a gentle jingle, screeched in protest as it was ripped from its bracket and tossed back onto the patisserie floor.

Dominique's mouth went dry. She attempted to swallow. Dread sat in her throat. What if Francois was still inside, cleaning up after his morning bake? The patisserie was his livelihood, his home, his passion. He wouldn't allow anyone to take it away from him.

The soldiers jostled to be first inside.

"I don't cook for Boche! Get out!" Francois yelled.

Desperate for a better view, Dominique went to yank the curtains back.

"Non!" Marie grabbed her hand. "Non, Dominique. It's not safe."

Thwack.

"Aargh!" Francois cried out in pain as the soldiers shoved him into the street. He fell to the hard cobbles, blood pouring from his face.

"He's hurt," Dominique gasped.

The soldiers re-emerged from the patisserie, hands and mouths stuffed with croissants and baguettes. Surely, they had all they wanted. Dominique silently urged them to leave. She wanted to rush down and tend to Francois. But the soldiers hadn't finished. They weren't content and took turns to kick the baker; in the kidneys, ribs, and back; from all sides like he was a loaf of bread. They laughed raucously as a soldier kicked him in the head.

Francois groaned loudly before going deadly quiet, a pool of blood forming beneath him.

"They've killed him." Dominique shook her head. It couldn't be true. "Poor Francois, an innocent man who only wanted to help people. How could they do that? All for a piece of bread."

"He might be just pretending, Dominique, playing dead so they'll leave him alone," Marie suggested. "Look they're moving on."

Dominique's sigh of relief was short-lived. The soldiers lost interest in Francois, but they turned into Rue Brancion and were headed their way. The girls pulled back from the window.

"What should we do?" Marie's question came out as a high-pitched squeak as her eyes widened. "Have we got time to make it to the cellar?"

Marie's worried look made Dominique feel brave. She could keep them safe. She had to.

"Non," she replied with as calm a tone as she could muster while her mind raced to find a solution. "The wardrobe." She pointed to the tall oak cupboard that sat in the corner, strong and sturdy like the oak trees Le Quesnoy was synonymous with. "If they get inside the house, we can hide at the back of the wardrobe, behind the clothes. They're women's clothing, the Boche aren't going to be interested in them."

It sounded plausible. Dominique hoped they wouldn't need to prove it was.

The shattering of glass drew them back to the window. Madame Severin's abandoned house was the next target of the soldiers with more joining the rampage. One shoulder-charged the front door, breaking the door latch as he smashed his way inside. She'd probably left it unlocked. Hopefully the Severin family had taken or hidden everything precious when they left.

The soldiers barged inside the homestead which sat wedged between two others. Dominique hadn't seen the other neighbours leave and imagined them cowering in their cellars.

Wooden chairs were thrown out the open door and through the smashed windows, sending shards of glass across the street. Those without wine soon found Madame Severin's supply and exited the house swigging from bottles they'd smashed the tops off, red drool dribbling from their chins. A soldier laughed gleefully before munching from the hunk of cheese he had skewered with the bayonet attached to the head of his rifle. He alternated mouthfuls of cheese and bread, washing each away with another swig of wine.

Dominique could see the soldiers' faces now. They were clean shaven young men. If they hadn't been dressed in their green-grey uniforms with a malevolent spike on the top of their helmets, they could have passed as friendly French soldiers. Somebody's son, brother or husband. But the triumphant cheers and evil laughter as they ransacked houses painted a different picture. They were no longer a bunch of young drunk men innocently partying their way through town but Germans, intent on wreaking havoc, trying to prove they were superior, with the rights to do whatever they chose, bereft of respect for the Quercitains.

When Madame Severin's house no longer looked habitable, the soldiers moved on to find their next victim. They looked up and down the street and then directly at the Favier house. Dominique sucked in a breath, clenching her hands so tight her knuckles went white. She edged slowly back from the window, avoiding any sudden movement that might draw their attention.

"Don't let them see us," she whispered.

Remy growled. His protective instincts raised his hackles.

"Ssh, Remy, ssh." Dominique clamped her hand over his muzzle.

The seconds that ticked by felt like hours. Was their house about to be ransacked? The house had stood in the same spot for centuries; was it no longer able to protect them? Dominique eyed the wardrobe. Her heart thundered in her chest. The Germans had smashed Madame Severin's chairs as if they were matchsticks. How was an oak wardrobe going to be safe? An image of Simone's terrified look loomed large in her mind. What if the Germans found them, dragged them from the wardrobe and did to her and Marie whatever it was they'd done to the refugees?

Dominique listened; her ears keened for any noise that signalled the Germans had crossed the threshold into their home. She closed her eyes, screwed up her face. Perhaps she should have listened to her mother. They could have escaped through the tunnel that went from the cellar to the ramparts. She could have skirted back around to Nathalie's.

It was too late now.

For whatever reason, fortunately, the Germans didn't cross the road. The Favier family home was spared on this occasion.

"Look, Dominique." Marie pointed at the retreating Germans. "They're leaving."

They watched from the safety of the window as the soldiers left Rue Brancion wandering back past Francois who hadn't moved.

"Französischer abschaum!" The last of the soldiers gave Francois a final 'just-to-be-sure' kick as he yelled his insult.

The girls stayed where they were as the harrowing noises slowly abated putting a distance between them and the attackers.

"They must have left town." Dominique let Remy jump down and slowly unfurled her legs which had gone numb beneath her.

She stood and shook herself. The moment felt surreal. Did she witness what they'd thought? She leant back to peer out the window to check on Francois. He had rolled up to a sitting position, holding his head in his hands.

"Francois is still alive." Dominique rushed to the door. "We must go and help him."

Dominique and Marie scrambled to the end of the street, dodging the debris that littered the cobbles. They peeked around the corner, down towards Porte Faroleaux and back towards the town hall to check there were no lingering Germans, before going to Francois. He groaned with agony as they helped him stand. One under each arm they escorted him hobbling back to Dr Favier's surgery. They were lowering him into a chair when Henri came through the door.

Lucie, Louis and Victor soon followed.

"Henri." Lucie rushed to her husband's side. "Where have you been when I needed you?"

"I'm sorry, my dear." Henri kissed Lucie's cheek. "I've been at the hospital. I had to shelter there until it was safe to come home."

"It was terrible." Lucie looked like she was about to faint. "The Germans. They were going to get us."

With one eye on Francois, Henri took Lucie's hands in his.

"It's alright, my dear," he said. "They've gone now. I'll just tend to Francois and be right with you. Marie, please make my wife a hot drink to calm her nerves. Boys, take your mere to the sitting room and make her comfortable."

"Dominique?" Lucie's look went from helpless to angry. "We need to talk about your daughter. She doesn't listen to anything I say. Endangering us all."

"I didn't ..." Dominique protested. "We were ... I found Remy, kept him safe."

"What's done is done," Henri said. "Let me tend to Francois and we can discuss this later."

Henri turned his attention to the injured baker, making it clear there would be no more conversation at this point.

"Dominique, fetch me a clean cloth and some water to clean these wounds."

Knowing it would be easier to gain her pere's support, she did as he asked.

Once the blood was cleaned away, Francois didn't look quite so bad. His swollen right eyelid was stained indigo and swelled shut. Henri removed Francois' torn shirt before helping him onto the examination table. His torso was covered in red welts, slowly darkening as the bruising emerged.

Henri's gentle examination still prompted groans of pain.

"I think you may have cracked ribs, Francois. You'll need to take it easy for a while. No heavy lifting." Henri moved to the foot of the table. "Any pain to your legs and feet?"

"He was limping, Pere," Dominique stepped up beside Henri. "I think his right ankle might be broken."

"Or badly sprained? Let's not be overly dramatic, Dominique. We examine the patient, learn the facts and draw reasoned conclusions."

Not like my mere.

"Aargh!" Francois's face screwed up in agony as Henri gently untied and loosened laces to wriggle the boot off his right foot.

"Remove his left boot, please, Dominique," Henri instructed.

Dominique jumped at the opportunity to assist. It was a first. Her pere used to ask Eugenie, then Marie. Now it was finally her turn. There were some advantages to the German attack. She proceeded carefully, watching Francois's face for any sign she was being too rough.

Comparing the two, it was easy to see the swelling in the right foot, but Francois was able to wiggle his toes and there were no obvious bones protruding so Henri concluded it was a bad sprain.

"We should be able to borrow some crutches from the hospital, but you will heal faster if you have a few days bed rest."

"Who will do my baking?"

"It sounds like Dominique might need a job to keep her out of trouble." Henri looked sideways at Dominique. "Perhaps she can help you."

It was easy to assume the Germans had left town, that's what Dominique wanted to think; except that they would be persecuting those who lived to the south, or even worse they could be on the tail of the Belgian refugees. Nobody deserved their ill treatment more than once. Nobody deserved it at all.

The townsfolk gradually emerged from wherever they'd been sheltering. They gathered in small groups in the battered streets, checking on their neighbours and inspecting the damage. Dominique and her pere joined those congregating outside the Severin homestead, peering through the damaged frontage.

"Are we safe?"

"Have they gone?"

Slamming doors, yelling children, noises, which on any other day would have been ignored, had the townsfolk twitching nervously, scanning the street, wide-eyed and alert to any danger.

"I'll kill them if they come back."

"Look what they've done."

"Poor Madame Severin. It was just as well she'd left. Imagine what they'd have done to her, if she'd still been here."

The house was battered and beaten but not destroyed.

"We'll board up the windows, fix the door," Henri suggested.

"But what if they've trashed the inside as well?" a concerned neighbour asked.

"We'd best check that out too."

Dominique followed the small delegation that stepped over the smashed front door and entered the house. She probably should have stayed outside to help the others sweep shards of glass from the cobbles but a fear she was trying to batten down needed to be reassured. If the Germans came back, if they got inside their house, could she still be safe?

The disarray did nothing to quell the fear. Furniture, or what was left of tables and chairs, was strewn across the room. Half eaten, discarded food scraps were trampled into the flooring or splattered against the walls and ceiling hanging in precarious splodges. Dominique sucked in a breath and swallowed the lump threatening to choke her. The stench was unbearable. Not of food because it hadn't had time to rot or go rancid but of urine and faeces. The Germans hadn't bothered to find the toilet. They'd relieved themselves where twenty-four hours ago Madame Severin would have been eating her lunch. Trails of urine left dark stains down the walls. The drapes, torn from their rails were smeared with faeces. Dominique gagged and ran into the street. The contents of her stomach added to the mess outside.

"Best you get to work." Henri rubbed his daughter's back. "Take your mind off it. Collect the bits of wood and take them to the woodshed."

Robotically Dominique followed her father's suggestion. She tried not to imagine what the splintered pieces of timber she gathered into her arms had previously been; a chair, the frame of a window or a door that should have kept intruders out.

A neighbour added a final few pieces to her load, tucking them under her chin. "It's hard to unsee what you've already seen, isn't it?"

"Oui." Dominique's reply was barely a whisper as she carried the wood out to the shed that jutted out from the high brick wall at the back of the yard.

They'd begun the job of restocking the shed after the last long cold winter but there was still plenty of wood to be gathered. At least the Germans had helped with that task.

Louis and Victor were back playing in the garden as if nothing had happened. Remy running about with them, as fast as his short legs would allow.

"Peow!" Louis threw a still-green walnut directly at Victor, yelling triumphantly when he hit his target. "Gotcha! You're dead!"

"Louis!" Dominique stormed over to her brother. "That's not funny."

"But I'm a French soldier," Louis protested. "And I just killed a German."

Dominique opened her mouth to speak but what could she say? Nothing. Not when she wanted to kill a German too. Not just one but every one of them that threatened to hurt or destroy everything precious to her.

Chapter 6

Dominique was meant to be asleep but tiptoed back downstairs to get a glass of water. When she heard her mother mention her name, she stopped on the landing, close enough to their slightly ajar bedroom door to be able to hear but next to the stairwell so, if necessary, she could pretend she was innocently passing by.

"We must send Dominique away, Henri. It isn't safe for her to stay here."

"Where would we send her, Lucie?"

"She could join Eugenie. I'm sure my aunt wouldn't mind."

There was a deafening silence Dominique itched to fill with a scream of protest. It would be wonderful to see Eugenie again, but how could she abandon everyone here? Nathalie with her sick pere. Francois with his injuries. Gabriel who may return and not know where to find her.

"Please, Pere, don't make me leave," she whispered.

"The Germans have gone, Lucie. The fighting has moved south. The town should be safe now."

"South!" Lucie sobbed. "Will they reach Paris? Will Eugenie be safe? Should we get her back here?"

"Oui! Oui!" Dominique covered her mouth with her hands to stifle her excitement. Eugenie home, instead of her going away, that would be wonderful.

"The best thing we can do, Lucie, is try to get some rest." Henri's sigh was audible. "Everything will look different on a new day and perhaps there will be some more information on which to base our decisions."

"We still need to keep Dominique out of trouble. She won't listen to a thing I say."

"She is going to help Francois in the patisserie. Until he is back on his feet. She'll have to be up at the break of day and will be so exhausted after a day of baking, she won't have any energy to get into mischief."

"Mischief? I don't get into mischief," Dominique grumbled as she continued down to the kitchen. "I can't help if I'd rather be out lending a hand than sitting doing embroidery."

Her pere was right though, she'd better hurry back to bed to get some sleep so she'd have plenty of energy to help Francois.

"Bonjour Francois." Dominique tried to sound as bright and cheerful as the doorbell that would have announced her arrival if it hadn't been torn from its perch. "Where would you like me to start?"

She glanced around the bakery expecting to see the disarray left by the Germans, but the tables, trays and baking pans all looked to be back in their rightful space. Francois had even managed to get the fire started so the oven was heating up.

"The neighbours put everything right for me," Francois explained as his hands deftly worked a fresh batch of dough. "With my crutch I can hobble around here."

"Oh, but Pere said I am to help you out for the day."

Francois rubbed his chin with the back of his floury hand. "You could take the trolley to the mill and get another sack of flour. That would be helpful."

"Oui, oui." It was the perfect job, allowing Dominique to inspect the damage across town. She grabbed Francois's rickety trolley from the corner. "Au revoir. I'll be back soon."

With a wonky wheel it was hard enough to push the trolley across the cobbles, without adding the weight of a sack of flour.

"Oh, well, you've got to take the good with the bad, Dominique." She mimicked her father's saying and deep tone of voice.

Everyone was out and about. The town almost appeared normal except there was a tension in the air. The townsfolk were on edge, glancing over their shoulders as if they expected someone was following them, peeking around the corners to check the way ahead was clear. Around the town square women went in and out of shops, each time emerging with their baskets laden with more supplies.

"Bonjour, Madam Gadron." Dominique's cheerful demeanour was met with a silent scowl from the mother of one of her school friends.

When Dominique leaned closer to peer into the woman's basket, she pulled it protectively into her side and shielded the groceries with her arm as if Dominique had been about to pilfer them. Dominique shrugged off the perceived accusation and continued around the square. From what she'd seen, the basket held nothing exciting, only staples like rice, coffee and butter.

There was a queue at the mill which Dominique assumed was normal until she joined the others lining up.

"I'm going to get as much as we can carry," said a woman with three young children in tow.

"Oui, we need to stockpile," another woman nodded in agreement.

"We can barricade ourselves in and have food to survive."

"Survive what?" Dominique asked.

The group of women stared wide-eyed at her, incredulous at her question.

"When the Germans come back, of course."

"But they've gone south." Dominique repeated what her father had said. Surely, he knew more than these women.

"Nothing to stop them coming back, child."

"They'll want to protect their backsides."

"Oui, or someone else will be on their tail."

It all sounded quite rational, but that would mean Dominique's father was wrong. Had he ever been mistaken before?

People exited the mill straining under the weight of the flour bags they carried, and the queue edged closer, its orderly state deteriorating into a jostling cluster of women desperate to get inside and claim their share. When Dominique finally made it through the door, she was shoved back against the wall.

"Watch out. That's mine." A woman pushed past her to grab one of the few remaining bags of flour.

Dominique gasped. She couldn't believe the scene before her. Her moment of inaction saw another sack disappear from the diminishing stores. She had to act or miss out. She rushed forward, using the trolley as a barrier, she lay claim to the last sack. Nobody helped her lift her heavy bounty and hitch it to the trolley. She was certain before yesterday, they would have. It seemed like the Germans had drawn a line that would define her life – the before and the after. So far, she preferred the before.

She swallowed, tried to dismiss the guilt that had her looking everywhere but directly at the people who would miss out. She'd only done what others had done. She wasn't being selfish. The flour was for Francois and if a baker was left without essential ingredients, then so many more would go hungry.

"Please charge this to Francois the patisserie's account." She raised her voice so the woman behind the counter could hear over the fracas that echoed around the mill. "When will you be getting more supplies in?"

"When?" The woman scoffed and looked sideways at Dominique. "*If*, child, *if*. The Boche have destroyed the crops, trampled right through the fields as if they were a main road or burnt them, just because they could."

Dominique stood wide-eyed and stunned, glued to the spot until she was prodded in the ribs from behind.

"Hurry up, will you," a woman growled. "I've got to get to the butchers, before he's got nothing left too."

On her walk back to the patisserie, Dominique saw the townsfolk in a totally different light. They were like worker ants scurrying about, amassing supplies to be stashed away, hidden from sight. Were they to be shared with the colony? She didn't think so.

Dominique delivered the sack of flour to Francois along with the bad news about the shortage of supplies.

"There will be other mills," he replied philosophically. "Here, test my latest batch of croissants."

That was why Dominique liked Francois, he always had delicious baking that made any problem pale into insignificance. She bit the end of the flaky pastry, closed her eyes and let the tastes melt into her mouth and her worrisome thoughts about the Germans dissolve.

"Magnifique!" she purred between mouthfuls.

Dominique licked the tips of her fingers, savouring every morsel of the croissant.

"What would you like me to do now, Francois?"

"I've finished baking for the day," he replied. "We just need to clean up and then you should go home and help your family."

Dominique spent the next hour with her hands in soapy water washing bowls and utensils. Her fingertips were wrinkled like an old woman's by the time she'd finished. She swept the floor, throwing the sweepings into the backyard as Francois had directed. The crumbs had barely hit the ground when several sparrows flew down from the fence and pecked at the bounty.

Before, Dominique would have assumed their chirps were a song of gratitude but after this morning, she saw things in a different light. The way their eyes darted around; the birds were more like the women at the mill warning others away from their cache.

"It's alright, little birdies, there will be plenty more. You don't have to panic."

The postman was about to put letters through the slot in the front door when Dominique arrived home.

"I can take those, Monsieur Pottier."

Startled, he dropped the letters.

"Sorry, I didn't mean to frighten you." Dominique retrieved the mail from the cobbles.

Her heart skipped a beat when she recognised Eugenie's handwriting, but her excitement was short-lived. The envelope was addressed to her father. She rustled through the rest of the mail, surely there was another one for her. Eugenie promised she would write every week. Nothing. Was Eugenie like everyone else? Thinking only of herself since the war broke out?

Dominique pictured her sister. Hers wasn't a face that gave any hint of selfishness; with eyes that sparkled with happiness, and a demeanour that exuded kindness and caring. They'd had their moments, screaming and yelling at each other but all sisters did. Theirs was a bond that even a war couldn't break.

Then it dawned on Dominique. Eugenie had written to their father, not their mother and her as she usually did. Something must have happened. Was she coming home? Was she getting married to Andre? Had the Germans made it to Paris already and she'd been injured? Possibilities raced through Dominique's mind as she stood, still in the street, frozen to the spot.

"Is it bad news, Dominique?" Monsieur Pottier asked, jolting her out of her reverie.

"Oh!" It was Dominique's turn to be startled. "Non. Well, I hope not."

"That seems to be all I'm doing nowadays." The postman's shoulders slumped and not just under the weight of his mail bag. "Delivering bad news."

"I'd better take it inside to find out." Dominique forgot to say goodbye, hurrying through the door without a backwards glance.

She found her parents in the dining room, seated at the table, a table laden with food like it was immune to the apparent shortages outside.

"It's a letter from Eugenie." Dominique waved the envelope in the air. Offering it, eager to hear good news but retracting it in case bad news would escape its folds.

"Hand it over, child." Henri's command wasn't to be ignored.

She placed the letter on his upturned palm before she crossed her fingers behind her back.

Henri didn't dally as Dominique would have, he hooked his thumb under the envelope's flap and retrieved the letter. He would no doubt deal with whatever news the letter brought with his usual calmness, while Dominique had to brace her knees together to stop them trembling. Eugenie's scent wafted from the pastel pink writing paper. It was almost like she'd returned home. If only she had.

Dominique watched her pere's face, hunting for clues as his eyes scanned the message. He reached the end, folded the paper and placed the letter back into the envelope. Seconds ticked by. The silence was deafening. Eventually, with his hands steepled, his elbows resting on the table, Henri looked directly at his wife.

"What is it, Henri? What is it?" Lucie implored.

It was too late for crossed fingers. Dominique brought her palms together in front of her chest. If luck wouldn't help Eugenie, then maybe prayers would.

Henri cleared his throat. "Eugenie has made a choice you are unlikely to agree with, my dear."

She's getting married. Andre has proposed. Oh, I hope it was on top of the hill at Montmartre or on the banks of the Seine, perhaps on lovers' bridge. Somewhere romantic. They could get married in Notre Dame cathedral. I could be bridesmaid.

"What are you smiling for, Dominique?" Lucie scalded. "You look like the cat that stole the cream."

"I'm just excited for Eugenie's news, Maman, that's all."

"Well, be quiet, child and let your pere tell us what it is."

Dominique itched to protest but instead took a deep breath and stood quietly looking at her Pere.

"She's volunteered to be a nurse in a military hospital." Once he'd relayed the news, Henri leaned back and took a deep, satisfied breath as if he was proud of his daughter's decision. She was after all following in his footsteps. Another of his offspring to venture into medicine.

"Non! Non!" Lucie gasped and clutched her hands to her chest. "She can't. This isn't what I had planned for her."

"She's going through training first. She'll be based in Paris, far away from the fighting. The war will likely be over before she even gets close to the front," Henri attempted to console his wife.

Dominique bit the inside of her cheek to quieten herself. She couldn't say that her mere wasn't worried about Eugenie being injured, perhaps she was, but she was more concerned that her eldest daughter was choosing medicine instead of a husband that could provide for her, allow her to be a lady of leisure, accord her the lifestyle her mere thought she deserved.

"Non! Non!" Lucie appeared inconsolable.

"It'll be alright, dear." Henri moved to stand behind his wife, he placed his calming hands on her shoulders and kissed the top of her head. "Everything will be alright."

Dominique picked up Eugenie's letter and inhaled her scent while she silently thanked her sister for paving the way, carving a life path that was different from what was expected, thus allowing Dominique to do the same, when she eventually decided where life would take her. There was some good to come out of this war after all.

**

"I must return to the hospital, my dear." Henri drank the last mouthful of his cup of coffee. "Dominique, stay with your mother, keep her company."

Dominique wanted to protest but kept her thoughts to herself. "Oui, Pere."

Her father's departure left a silent void, Dominique needed to fill.

"Everyone is stocking up on food, Maman. We should too."

"Food. How can you think of food at a time like this, Dominique?"

"If the shops end up with nothing on their shelves, then we won't be able to enjoy dishes such as these." Dominique waved her hand across the leftovers remaining on the table.

"Food is Marie's concern, not mine. I must go and write a letter to Eugenie, convince her to change her mind about this stupid notion to become a nurse."

Lucie sighed, stood and left the room. It was a relief. Dominique's presence wasn't required after all.

"Shall I clear the table now?" Marie came through from the kitchen.

"Oui. I'll help you," Dominique offered.

"No need for that, Dominique, it is my job."

"But I need to talk to you." Dominique ignored Marie and stacked the plates to carry them to the kitchen. "When I was in the square this morning everyone was buying up supplies. All the flour at the mill was gone. I got the last sack for Francois. What will we do if we run out of food?"

Marie laughed. "Trust you to be thinking about your stomach, Dominique. There will be more arriving. The Germans have passed through, everything will go back to normal. You'll see."

"I hope you're right."

"Besides there is plenty in the garden, fruit and vegetables," Marie replied. "The chickens give us eggs. We can get milk and meat from the farmers on the outskirts of town. Your meals mightn't be as grand as you're used to, but my family have survived for a long time on a lot less. We'll make do."

Chapter 7

25 September 1914

For the next month it was as if the view from Dominique's bedroom window was an oracle card predicting how the day would unfold. If the road to Englefontaine revealed a steady stream of Germans, marching on foot, riding horses or driving trucks piled high with ammunition boxes, then it was assured that someone somewhere would be suffering.

Stories filtered through on whispered chains or if they favoured the Germans were shouted out through the streets, the town crier forced to relay their messages for fear of being beaten. Dominique was on her way to visit Clemence and Alphonse when she heard today's announcements echo through the streets.

"The Council of War has reached its verdict. Augustine Delbecque, Priest from Maing to be executed."

"He's a priest. What could he have possibly done wrong?" Dominique muttered as she hurried to the cottage beside the brewery.

Clemence was busy sweeping the wooden floor beneath the kitchen table. She neither saw nor heard Dominique unlatch the gate, walk up the short path and knock on the open door.

"Bonjour, Clemence." Dominique's greeting carried its usual cheerfulness, but it still made her half-sister jump.

A flick of the broom scattered the pile of sweepings. "Oh, Dominique, look what you've made me do. I'll have to start again now."

"Not my fault you were a million miles away." Dominique leaned in and kissed Clemence on each cheek. "What were you thinking about?"

Clemence cupped her hands over the end of the broom handle and rested her chin on top. "Germans."

"You shouldn't give them the time of day," Alphonse came down the staircase, pulling his braces onto his shoulders. "Bonjour, Dominique."

"It's hard not to." Clemence sighed and shook her head. "Their impact is everywhere. Even in the hospital. They just look like any other young soldier when they're lying there, injured, out of uniform, bandaged."

"Did you hear the latest news?" Dominique asked.

"Non," Clemence sounded weary. "What message are they making the town crier call out now?"

"Augustine Delbecque, Priest from Maing to be executed," Dominique imitated the town crier's chant. "Why do they have to execute a priest? What could he have possibly done wrong?"

"Nobody is safe, Dominique," Alphonse answered for his wife. "Abbot Giloteaux was slapped and fined, just for refusing to salute a German soldier."

"Apparently, the priest had a letter from the Governor of Dunkirk," Clemence added.

"They don't need an excuse." Alphonse waved his fist angrily. "In Querenaing, they reckoned shots were fired at them, so they lined up a whole lot of civilians and executed them."

"Alphonse," Clemence put a calming hand on her husband's forearm. "Dominique is too young to hear of such atrocities."

"It's alright, Clemence. I saw what they did to Francois. All for a baguette."

Alphonse ignored Clemence. "I'd make damn sure I hit them if I was going to fire shots. Kill the damn lot of them."

"You must be careful, Dominique," Clemence warned. "It might be safer to stay home."

"I can't hide inside the sitting room, like Maman." Dominique knew Clemence agreed with her even though she remained quiet. "I need to be out helping, like you, Alice and Eugenie."

"Thank goodness you are not old enough to volunteer like Eugenie. Nursing is bad enough in the hospital without being at the front where she will be sent." Clemence swept the crumbs back into a heap in front of her, swapped the broom for a half brush and shovel and scooped up the sweepings. "Have you had a letter from her recently?"

"Oui, one arrived just the other day." Dominique's face lit up as if she was reliving the excitement she felt when the letter arrived. She smiled from ear to ear as she relayed Eugenie's news to Clemence and Alphonse. "She's finished her training and is just awaiting her orders as to where she will be stationed. Andre has been posted away. She's hoping to be going somewhere near him."

"Andre?" Alphonse arched his bushy dark eyebrows. "Who is Andre? And why haven't I heard about him before?"

Dominique giggled. "You sound like Pere. Andre is Eugenie's beau. He was working in the shoe factory before he enlisted."

"The shoe factory," Alphonse repeated. "That doesn't sound like prospective husband material your Mere would approve of."

"His pere does own the factory," Clemence added.

"Well, that makes it alright then," Alphonse teased.

The gate latch clunked again, interrupting any further conversation.

"Who could that be now?" Clemence leaned out to look.

The young boy standing on the doorstep had to catch his breath before he could speak.

"Hurry … you're needed … at the hospital … lots of people … hurt … burned."

"Soldiers?" Clemence asked. "More Germans?"

She looked reluctant to hurry anywhere if the new patients were Germans.

"Non," the boy shook his head. "Orchies. The Boche burnt it to the ground."

"Orchies?" Clemence sounded doubtful. "Why are they bringing them here? Valenciennes is much closer."

"Full up," the boy replied. "Too many injured for Valenciennes."

"You'd better go, Clemence," Alphonse said. "I've got to get to the brewery too. German soldiers demanded nearly all my supplies the other day. Lucky, I had some hidden away."

Clemence took off her apron, hung it over the back of the chair, kissed her husband and headed for the door.

"I'll come with you to the hospital," Dominique offered.

Clemence hesitated, looked as if she was about to tell Dominique she was too young, but she remained quiet. She probably knew any refusal would be like a red rag to a bull.

"Raus hier!" A German Soldier stood in the hospital doorway, barring the entrance. He waved his rifle, casting the new arrivals aside. The message was clear; the burns victims weren't welcome.

Alice appeared around the corner just as Clemence and Dominique reached the gathering throng.

"Quick! Bring them this way." Alice hooked her arm around the waist of an elderly man, offering support as he limped along, his hair singed, his clothes charred.

Desperate for help, the new arrivals didn't question her instruction and turned to follow her.

"Here, link hands," Clemence held her hands out to Dominique. Together they made a seat, relieving a mother of the weight of her child, before she collapsed under the strain.

The child whimpered, almost imperceptible.

"We'll have you back playing with your friends, in no time."

Dominique tried to reconcile Clemence's attempt to cheer the boy with the skin blistering on his forearms. She had to turn her face away, to inhale air that was free of the stench of burning flesh and hair.

They headed towards the back of the hospital. The Lowendaal barracks looked as damaged as the Orchesiens, but the building was better than nothing. One end of the barracks was still intact, its roof would provide shelter, the beds somewhere to rest while wounds were tended to.

"In here." Alice pushed the door open. "Find a bed. Rest. We'll get to you soon."

Clemence found the closest bed and she and Dominique lowered the boy onto the mattress.

"Merci, merci." His mother thanked them, more concerned about her son's injuries than her own.

"Dominique!" Alice strode up to the bed. "You shouldn't be here."

"But ... I can help."

"You should be in school."

"It's Samedi, Alice, the weekend, there is no school."

Alice sighed wearily. "We're so busy I don't even know which day it is."

"So, let me help," Dominique begged.

"You have no training." Alice's eyes darted around the makeshift ward as if she was assessing the patients' needs. "You'll just get in the way."

"I won't. I promise." Dominique directed her usual look of innocence at Clemence, her eyes imploring her to come to the rescue.

"I can look after her, Alice," Clemence volunteered. "She can run errands for me. We are short staffed."

"I'm too busy to argue with you," Alice harumphed, shook her head and walked away. "Make sure you stay out of trouble."

Clemence ensured Dominique had no chance to annoy Alice. As they worked their way around the makeshift ward, she fired out orders.

"Take these to the rubbish," handing over clothes that were beyond repair.

"Fetch me some more bandages."

"Help this man to have a drink of water."

"Hold this girl's hand while I attend to her mother."

That didn't stop Dominique from asking questions though. Each time she finished an errand she fired another question at Clemence.

"Why are these patients not in the hospital?"

"It's full up."

"With soldiers?"

"Oui."

"Are there more French soldiers?" The thought that Gabriel may have arrived without her knowing was always at the back of Dominique's mind.

"Non, German."

"Is that why Alice is so grumpy?"

"She's a busy nurse."

"So are you and you're never as grumpy as her."

Clemence paused as if she didn't know whether to agree with Dominique or not.

"She's just serious," she eventually replied. "She's very dedicated to her job."

"So are you." Dominique stopped. She stood, hands on hips, waiting.

"We weren't as lucky as you. Our mother died when we were both quite young. Alice was older, she had to grow up quick. She was forced to leave her childhood innocence behind."

Dominique glanced around the room at the wounded children. What was the world going to be like when these children grew up? They'd certainly been robbed of their childhood.

"Just like these children."

"Oui, and she's under added pressure today with the train arriving." Clemence sucked in a breath and clamped her mouth shut as if she'd said too much.

"Train? What train?"

Clemence shook her head and focussed on the bandage she was applying. Dominique knew she'd got all the information out of Clemence she was going to get today.

"Is that everyone seen to, Clemence?" Alice bustled up beside them.

"Oui. All the wounds have been cleaned."

"Good. I'd better get back to the hospital. You stay here and keep an eye on them. Thank you for your help, Dominique, you should head home now."

"Au revoir, Alice. Au revoir, Clemence." Dominique waved and left the barracks before her half-sisters could question her acquiescence. She knew they'd be shaking their heads and sighing, knowing full well she had no intention of going home. How could she? Not when there was a train arriving.

Instead, she headed to Nathalie's who most certainly would want to see the train as well. She rounded the corner and was about to cross the road to the mayor's house when she heard shouting, a cacophony of accents and tones, none of which sounded friendly.

"Kommen! Nun!" A German officer stood to the left of the open front door in a threatening stance. His spine ramrod straight, hands clasped behind his back, a scowl curling his mouth into an ugly sneer as he yelled commands that weren't to be ignored.

Achille Carlier was hauled from his home. Between two burly German soldiers, he looked like a dead weight, his shoes dragging on the ground, clomping down the stairs.

"He's recovering from a heart attack," Dominique muttered, wanting to demand they take care.

The mayor was manhandled into the rear seat of an army vehicle emblazoned with the German flag, closely followed by the officer.

The vehicle skidded on the gravel driveway, flicking a torrent of stones back at the house like bullet fire. Dominique huddled in an adjacent doorway until the car drove past. Once it had disappeared out of sight she ran to the front door where Nathalie and her mother were consoling one another.

"Nathalie! Nathalie, why are they taking your pere?"

"They're holding him hostage," Madam Carlier replied between sobs.

"Whatever for?"

"I assume it's because of the train." Nathalie passed her mother a handkerchief.

"It's going to the hospital," Dominique volunteered what she knew.

"Well, it's going to the train station, to pick up the German soldiers who are patients at the hospital."

"Oui, oui, you knew what I meant." Dominique rolled her eyes; Nathalie was always so precise. "But what's that got to do with your pere?"

"He's insurance," Madam Carlier said.

"To ensure nobody sabotages the train or the track," Nathalie added. "As if Pere would have anything to do with that."

"We'd best go then," Dominique reached out to take Nathalie's hand. "Do what we can to make sure they release him unharmed."

"You can't girls. It's too dangerous. If the Germans were to punish you too ..." Madam Carlier shuddered with the thought.

"We'll stay out of their sight. Hide in the trees on either side of the track." Dominique had it all worked out. "We'll keep an eye out for anyone that looks like they're up to no good. Well, anything that hinders or harms the Germans would be good, but not until Mayor Carlier is released."

"Oh, girls," Madam Carlier shoulders slumped in defeat. "I know anything I say will fall on deaf ears but please, please be careful."

Nathalie pecked her mother on both cheeks and she and Dominique hurried out to the footpath. They scooted to the end of the street, deciding the quickest route to the Gare du Quesnoy which sat to the north of the town. Whenever they saw anyone on the streets, they slowed their pace, walked, hand in hand, chatting away as if they were just out for a stroll.

They heard the train pull into the station before they saw it, its screeching brakes grinding the engine to a halt, steam and smoke pouring from its stack.

"I wish I could go on a train one day." Dominique remembered Eugenie's excitement when she set off for Paris.

Today's train was headed in the opposite direction but if Dominique ignored the German soldiers that disembarked from its carriages to stand sentry on the platform, she could still imagine an adventure lying in wait at the end of the tracks.

"Not this one." Nathalie brought Dominique back to reality. "Look there's Alain and Benoit sneaking around. I wonder what they're up to."

The boys, the same age as Dominique and Nathalie were on the other side of the station where there was another garden, with plants that mirrored those beside the girls; lavender with fragrant heads wafting in the breeze, lilac bushes past their spring best but still green and lush. The beauty of the gardens contrasted with the scene unfolding before them.

"Look, there's the car."

It stopped in front of Alain and Benoit and Achille Carlier was dragged from the back seat and ordered to stand on the platform. One German soldier stood beside him; a pistol pointed at his temple.

"Don't look, Nathalie." Dominique raised her palm in front of Nathalie's face, but Nathalie brushed it away.

"My pere's not afraid and neither will I be." Nathalie pointed, not to her father but at Alain and Benoit. "Look. The boys."

Dominique gasped as the butt of a soldier's rifle was slammed into Benoit's side. He cried out in pain and Alain raised his arms to protect himself from a similar punishment.

"Abhauen!" the soldier yelled, brandishing his rifle to indicate they should leave. "Abhauen!"

Wide eyed, the boys scurried away, Benoit hugging his ribs. The soldier scanned the area, and his eyes met Dominique's. She sucked in a breath, turned Nathalie towards the plants and bent over to sniff the lavender, hoping the innocence of two girls smelling flowers would save them.

The hairs on Dominique's arms and nape stood as rigid and alert as the soldiers on sentry. She looked at the heads of lavender but could only see a purple blur. Unsure whether to scream or cry, flee or stay put, she stood bent at ninety degrees, her legs trembling, for what seemed like forever but was likely only a matter of seconds.

Fortunately, her ploy was not tested as other vehicles arrived. They came from the direction of the hospital, trucks and ambulances in a convoy that pulled up beside the station. Dominique kept one eye on the mayor and one on the convoy as patients exited the vehicles.

Nathalie's pere stood still, he barely blinked, his face frozen into a mask that kept his thoughts about the Germans hidden. Perhaps that was the better course of action, instead of protesting loudly like Francois, or suspiciously like Alain and Benoit and getting beaten for your efforts. Or was he just bracing himself for whatever ordeal they would subject him to? Were they so brutal, once he'd served his purpose, he too would be beaten?

"They must be running out of soldiers," Nathalie whispered. "These ones will be going back to fight when they're better."

Most were back in their uniforms with the addition of head bandages, slings or crutches depending on their injury. One by one the patients filed into the train carriages and the vehicles that had delivered them to the station departed.

"Hopefully, the war will be over before that happens," Dominique replied.

It wasn't until the last patient had boarded and the train built up its steam to leave that the pistol pointed at Mayor Carlier's head was finally lowered. He staggered, seeking the support of a seat, as if he'd used all his energy to stay calm and he had nothing left to hold himself up.

Dominique looked heavenward and silently thanked whoever had kept him safe. Her legs felt wobbly too as she embraced Nathalie.

"He's safe," Dominique sighed with relief. "Let's help your pere get home."

She decided in that moment that anything she did to hinder the Germans would be so subtle they wouldn't even know it was subterfuge.

Chapter 8

7 October 1914

The thought that it was only Wednesday and Dominique had two more days of sitting on an uncomfortable wooden seat, in the confines of the classroom, struggling with algebraic formulae she had no idea how and when she would ever use again, left her fidgety, eager to run bare foot on the grass or dip her toes into the pond beyond the ramparts.

A glance at the clock hung high on the wall above the blackboard signalled the bell was due to be rung. The seconds ticked slowly by; the clock's big hand as reluctant as Dominique to stand up straight. She gazed out the window, imagining that all daylight would be gone by the time they were allowed to leave.

"Finally!" Dominique called out in relief as the bell ended the silence that was meant to keep the students focussed. An out of tune collection of raucous sounds filled the classroom. Chairs scraped across the floor, desktops were open and shut with a bang and excited conversations increased in volume as plans were hatched for after school activities.

"Come on, Nathalie, let's go for a walk. I need fresh air and sunshine."

"Shall we go watch the pelota in the square?" Nathalie suggested.

"Umm, I'm not sure." Dominique pretended she needed time to ponder the decision, but she knew Nathalie wanted to watch the boys play, or more precisely, one in particular.

The pink of Nathalie's cheeks heightened whenever Jean-Philippe was about, and she went scarlet when he spoke to her. It was the only time Dominique had known her friend to be speechless.

She broke into a smile and nudged Nathalie. "Of course, we can. Let's go."

With no music being played at the band rotunda next to the square, the hexagonal stand provided the perfect place for the girls to sit and watch the game. Dominique removed her shoes wiggled her toes, welcoming the sun's warmth.

Two teams of five had already started hitting the small black pelota ball backwards and forwards, throwing it with their gloved hands. Victor and Louis had joined the game, one on either team. They were the youngest, but their competitiveness meant they were more skilful players than some of the older boys.

Nathalie squealed with delight when Jean-Phillippe's shot flew past Louis ending the rally. Focussed only on the ball, Louis ran straight towards a line of German soldiers marching into the square.

"Louis!" Dominique was unsure how the soldiers would react. "Come away."

A black ball wasn't worth her brother bearing the German's wrath. The regular stomping of their footfall on the cobbles announced their arrival at the door to the barracks.

"What are they doing back?" Dominique hoped Nathalie would have the answer.

The soldiers ignored the children, unhitched their packs and went inside as if the barracks had been theirs all along.

"Looks like they're here to stay," Nathalie observed. "Perhaps I'd better head home."

"Me too." Dominique put her shoes back on, stood and brushed down her skirt. "Victor. Louis. We have to leave."

"We've time for one more round." Louis bounced the ball, getting ready to launch it at the other team. "Scores are equal. One more rally to show who's the best. The ball won't get past me again."

"We'll see about that." Jean-Phillippe swayed from side to side, ready to hit the ball whichever way it bounced. "Come on then."

Thwack! Louis took up the challenge, lobbing the ball towards the corner furthest from Jean-Phillippe. The older, taller boy reached across and hit it back with ease. *Thwack!* Louis barged in front of his teammates and hit the ball back. Backwards and forwards it went between the two, as if they were the only ones on the court.

The other children lined up around the square cheering them on, clapping and yelling so loudly they didn't hear the entourage of horses and vehicles arrive. The game continued, the excitement building. A soldier forced his way through the perimeter, his horse cutting a path as children scuttled to safety. He stopped behind Louis, distracting Jean-Phillippe who let the ball drop to his feet.

"Oui! I won!" Louis yelled, still unaware of the soldier behind him.

When he finally realised that all eyes were not on him and he wasn't receiving the accolades he expected, he turned to see who or what had taken the attention away. Louis gasped and stumbled backwards at the sight of the horse towering over him, ears back, black eyes staring. The ominous presence of the soldier overshadowed any triumph in a game of pelota. Louis quietly retreated to stand beside Dominique.

Unsure what to expect from the enemy in their midst, the crowd chose not to wait around to discover their intentions and quickly dispersed heading in different directions. Dominique grabbed her brothers' hands, one on either side. They might have been bravado with the big boys, but they were still her little brothers, and she needed to get them home safe.

There was no time for goodbyes. The trio ran across the square. Rue du Lombard veered off to the right. Dominique could tell Louis had expended his energy in the game, so she stopped at the corner to let him catch his breath. She glanced back, hoping the Germans were still at the barracks and the interruption to their game was just a show of power.

The entourage hadn't stopped though. They were headed in the same direction as them. The clip clop of the horses' hooves echoed on the cobbles. It used to be a sound Dominique found comforting. Not anymore.

"Quick!" She yanked on Louis's and Victor's hands and took off. "They're coming this way."

The trio turned at the first corner, left into Rue Brancion, panting as they ran up the small rise, not stopping until they'd ducked inside the door and pushed the lock across.

"Phew! Lucky, we live so close." Dominique leaned back on the door and caught her breath.

"What's lucky?" Henri came out from his office. "Have you been getting into trouble again?"

"Non!" the children protested in unison. "The Germans ..."

Thump, thump, thump.

Dominique jumped away from the door which rattled behind her.

"Offnen!"

"Come, children, away from the door," Henri ushered them towards the stairs. "To your bedrooms."

"Offnen!"

Thump, thump, thump.

Louis and Victor followed their father's orders, but Dominique went only so far as the top of the first flight of stairs. She crouched, kneeling on the top step, within hearing distance and just able to see her father slide the lock back across and open the door.

"Make way for Kommandantur Lubbert to inspect accommodation." The demand was in English but with a sinister German accent.

"What do you mean?" Henri asked as the uniformed man barged past him and inspected the entrance way to ensure it was clear for the officer who followed.

"Salute Kommandantur Lubbert!" The soldier saluted the officer and signalled for Henri to do the same.

Dominique squeezed her eyes shut. All she could imagine was the beating Francois received for not following the German's orders.

"Do it Pere, do what they say," she whispered.

She sucked in a breath and opened one eye, sighing with relief when her father lifted his hand to salute.

"Mayor Carlier has listed this dwelling as accommodation suitable for officers," the soldier who spoke English continued. "Kommandantur Lubbert will inspect."

"But ..." Henri hesitated.

Mayor Carlier would never want us to have Germans in our home, Dominique itched to finish her Pere's sentence.

Lubbert, a broad-shouldered man with a downturned mouth that looked incapable of forming a smile, strode past Henri without wiping his boots on the mat.

"This is not a request." The soldier stood opposite Henri, a mere six inches between them, and glared at him. "This is an order to be obeyed or risk punishment."

Henri stepped back out of the way and then followed the Germans as they disappeared from Dominique's view. Her mother's scream told her where they'd gone. The sitting room.

"It's alright Lucie," Henri tried to placate his wife. "We'll be safe as long as we do what these men want."

"And what do they want?" Lucie's question was high-pitched and full of panic.

"Apparently we are to accommodate some officers."

The shattering of a cup and saucer on the floor told Dominique her mere was less than happy about the intrusion into their home.

"Schlafzimmer?"

Dominique sucked in a breath, Lubbert's tone made whatever he'd said sound like a threat. Was her mere in danger? Should she run down the stairs and distract the Germans?

"Where are the bedrooms?" The English-speaking soldier asked.

Dominique wasn't sure if schlafzimmer and bedrooms were the same thing, but she scurried up the flight of stairs instead of down when she heard the clomp of boots coming in her direction. The soldier was the first to reach the landing, one hand on the pistol holstered at his waist. He pushed open the door to her parents' bedroom.

"That's our bedroom," Henri tried to lay claim to the room as if it would make a difference.

"Ein schlafzimmer," the soldier reported to Lubbert before crossing the landing to inspect the other bedroom with windows that looked down over Rue Brancion. "Zwei schlafzimmer."

"What's upstairs?" the soldier demanded.

Dominique pulled back from the wrought iron spindles holding up the banister, keeping out of view and silently praying they wouldn't come upstairs.

"My children's rooms," Henri answered.

Dominique looked heavenward and flopped back on the stairs when she heard footsteps head in the opposite direction, down the passageway to the rear of the house. At least her and her brothers' bedroom seemed safe.

"Drei schlafzimmer." The soldier's call echoed down the hallway before he rejoined Lubbert on the landing. "Kein blick auf die straße."

The pair conversed in German before the soldier relayed to Henri the decision that had been made.

"You will sleep in the back room. You will accommodate an officer in each of these front rooms. They will arrive in the morning. Understood?"

Dominique was back on her haunches peeking through the spindles watching her father's response. He raised his finger, opened his mouth to speak, then his shoulders slumped, and he remained silent as if he realised any protest would fall on deaf ears.

The Germans left as suddenly as they had arrived. No sooner had they gone and Henri summoned the family to the sitting room.

"From tomorrow we will have two German officers staying in the house." Henri stood beside Lucie; his reassuring hand rested on her shoulder.

"But how can they force us to do that?" Lucie demanded, clearly not placated by Henri's calmness.

"They're everywhere, Mere." Dominique reported what they'd seen. "They've taken over the barracks by the pelota court."

"Oui," Henri sighed. "It appears they've taken control of Le Quesnoy. We are now living in occupied territory."

"What will that mean for us?" Lucie dabbed a lace handkerchief at the corners of her eyes.

"It will be better to stay out of their way," Henri answered. "Children, play in your bedrooms or in the back yard. Don't do anything to aggravate them. Understand?"

Louis and Victor looked terrified; their eyes bulged as they nodded in unison.

"Unfortunately, we will have to vacate our bedroom as well." Henri straightened as if he was bracing himself for Lucie's reaction.

"Non! Sacrebleu!" She protested, waving her arms about. "My clothes, my jewellery, my precious things."

"We're just going to sleep in the room at the back of the house. Dominique and Marie can move all your things. You'll have a lovely view of the garden."

"Non! Non! Non! How can they? What else will they do?"

Dominique's stomach churned. *What else will they do, Pere?* She silently repeated, anxious for his answer.

"It won't be for long. You'll see. The French will soon defeat them and turn them back to their own country."

Dominique frowned and looked askance at her pere. His response wasn't what she wanted. He didn't answer the questions. Did he not know, or did he think his family knowing would serve no purpose? Was he trying to protect them? From what? If her pere wouldn't say, then Dominique would have to find out from other sources. She needed to talk to Nathalie.

Dominique and Marie moved everything from the front bedroom to the bedroom at the back of the house. Lucie wouldn't lift a finger to help the Germans. She flitted in and out of the room an hour later to inspect.

"Change the linen," she demanded. "Get the old grey bedspread from the cupboard and swap it for this one. They just need a bed, the essentials, not luxury."

"I can do it." Marie waited until Lucie went back downstairs. "You go see Nathalie and find out what you can, before the soldiers arrive tomorrow."

"Merci, Marie." Dominique didn't wait for the offer to be made a second time.

She grabbed a jacket from the hook inside the front door and left before anyone could tell her she shouldn't be out and about on the streets.

Rue Brancion was bare, not a person nor an animal in sight. She glanced in the window of Francois's patisserie, hoping to see his familiar face. The shop was empty. The streets were eerily quiet. Window shutters were closed. Whether the townsfolk were hiding inside or had left town was unknown. Dominique tried to pretend nothing had changed but the silence made it difficult.

A dog barked. Dominique flinched, her eyes darting about. Perhaps she should have stayed at home. She reached the town square. Sentries were posted on each corner; their grey uniforms merged with the concrete buildings. She imagined them all looking at her, their blue eyes icily cold, their rifles ready to shoot any perceived threat. Would they see her as a menace? Would they be a danger to her? She pulled her jacket tight across her chest, pressing her elbows into her sides. She needed them to think she was younger than her sixteen years, merely an innocent child running an errand.

The quickest route to Nathalie's was straight across the square but Dominique's feet refused to take her. The Carlier house seemed too far but she was over halfway now. It was too late to turn back.

French soldiers occupied the yard in front of the mayoral chambers the last time Dominique had been there. If only they could be there again. She held her breath as she reached the corner, clinging onto the slimmest of chances her wish might be true.

"Damn!"

German soldiers patrolled the area. A sea of grey, like a threatening storm, dark and ominous, impenetrable. Dominique pulled back before they saw her. She huddled in a doorway, out of sight, while she pondered her options.

Mayor Carlier's Brouhout car was still parked outside. Nathalie and her family should still be at home. Madam Cacheux would be in the kitchen.

"I'll skirt around the back. Come in through the kitchen." Dominique jumped when she realised, she'd given voice to her plan. "Don't be paranoid," she whispered. "Nobody heard you."

She crossed Rue Strasbourg, trying to pretend nothing was amiss while her heart thundered in her chest. She kept her head down until Rue Strasbourg met Rue Goa and then darted down the road that ran behind the Carlier house. The furrowed bark on the trunk of an oak tree in the backyard provided a brief respite until Dominique was sure she could reach the kitchen door without being seen. She darted across the lawn, not stopping to take a breath until she was inside.

"Dominique!" Madam Cacheux looked as shocked to see her as Dominique felt being there. "What are you doing here? It is not safe to be out and about."

Dominique tiptoed to the door that led to the rest of the house and put her ear against it. The voices she heard were muffled but they bore deep masculine tones and spoke German not French.

"Is Nathalie still here? Is Mayor Carlier still in control? Have *they* taken over?"

"Come away from the door, Dominique." Madam Cacheux wiped her hands on her apron. "Kommandantur Lubbert has set himself up in the meeting room. They've demanded a cup of tea."

"You should put poison in it." Dominique's pulse raced. What if they could fight the battle from the inside, win the war that the soldiers were struggling to? Nobody would think she was a child if she arranged it.

"Dominique," Madam Cacheux placed a calming hand on Dominique's forearm, making sure she had her attention before she continued. "We are not going to poison the Kommandantur. I am sure they will be wise to such tricks and likely require someone French to drink first to prove it is safe. I don't want to be that person."

Madam Cacheux was right and if it wasn't her, it would be Nathalie's pere that became the guinea pig. They'd already threatened him with punishment.

"Where's Mayor Carlier?" she asked, concerned for his health.

"The councillors are meeting elsewhere," Madam Cacheux replied. "At Monsieur Menu's café I believe. Nathalie is in her room. If you wait until I take the cup of tea through, you can sneak up the stairs without them knowing. Just be very careful."

Dominique paced impatiently until the tea was brewed and cups and saucers assembled on a tray.

"Your impatience will get you into trouble, child," Madam Cacheux warned. "Wait until I reach the meeting room before you leave the kitchen."

Despite being annoyed at being referred to as a child, Dominique heeded the cook's warning. She waited for the clunk of the tray on the meeting room table before she tiptoed upstairs to Nathalie's bedroom.

"Dominique!" Nathalie jumped up from her bed. "What are you doing here? It's not safe."

"Oui, people keep telling me." Dominique's energy sagged as she flopped down on Nathalie's bed. She hadn't realised how tense she'd become. She slowed her breath, inhaling and exhaling before she spoke. "We must provide beds for two German soldiers. I had to know why your pere would offer our home to them."

Nathalie's eyes fixed on the door as if she was scared someone was going to burst through it.

"The Kommandantur has taken over my parents' room." Nathalie spoke quietly, almost monotone, like she was resigned to the fact. "They have to sleep in Gabriel's room."

"You have Lubbert in your home!" Dominique pictured the German's downturned mouth and dismissed her own worries.

"Pere had no choice. They threatened him. We were so worried he would have another heart attack."

"Is he alright?" Dominique stood and hugged her friend.

"The councillors are meeting at the café, discussing how Quercitains should deal with the German presence."

"We can't let them get away with it." Dominique held Nathalie's hands as if jointly they would have a combined strength to fight. "We can't."

Chapter 9

"Now straight to school and straight home again," Henri instructed Dominique, Louis and Victor as they arrived in the entrance way with their satchels.

"Oui, Pere." Dominique gave the expected response unsure she would abide by his direction.

Henri pulled back the lock and kissed his children one by one on the forehead as they stepped into the street.

Dominique came face to face with two soldiers who stood pointing at the plaque on the front of the building. A shiver ran down her spine and her jaw clenched. The urge to bare her teeth like a wild dog was strong. She'd never been this close to a real live German.

The one on the right wore glasses and with his cap stood not much taller than Dominique. She looked him up and down, following the polished buttons on his jacket, and imagined its high collar would be itchy on his neck. He wasn't broad like Lubbert, not even as muscled as she imagined Gabriel was, almost puny and not designed for fighting at all. He was clean shaven except for his moustache. She judged that to be an attempt to make him look older, give him a seriousness his blue eyes betrayed.

"On your way, Dominique," Henri prompted.

Her assessment of the perceived enemy was cut short. She glanced at the other soldier, saw him eyeing her and quickly turned to catch up with Victor and Louis. She shook her head, trying to rearrange her thoughts and gain some clarity. Nothing made sense. The soldiers looked like any other young men, but they weren't. She'd witnessed what they were capable of. Were the two men who were going to be sleeping downstairs from her like the other German soldiers, the ones who beat Francois, ransacked Madam Severin's house, threatened Mayor Carlier and executed an abbot? The answer scared Dominique.

The trio reached the end of Rue Brancion just as more soldiers emerged from Francois's patisserie, their arms laden with baskets of baguettes, croissants and loaves of bread.

"Wait!" Dominique stopped her brothers. "Wait until they've gone."

Francois limped from the bakery, shaking his head, waving his fist at the backs of the soldiers.

"Sacrebleu!" Francois's shoulders slumped, as if the fight had drained from him.

"You keep going, Louis and Victor." Dominique didn't want her brothers to bear witness to whatever damage the soldiers had inflicted. "I'll catch up. I'll just check on Francois."

She waited until the boys were out of earshot and hurried to the baker's side.

"Are you alright, Francois? Did they hurt you again?"

"Moi, and everyone else," Francois replied.

Dominique scanned him for injuries but there were no fresh visible wounds. "Where did they hurt you?"

"They've taken all my baking. There's nothing for anyone else." Francois sighed. "No croissant for you today, Dominique."

"Tomorrow, Francois, tomorrow will be different."

"Non!" He rubbed his forehead. "The Boche have demanded the same tomorrow. And the day after. Their troops must be fed, they said. They do not care about the Quercitains. They're not going to shoot us. They're going to starve us to death."

"We'll think of something, some way around their demands."

The school bell ringing dragged Dominique back to the present. She saw her brothers had reached the school gate and were about to enter.

"Oh, non, I'll be late for school." Dominique hurried off. "Don't give up, Francois."

"Nathalie, you must tell your pere," Dominique waited until the teacher was busy at the blackboard before she leaned toward Nathalie and murmured. "The Germans demanded all the baking Francois did this morning. There is none left for the townsfolk. We must do something."

"He knows," Nathalie whispered, her eyes still on her schoolwork. "It wasn't just Francois's baking they took; it was all the patisseries."

"The Kommandantur is fat enough." Dominique puffed her cheeks to mimic Lubbert. "He doesn't need our food."

"Pere and the councillors will be visiting Francois and the other bakers now." Nathalie glanced around the classroom, ensuring no-one was paying attention to them before continuing. "They're organising a second bake."

"But won't the Germans just take that too, if it's sitting in the patisseries?"

Nathalie tapped the side of her nose with her forefinger. "It won't make it to the shelves. It is to be delivered to the hospital courtyard where the townsfolk can collect it."

"Surely the Germans will find out?"

"Non, it will all happen under the cover of darkness."

A delighted chuckle escaped Dominique, one that drew the attention of Mademoiselle Forestier. Dominique quickly covered her mouth with her fingers and tried to pretend it was a hiccup.

"Excuse moi," she apologised to maintain the ruse.

The teacher was beside Dominique's desk in a flash. Her wooden pointer waving about, seeming to seek out Dominique's knuckles which had been safely stowed under the desk.

"Your work, Dominique! Practice your handwriting or you will never amount to anything."

"Oui, mademoiselle."

I don't need handwriting to amount to something. Just you wait and see.

Curiosity about the Germans staying under her roof and the need to protect her brothers had Dominique hurrying home straight after school. The delicious aroma from Francois's afternoon bake wafted into the street as they passed, even though his 'closed' sign was up and the blinds down. She could almost taste the croissants, feel the flaky pastry dissolving on her tongue. She'd have to find a way to get to the hospital courtyard tonight.

The postman was about to push some envelopes through the slot in the door as they arrived home.

"Monsieur Pottier," Dominique called out as Victor and Louis pushed past to get inside. "I'll take those."

"No letter from your sister this time." The postman handed over the mail.

"She'd better write soon. Her news from beyond the ramparts gives me hope." Dominique flicked through the envelopes in case he was wrong. "And I've got so much to tell her, but I don't have an address to send my letter to."

"It doesn't matter. Your letter wouldn't make it to her even if you knew the address."

"Why ever not?" A frown crinkled Dominique's forehead.

"The Germans are not letting anything come in or out."

"Why ever not?" Dominique repeated her question.

"My instructions are clear." Monsieur Pottier's ashen face told Dominique he'd been made aware of the implications of disobeying. "All letters from free France are to be marked 'Place of Destination Invaded' and returned to sender. All letters to free France are to be handed to the Germans."

"They might still send them," Dominique said with more hope than she truly felt. "If there's nothing of importance to them inside."

"Send them to the incinerator," the postman replied despondently.

"We'll have to resort to carrier pigeons to get our messages out." Dominique laughed but it was an option to be considered if nothing else would work.

"They've thought of that too." Monsieur Pottier shook his head. "They've sent a notice around. The use of carrier pigeons is prohibited. Offenders will be punished. Five years' imprisonment and a fine. Or even the death penalty."

"Oh, non. What will the people do with their birds? I hope the Boche don't want to eat them too," Dominique swallowed. "... or force us to."

"Not at this stage. The pigeon owners must keep them locked away." The postman hitched his mailbag back onto his shoulder. "I'd best be off."

As Monsieur Pottier was about to walk off, it dawned on Dominique that he would be the perfect person to let people know about the secret bake. He'd know which townsfolk to trust and who would likely reveal the scheme to the enemy.

"Monsieur Pottier." Dominique glanced up and down the street before she spoke. She chose her words carefully, not wanting to impart information that could jeopardise everything. "There's a special supply of bread just for the townsfolk. If you know of anyone in need, tell them to contact me."

"Merci beaucoup, Dominique." The offer raised the postman's spirits, and he smiled. "Au revoir. Take care."

Dominique didn't expect to see her mother enjoying a cup of coffee with the Germans, but her curiosity needed them to be somewhere in the house. She was disappointed to learn from Marie that they'd merely inspected their rooms, dropped off their belongings and gone away again.

She crept upstairs with the intention of discovering more about them. It felt strange to be sneaking about in her own house. She seemed to be doing it with greater frequency of late. The door to what used to be her parents' bedroom was closed. Dominique turned the doorknob, first one way and then the other but the door didn't budge. It had never been locked before. The key always sat in the keyhole. The knowledge that it could be secured if needed was comforting enough. But now it was locked, by someone who shouldn't have the right to bar them from their own property.

"What are you hiding, soldier?" Dominique folded her arms across her chest while she pondered the answer.

She tried the door handle again, perhaps she hadn't turned it far enough, but the door remained firmly shut. She knelt and peeked through the keyhole. Everything appeared normal, not the same as when her parents occupied the room, but with the ugly grey blanket her mere had insisted upon. A canvas rucksack on the bed looked as if it had been carelessly abandoned.

Dominique sighed, sagged down to the floor and leaned her back on the door.

"Perhaps you have nothing precious. You're just a soldier." Even as she said the words she knew they couldn't be true. Everybody has something or someone they hold dear. She would just have to delve further to find his secrets.

"What are you doing sitting there, Dominique?" Louis arrived at the first-floor landing, tossing a ball from one hand to the other.

"Don't throw balls inside, Louis." Dominique's reprimand took the attention away from her. She wasn't going to explain to her little brother what she'd been doing. She stood and brushed down her skirt.

"I'm not throwing, I'm juggling," Louis protested.

"Well, if you drop your juggling ball and it breaks one of Mamon's ornaments, you'll be in trouble."

Louis's eyes went wide. He grasped the ball and hugged it into his chest as he ran up the second flight of stairs.

Dominique heard his bedroom door slam. With Louis out of the way, she headed across the landing to try the other bedroom door, hoping the second soldier wasn't so worried about his privacy.

"Très bien!"

This door wasn't locked. Like a cat that had just discovered a bowl of cream, with a big smile Dominique crept into the bedroom and eased the door closed behind her. This soldier had already unpacked. A small photograph in a silver frame sat on the bedside table. Even out of his uniform she recognised the second soldier, the one who'd looked her up and down. He posed sitting with two children, one on either knee, boys, twins, about the same age as Louis and Victor. *He had a family.* The thought was comforting, as if he would be kinder because he had children of his own.

Dominique replaced the photo frame, tweaking the angle at which it sat to ensure her visit couldn't be detected. She quickly checked the drawers and the wardrobe. She had no idea what she hoped to find so wasn't disappointed when all she saw were undergarments neatly folded in the drawers and shirts and trousers hanging in an orderly fashion in the wardrobe. A pair of slippers and a pair of highly polished dress shoes sat in a line on the floor of the wardrobe, as if they too were soldiers reporting for duty. There was nothing out of the ordinary, she likely would have found the same items if she bothered to snoop in her pere's wardrobe.

It was dark outside by the time Dominique heard deep voices, speaking in a foreign tongue, echoing up the stairwell. She'd been reading a book or at least attempting to do so by candlelight. A breeze sneaking in through a crack around the window frame made the flame flicker across her pages, casting shadows over the words she'd been struggling to concentrate on.

Still dressed, she climbed quietly out from beneath the bedcovers, picked up her shoes and carried them out of her bedroom, tiptoeing along the passage so as not to disturb her sleeping brothers. At the top of the stairwell, she paused, turned her ear to listen for the click of keys turning. Once to unlock, again to lock and then repeated for the other bedroom. Satisfied the soldiers had retired for the night, Dominique crept down the two flights of stairs avoiding the squeaky boards which would give away her presence.

She reached the entrance and let out a sigh of relief as she slipped her feet into her shoes and took her jacket from the coat stand.

"Where are you going, Dominique?"

Dominique jumped in fright, then froze while replies to the question raced through her mind. None of them seemed viable. She was so busy searching for answers that she failed to consider who'd asked the question and why. Slowly, it dawned on Dominique that it was Marie standing behind her. Her pulse eased as she turned to face her.

"Bonsoir, Marie." Dominique smiled.

Marie too, was dressed, a cape over her shoulders and a wicker basket in the crook of her elbow.

"Are you going to get bread?" Dominique murmured a question instead.

"Oui, Mayor Carlier arranged a secret bake for the townsfolk."

"I was headed there too."

"No need," Marie said. "You head back up to bed. You've got school in the morning."

"You sound like Maman," Dominique groaned. "It'll be safer on the streets if there are two of us. These soldiers," Dominique pointed upstairs, "might be in bed asleep but I'm sure there'll be others out."

"Oui, you are right." Marie nodded. "I was a little worried but thought I could say I was a servant returning home at the end of my day."

"Come on then." Dominique slid the door lock quietly back. "We'll get there and back before anyone is any the wiser."

The pair slipped through the door into the darkened streets. The howl of a dog pierced the quietness and made Dominique and Marie clasp hands. Together they crossed the cobbles, pausing at the corner to ensure the soldiers patrolling Porte Fauroeulx weren't looking their way before they headed towards the town square. Sentries were posted on each corner, rifles over their shoulders, eyes and ears alert to any movement beyond the sphere lit up by their gas lamps.

"Best we avoid them." Marie pulled on Dominique's hand urging her to turn into a side street and avoid the square.

Forgetting to check the street first, they came face to face with a couple.

"Aufhoren!" Despite the German's angry sneer his command was slurred. His blonde fringe drooped down over his forehead, his tie hung loosely around his neck, the buttons of his shirt undone. He held a half empty bottle of wine in one hand, his other hand was draped over the shoulder of a woman.

"Madam Blaise?" Dominique couldn't keep her disbelief from her voice. "What are you doing?"

"I could ask the same of you two." Madam Blaise glared at Dominique and Marie; her red lipstick drawn into a harsh line.

"You're too young to be about the streets at this time of night. Best you head home."

"We were just ..." Unsure what excuse to offer, Dominique left her response hanging.

"Come on, Ludolf." Madam Blaise leaned into the German soldier and encouraged him to move on. "These children mean no harm."

The couple stumbled past, forcing Dominique and Marie to back up against the building bordering the street. Dominique leaned back against the cold brickwork

"Phew, that was close," Marie sighed. "We'll have to thank Madam Blaise."

"What ... whatever for?" Dominique stuttered, unable to believe that a woman behaving that way with a German soldier should be thanked.

"She probably saved us from that soldier."

"But what was she having to do in return?" A shiver ran down Dominique's spine. She didn't want to know the answer. Madam Blaise looked nothing like the woman Dominique thought she was. Her husband had enlisted, and she'd been cleaning people's houses to make ends meet. Surely that was enough.

"She knows what side her bread is buttered on." Marie sounded much older and wiser than her seventeen years.

The mention of bread jolted the pair back into action. They hurried along the streets, careful to stop at each corner and check the way was clear. On Rue de Strasbourg the rumble of a vehicle made them duck into the darkened corners of a door alcove, the shadows concealing their presence until the car, emblazoned with a German flag, drove slowly past.

"I think we'll have to go through the rampart tunnels next time," Dominique suggested when they were finally able to continue their journey.

"Oui, it might be safer."

A beam of yellow light squeezing under the hospital's front door, signalled they'd arrived. Dominique glanced up and down the street, checking no one was about before she edged the courtyard gate open.

A small group of townsfolk were huddled around a table in the corner, where Nathalie stood handing out baguettes, croissants and loaves of bread.

"Nathalie!" Dominique wasn't sure she could take any more surprises tonight. She didn't bother to ask what her friend was doing, that much was obvious, and she could understand why. It was important to help, to bolster the morale of the townsfolk, if they had no food, they wouldn't have the strength to fight back or at least resist destruction. Dominique went to help.

Chapter 10

22 October 1914

"Bonsoir, Dominique."

Clemence's greeting made Dominique jump. The loaf of bread she was about to hand over to a stooped elderly man who'd hobbled to the hospital courtyard dropped from her hands.

"You're going to have to stop coming. It's no longer safe," Clemence cautioned.

"I come via the tunnels, not the streets. I'm very careful, so there's little chance of being caught." Dominique defended her nightly outings.

It was strange scurrying through the tunnels under darkness. She'd been petrified the first time, her candle casting eerie shadows on the bricks. As a child the tunnels were a place of fun, games of hide-and-seek in the small alcoves, daylight shining through the air vents. The still of night amplified every sound. Dominique imagined rats scuttling over the earthen floor. Cobwebs remained hidden until her hand or face brushed through them. She knew, if you stopped long enough and listened carefully, vibrations would tell you how close the attacking enemy were. The method had been used for centuries but Dominique wasn't brave enough to pause, besides the enemy had already arrived.

"It's not the streets I'm worried about, it's here at the hospital." Clemence sighed, her cheeks drawn, almost gaunt, like she'd aged ten years since the war began. "The Boche are taking over the hospital."

"You'll have to nurse German soldiers?" Dominique's eyes went wide.

"Oui, but first we need to get the British and French patients out of here. Anyone that can walk through the doors has to leave for their own safety."

"How many are there?" Dominique let Nathalie finish the distribution and moved away with Clemence.

"About twenty," Clemence replied, "but one British and three French are barely conscious so they won't be going anywhere."

Dominique shivered. It wasn't the chill of the night that seeped into her belly, it was the dread of what the Boche would do next, how they chose to exert their power, demonstrate their ability to destroy whatever or whomever they chose.

"What will happen to them? Will the Germans kill them? Send them to a prisoner of war camp?"

Despite the curtailed mail delivery, stories filtered through. It seemed the options were a fast death by gunshot, a slow painful death by starvation at a prisoner of war camp or being made to work until you died of exhaustion.

"Don't worry, we won't let anything happen to them." Clemence straightened as if buoyed by the thought of outwitting the Germans. "We have a plan."

"Can I help?" Gabriel could just as easily be an injured soldier at another hospital and Dominique hoped someone would do the same for him.

Clemence shook her head. "It's too dangerous, Dominique."

"Someone has to help them."

Clemence lowered her voice to a whisper. "Sister Jeanne, Alice and I will get the sixteen men fed, dressed and out of the hospital. Alphonse will get them to the Foret de Mormal. Others will get them from there to freedom. The four remaining will have to go into the stable with all the local patients."

Alphonse. Dominique knew he wouldn't stop her from helping, unless Clemence had already told him to say no.

"Seems like you've got it all under control then," Dominique made her submission sound sulky so Clemence would be convinced she wouldn't pursue the matter. "I'd best get back to the bread distribution."

"We do need some clothes for them." Clemence followed Dominique back to the table. "Wearing their uniforms will be like having a target on their backs. You could ask the townsfolk collecting bread if they have any clothes they can donate. Shirts and trousers, socks and underwear."

Dominique smiled. "I'm sure the women with family who've gone to battle will be willing to donate. They'd want others to do the same for their husbands, sons and brothers."

"Merci boucoup, Dominique." Clemence kissed her cheek and headed back into the hospital.

By the time the remaining bread had been distributed, Dominique and Nathalie had offers of clothing sufficient to equip the sixteen who would be leaving tomorrow. If the donors couldn't drop the clothing at the hospital, the girls arranged to collect it from their homes. With school and a visit to Alphonse at the brewery as well, it was going to be a busy day.

Dominique had a restless night. Sleep eluded her as mental lists of what to collect from where, when to go, and how to get everything to the hospital without drawing the attention of the Germans formed, were discounted as impossible or too dangerous, and reformed.

The German soldiers were still at the breakfast table when she came downstairs. In the few weeks the men had been living under the Favier roof, she'd ascertained their names were Wolfgang and Hans. The names seemed appropriate. Wolfgang remained aloof as if he considered himself above the French. He looked at them with disdain through his wire rimmed glasses. Sometimes he eyed them up and down and spoke to Hans in a menacing tone with an evil laugh.

Dominique didn't trust Wolfgang. There was always a pistol in a holster at his hip. She imagined he wouldn't hesitate to draw it and would pull the trigger without a second thought for the consequences, the suffering he would cause. She tried to stay clear of him.

It was Hans who confused her. Much to her mere's consternation he tried to interact with Louis and Victor daily. He showed Louis how to juggle, not just two but three balls.

"I've been practicing." Louis grinned proudly, pushed his chair back from the table and pulled his juggling balls from his pocket. "I'm much better now."

He stepped back from the table and threw the first ball skyward, followed it with the second and then when the first landed in his left hand he sent the third ball up.

"Louis!" Lucie growled. She sat rigid at the end of the table, her eyes bulging.

Louis ignored his mother. His concentration was on the balls, his eyes following their movement.

"Gut gemacht." Hans applauded when he finished.

Louis puffed his chest out and smiled knowingly, lapping up the praise.

"Louis, get ready for school now," Lucie ordered.

He pouted as he glanced at his mother but followed her instruction. Hans reached out as Louis passed his chair. The soldier ruffled his hair and pulled Louis into his side for a hug.

Lucie gasped. The thump of her napkin, discarded on the table, made the china cup rattle in its saucer. She stood, her back straight, her chin held high.

"Victor and Dominique, leave the table. Now!" Lucie grabbed the twins by the hand, first Victor and then Louis, pulling him away from Hans and stormed from the room.

"But Maman," Louis protested, dropping his juggling balls.

Dominique retrieved the balls and hurried after her mother. She struggled to reconcile a German soldier who could kill a French man but be kind and gentle with ten-year-old boys and act as if he was proud of their achievements. He must be missing his own sons, the ones in the photo, she wasn't supposed to know about.

As soon as the afternoon bell rang, Dominique ensured her brothers were headed straight home, before she went in the opposite direction to Alphonse's brewery. She found him beside a vat pouring beer into glass bottles and waited until he'd finished filling a bottle before she announced herself.

"Salut, Alphonse."

Alphonse pushed a cork into the bottle; put it with the others he'd already filled and turned to face her.

"Salut, Dominique." He kissed her on both cheeks. "I know that look," he chuckled. "What are you after? You know I can't give you and your friends any bottles of beer, especially now the Boche are stealing my production."

"Non, I don't want anything from you, Alphonse. It's the other way around. I want to help you."

Alphonse raised an eyebrow and looked askance at Dominique. "Oui ...?"

"I can help you tonight. With the soldiers."

"You know about the soldiers?" Alphonse rubbed his bristly chin. "Of course you do. You seem to have a way of knowing everything that's going on. Such an innocent face, people trust you."

"So let me help you," Dominique tried to keep the pleading from her voice. "I could take them through the tunnels to the outskirts of town, so you don't have to bring your wagon into the hospital and raise the suspicions of the Germans."

"I was going to pretend I was making a delivery to the hospital," Alphonse justified his trip. "Swapping kegs for people, all under the cover of darkness and a tarpaulin over the *goods*."

"You won't fit sixteen men on your wagon though." It was a big wagon, but not that big. "You could take those with the worst injuries, and I could lead the others through the tunnels. Split the group up. Smaller groups are less likely to be seen. Increase their chances of a successful escape."

Dominique watched Alphonse mull over her reasoning only continuing when he began slowly nodding his head.

"I know my way through the tunnels as good as anyone," she added. "And I know the Foret de Mormal, all the best places to get shelter and remain hidden until the others come to get them."

"You know about the others?" Alphonse looked concerned as if Dominique was getting in too deep.

"Just that there are others, not who they are or how or when they will rescue the soldiers."

Alphonse sighed. "Just as well. It is too dangerous an association. The Germans are on the lookout."

"If I'm caught, I'll say I'm going to visit a sick aunt." Dominique let Alphonse know she'd thought of everything. It worked.

"I can see you are well prepared as always." Alphonse smiled knowingly. "And I imagine you will come along anyway, even if I say non."

"Merci, merci." Dominique gave her brother-in-law a hug. "What time shall I meet you?"

"Just after sunset."

"See you then." Dominique turned to leave before Alphonse had a chance to see sense and change his mind. "Au revoir, Alphonse."

Dominique excused herself from the table early. It was easy to do when their dinner was no longer the elaborate affair it used to be. Marie had created what she could from the diminishing food supplies available to the townsfolk.

The Germans ensured their own men were fed well and had no remorse if the butcher ran out of meat. He had to seek their approval to get a beast butchered, even then it was only one of the old, sick or very thin cattle. All the prime meat was reserved for the enemy.

The Favier family were fortunate compared to others. Their large back yard allowed plenty of room for fruit trees, a vegetable garden and a chicken run. The Germans demanded most of their eggs, but Marie snuck a few into a cache hidden in the cellar.

She'd used some tonight with the last of the jambon to make a quiche, with thin slices of tomato on top. Dominique enjoyed the quiche but noticed her despondent mere push the food around her plate. Usually, Dominique liked to avoid her mother's polite conversations, but the silence was worse. When her pere dined with them, he could draw her out, but he was at the hospital again. He said Doctor Flament requested his help, but Dominique assumed he would be busy ensuring the departing patients' wounds had clean dressings and the soldiers any medication they could spare.

"I'm going to visit Nathalie. We have some mathematics homework to do." It was only a small lie, better than causing her mere any unnecessary concern.

Lucie nodded. "Be back before dark." The request was more a gentle reminder than a rule not to be broken. It was as if the light inside Lucie had been dulled, a shortage of power, expunged by the Germans like everything else in the town.

"Oui, Maman." Dominique swallowed her guilt at further extending the lie. She hurried from the room before it made her change her plans.

When Dominique arrived at the hospital, Clemence was working her way up and down the long rectangular ward, ensuring each soldier received half a baguette, a slice of jambon and a thick wedge of brie. Rather than announcing herself and being sent home again, Dominique joined several aspirants, their nun's habits distinguishing them, who came in with the bundles of clothes the townsfolk had delivered during the day. Dominique added her collection to the pile and together they matched the soldiers to appropriate-sized clothing.

The aspirants' bashful giggling at the sight of half-dressed men drew the attention of Alice and Sister Jeanne. The pair strode purposefully across the ward; their presence curtailed the laughter and hushed any murmurings amongst the aspirants.

Sister Jeanne cleared her throat. "We shall finish this task. You take the dirty bandages, clean those able to be re-used, burn any that are too contaminated."

Dominique stood to the side, it wasn't an instruction she was bound to follow and for that she was grateful. She couldn't imagine she'd ever have the discipline to become a nun.

"It'll take longer," Sister Jeanne explained her decree to Alice as she waved the aspirants away. "But it removes any temptation for inappropriate thoughts."

"I can help." Dominique stepped forward. "I've helped my pere with patients." *Only Francois, but I still helped.* She was extending the truth a lot tonight.

"Dominique, what are you doing here?" Alice demanded.

Dominique opened her mouth to speak. Flustered, unable to tell the truth but struggling to find another excuse that would stop her half-sister from banishing her from the hospital, she stood gaping for several seconds.

"P-P-Pere missed his dinner," she finally settled on. "Maman was worried about him and sent me to check everything was alright."

"He's busy assisting Doctor Flament in surgery," Alice snapped back.

"The wagon is here." Clemence joined the group and interrupted the conversation. "Quick, we need to hurry." She took the last of the clothes, looked at Dominique and frowned. "Come, you'd better help me."

"Merci, Clemence. You've saved me again." Dominique did her best to look contrite as she helped Clemence dress the remaining few men. "Alice and Sister Jeanne are so serious about everything."

"They have to be." Clemence moved methodically from one man to the next. "Things are a matter of life and death in here. More so with the Germans breathing down our neck."

"I understand that, but they are such sticklers for the rules."

"Medicine has always been in Alice's blood, instilled and encouraged by Pere. But even with Pere's support, it's a man's world. She'll never be able to train as a doctor. She must work twice as hard to prove herself just to learn at the hospital. You should support her and not judge her."

Dominique swallowed. She didn't want people to judge her and yet she was judging others.

"You're right. I'm sorry. What else can I do to help?"

"They're all dressed and as ready as they'll ever be to leave." Clemence stood, stretched her spine to ease her tired bones and glanced up and down the ward. "You can give them a cup of coffee while we wait for Alphonse to unload the wagon. It might be their last for a while."

Dominique found the coffee pot and several tin cups and began delivering the drinks. She had to hold the cup for a young soldier whose hands had both been amputated, tipping the hot liquid carefully as he sipped. How was he ever going to manage beyond these four walls? She shook her head to chase away the thoughts and concentrate on the task at hand.

Alphonse arrived and gave Clemence a peck on the cheek.

"I was just making a delivery and thought I would check in on my lovely wife."

It was difficult to tell whether he was teasing or keeping up the ruse in case anyone would dob him in later. Some of the townsfolk had been known to let the Germans know of anyone breaking the many rules they were imposing; such was their desperation for additional rations.

With the aspirants still busy cleaning and burning bandages, the ward was empty except for those complicit in the escape plan.

"I brought ten kegs in." Alphonse kept his voice low as a precaution. "I reckon I can get ten out through the gates without raising any attention."

"What about the remaining six?" Sister Jeanne asked, concern peppering her normally calm voice. "We must get them all to safety tonight."

Alphonse glanced at Dominique. He raised his eyebrows, asking the unspoken question, was she still up for the task. She smiled and gave him the thumbs up. Her façade was merely that, a veneer like a soldier's uniform she'd donned for a mission. Her knees shook beneath her skirt. Her insides were writhing; she felt nauseous.

Was she wrong to think she could do this? Was she being too rash like everyone thought she was? What if they all got caught? What punishment would the Germans inflict? The soldiers would likely be executed. It would be her fault. How could she live with the guilt? Maybe she wouldn't live. The Boche might decide she deserved to die too.

"Dominique!" Alice, Clemence and Sister Jeanne called her named in unison, dragging her back from her thoughts.

She looked at Alphonse and then at each of the women glaring at her. He'd obviously revealed her plan.

"We'd better get going before it's too late." She turned and beckoned the soldier without hands to follow her. She had to act, not give the women a chance to stop her and make it impossible for her to surmount her doubts.

Chapter 11

The streets appeared empty. A waxing crescent moon rested comfortably among a spattering of fluffy clouds, reminding Dominique she could be home snuggled into her soft mattress. She took a deep breath, silently telling herself she could help these men, play her part in saving their lives. What she was doing was nothing compared to what the soldiers had to endure at the battle front.

Alphonse climbed aboard his wagon; ten men huddled under a canvas on the back, those with leg injuries, still reliant on a crutch or walking stick. He flicked his reins and set his horse on its way. Each clip clop of hooves on the cobbles set Dominique's nerves on edge. She imagined the noise was loud enough to wake the entire town.

She held the remaining six soldiers back, hiding in the hospital courtyard until she believed no Germans had come to investigate the night's activities. These six were good on their feet. They were dressed like the townsfolk, any chest and back injuries easily concealed beneath layers of donated clothing. Collars were turned up and hats pulled down to conceal head injuries, sleeves tucked into pockets to look like missing hands and arms still existed. They'd agreed, the British were to remain silent. Any utterance with an English accent would surely mean death for all.

Dominique swapped her skirt for a pair of almost too big trousers and tucked her hair up under a hat thinking she'd look more like one of the lads. If apprehended they could say they were just out for a hunt, desperate to bolster their food reserves before winter set in.

She wanted the escapees to think of her as one of them. No-one else seemed to want to listen to a sixteen-year-old girl, why would they be any different? For their own sakes they needed to trust and follow her.

As sure as Dominique would ever be that it was safe, she turned to wave them on. Sister Jeanne had gathered the men into a group and their heads were all bowed in prayer.

"May God bless you and grant you safe passage to freedom. Amen." Sister Jeanne looked up, her face calm and serene, her hands in a prayer position at her heart.

The Sister's peaceful demeanour enveloped Dominique. Her heartbeat quietened. She felt reassured everything would work out, that God would ensure their safety.

Dominique did a final check of the street. "The coast is ..."

"Stoppen!"

Two German soldiers stood in front of Alphonse's wagon blocking his way, their rifles pointed at his head. Alphonse had no choice but to pull on the reins and bring the wagon to a stop. He dropped the leather straps across his lap and raised his hands to show he was unarmed.

Alphonse. Don't hurt Alphonse. Dominique gasped and clamped her hand over her mouth to stifle her scream.

The escaping soldiers looked at her expectantly. She raised a finger to her lips to ensure they stayed quiet and whispered.

"Germans."

Some of the injured men straightened and looked around for a weapon, their soldiering instincts kicking in. Others cowered in fear, afraid of being caught and executed.

"Was ist in ihrem waggon?"

Dominique peeked around the courtyard wall to see one of the Germans pointing his rifle at the rear of the wagon. She didn't need to speak the language to know what he wanted. She squeezed her eyes shut, unwilling to contemplate explaining to Clemence her husband was killed by Germans. If she banished the image, surely reality would do the same.

"Just empty kegs returning to the brewery to be refilled," Alphonse said shakily.

His French fell on German ears, unable to be understood, the soldiers looked dissatisfied and surly. One of them marched towards the back of the wagon.

"Bier." Alphonse had their attention. He pointed to a flask sitting on the seat beside him and slowly lowered his hand to pick it up. With his mouth downturned, creating an exaggerated sad face, he pulled the cork and turned the empty flask upside down. "Bier gone."

Dominique's admiration for her brother-in-law grew. He was clever. He'd anticipated the Germans stopping him and was prepared.

"You want bier." He pretended to drink from a full flask, pointing from the soldiers to his make-believe drink. One of them licked his lips, the other grinned and nodded so Alphonse seized the opportunity and pointed at the hospital. "Hospital."

Dominique yanked her head back as they turned to look her way.

"Krankenhaus," the soldier pointed and nodded. "Ja, bier, krankenhaus."

The clip clop of hooves signalled Alphonse had been allowed to leave. The stomping of approaching boots set Dominique's heart thundering.

"Quick, they're coming. We need to hide." She ushered the escapees away from the gate.

"Into the chapel," Sister Jeanne suggested. "They'll never look there. I won't allow them to desecrate our place of worship."

The group hurried across the courtyard and into the chapel.

"Wait here. I'll return when they've gone or are too inebriated to care."

Candles on the altar flickered with the rush of air from the open door but returned to their calming glow when Sister Jeanne closed the door behind Dominique and the men.

"Bier! Bier!" The Germans demanded as they barged into the courtyard.

"In the hospital. This way." Sister Jeanne led the soldiers away.

Dominique sagged into the first wooden pew, drained of energy, disappointed at the lack of progress in her mission. Would she ever be able to help the British and French to safety? Some of the men knelt at the altar and silently prayed, their despair as obvious as hers.

It seemed like forever before Sister Jeanne returned. Dominique had nodded off but woke with a start when the chapel door edged open.

"It's safe to go." The Sister looked weary, and Dominique wondered what she'd had to do to clear the way for the escape.

"We'd better head out then or we'll miss the rendezvous with Alphonse." Dominique ushered the men back to the courtyard gate. "Head right when you get outside and follow me."

"Right?" Sister Jeanne queried. "Are you not using the tunnels?"

"Oui," Dominique hesitated at the questioning of her plans. "We'll access them at the base of the ramparts."

"It'll be quicker and safer to get to the tunnels through the barracks." Sister Jeanne pointed to the Lowendaal barracks. "The Germans aren't using them, not after they bombed them. Some of the Orchian burns victims are still there but the Boche aren't worried about them either."

"But how do you get from the barracks to the tunnels?" Dominique hadn't discovered this part of the underground network in her childhood play.

"In the cellar. There are some shelves on the left. Pull them back and there is a door into the tunnels."

Dominique didn't have time to ask how a nun would know this. The soldiers had a long way to go to reach the Foret de Mormal and for her to return before sunrise.

"Thank you. We'd best be off then."

"Bless you, my child." Sister Jeanne touched a hand to Dominique's shoulder, and to the shoulder of each of the men as they passed through the gate and crept across the road into the barracks.

Clemence was inside adding another piece of wood to the fire to keep the chill at bay for the Orchian patients. With the damage to the building from the artillery fire it was difficult to maintain any level of heat.

"Where's the cellar?" Dominique had no time for niceties. "We need to get into the tunnels."

"I thought you'd left ages ago." Clemence frowned as she pointed to a door beside the fire. "Why are you still here?"

Dominique rolled her eyes. "Germans."

Even in the dim light she saw the whites of Clemence's eyes grow with fear.

"Alphonse?"

"He got away." Dominique opened the cellar door. "He bribed them with beer."

"Of course he did." Clemence's smile was full of love and admiration for her husband.

The stairwell was pitch black. Dominique hesitated. Images of the Favier family tomb loomed, a concrete panel slid across for internment of the ashes of loved ones, never to return except in memories. If she stepped into the darkness of the stairwell, would it be the end of her life too?

"Can I borrow a candle?" Her hand trembled as she reached out to take Clemence's candle, not accepting no for an answer. She sucked in a deep breath, filling her lungs with air and her heart with courage. "Follow me."

She held the candle aloft, watched the stone steps emerge from the darkness. *You can do this. One step at a time.* Her feet mirrored her thoughts, slowly, carefully, she descended into the cellar, the escapees following behind. The last of the men must have taken another candle, its flame illuminated the path of those in front of him.

When they reached the cellar, the door at the top of the stairs clicked shut. There was no turning back.

"Quick, we need to move this shelf aside." Dominique stood back while the more able soldiers dragged the shelf away to reveal the door into the tunnels.

A damp mustiness seeped into the cellar as the door's ancient hinges screeched in protest.

"Doesn't look like it's been used for a while," one of the men observed.

A shiver ran down Dominique's spine. That meant spiders had plenty of time to claim the tunnels as their own, weaving networks of intricate webs. She was tempted to let the man with the other candle go first but imagined him getting lost, taking a wrong turn in the labyrinth and leading them all to death's door. If these barracks had access to the tunnels, then no doubt the Cernay and Tournefort barracks, now occupied by the Boche, also did.

This is no time to fear spiders. These men won't trust and respect you, if you let a tiny insect get the better of you. Self-admonishment pushed Dominique's fear aside and she stepped into the tunnel. The ground was uneven, stones jutted from the earthen floor, but their sharp edges had been smoothed by all the feet that had trodden the same path before her. She drew strength from this reassuring thought and pushed on.

The tunnel's arched brick ceiling was well above her head but several of the men had to hunch over, watching the floor and feet of others to judge where they were going. The expected spider webs were absent until an air vent created the right environment for the busy arachnids.

"Aargh!" One of the hunched soldiers walked straight into a web of silken threads. His yell bounced off the bricks and amplified through the tunnels.

"Sssh!" Fearful the man's cry would draw the Germans, Dominique hurried on until she was sure the candle flames wouldn't give their presence away.

They reached a junction, tunnels branched off to the left and right. Dominique crouched down, leaning back against the bricks, indicating the men should do the same. She needed to catch her breath, get her bearings, so she could decide which way to proceed. She closed her eyes, pictured herself as one of the homing pigeons flying overhead. She imagined the tunnel from the barracks heading in a direct line to the ramparts. Once inside the thick walls that protected the city, they needed to find another tunnel, one to take them to the fields beyond the town, out of reach of the Germans who would be posted to guard the entrances to the town.

Dominique looked back at the men. She'd forgotten they were wounded, recovering from injuries suffered in the trenches and battlefields. Several of the men leaned uncomfortably against the tunnel walls, their heads lowered, as if they'd already spent all their energy reserves. She let them rest. There was nothing to be gained pushing them to the point of collapse.

"How much further?" One of them asked in English, his hand pointing down the tunnel.

Unable to decipher his words but interpreting his gestures, Dominique replied. "Presque la."

She held her hands up, palms facing with a small gap in between. He nodded and seemed buoyed by the prospect.

Sitting beside Dominique, the amputee looked despairingly at where his hands should have been. He sniffed and blinked back his tears. Her eyes watered up in sympathy and her chest tightened. She felt his pain, loss, never being able to do something so simple ever again.

A rodent scurrying past them brought her thoughts back to the present, reminded her they were all alive. They had to be grateful for life itself, and they needed to push on to ensure they remained so. If the rat was here, they must be close to the end of the tunnel. She leapt up, eager to continue and just as keen not to have a rat running across her feet.

Another hundred yards and the tunnel branched off again. The cool night air wafted in, and a slither of moonlight invited them to turn and walk up a gentle incline to the exit. Bushes partially concealed the tunnel, their leaves still provided camouflage indicating the Germans hadn't discovered the escape route. Dominique used the cover to check the way was clear of the enemy. The next stage of the journey was across open fields, there were few places to hide if the Germans were out patrolling.

She scanned the paddocks. Several sheep huddled together. The burnt skeleton of a barn reached out as if begging to be saved. An owl hooted in the distance. A dog howled in reply. But there was no motion, no human silhouettes moving about. Dominique was unsure whether to feel relieved or suspicious. She couldn't let her guard down, there was too much at stake.

She inched out further and turned to look back at the ramparts. Atop the stone walls that protected the city, a lone sentry paced slowly backwards and forwards. His feet looked leaden; his head downcast as if he had to will one foot in front of the other. There was no hint of the alertness required of a guard on duty but perhaps he was just biding time, playing games by himself to stay awake and ready to shoot anything that moved. Dominique's thoughts seesawed. Was it safe to move on, or not?

They had no choice. Staying where they were wasn't an option.

"Run to the barn," she whispered to the men.

The group were like the rat scurrying across the earth. They zigzagged across the field, skirted hollows carved out by artillery fire, dodged the limbs of trees smashed to the ground, and crawled beneath the wire of a fence to crouch beside the charred remains of the barn.

Dominique caught her breath, inhaled and exhaled long and slow until her heart stopped pounding. The sentry was still pacing backwards and forwards, none the wiser of their presence. Their success spurred her onto the next stage of their escape.

A hedgerow of hawthorn and holly ran alongside the road that Dominique knew headed in the direction of the Foret de Mormal.

"We'll head to the road," she pointed. "Stay in the field behind the hedgerow, in case there are patrols."

Single file they followed the road, concealed behind the hedge until the clip clop of horse's hooves brought them to a sudden stop. Dominique crouched and indicated for the men to do the same. She tried to discern whether it was Alphonse. Which direction was the horse headed? Was it merely a single rider or did it have a wagon in tow? She sighed with despair. She hadn't a clue how to tell from the noise alone. Dam all the repetition of useless facts they forced her to do in school, why couldn't they have taught her something that would be useful? Knowledge that might save her life?

"Stay here," she whispered before creeping forwards to where the hedgerow stopped, and a low stone wall created an entrance to the field.

She froze, held her breath and waited until the horse appeared. She didn't expect its high-pitched whinny. She fell back, landed on her bottom, the prickles of a holly branch piercing through her trousers. Trembles began in her lips and chin and quickly spread to her entire body. If the horse belonged to the enemy and gave away her presence, all would be lost.

"It's alright, Bessy. We're nearly there. I'll give you a good feed of hay when we get home."

Alphonse! Dominique almost wet herself with relief.

"Alphonse." She stood and stepped out from the wall.

"Ah, voila! Dominique!" Alphonse simultaneously smiled with delight and glanced all around to ensure the area was clear of Germans.

"It is so good to see you." Dominique waved to the other men, signalling they should join them.

"I can take them from here," Alphonse offered. "I wouldn't like to explain to your pere if you're not home by morning."

Dominique huffed. Everyone kept reminding her she was still a child. She straightened and puffed her chest out. She couldn't change her age, but she could behave like an adult and deserved to be appreciated for her efforts.

"You've done a great job getting them here," Alphonse complimented her.

"Oui, merci beaucoup," the French escapees repeated in unison.

Dominique went from annoyed to proud. Perhaps she'd misinterpreted Alphonse's reference to her pere. She took a moment to realise that fatherly concern didn't stop when she was no longer a child. Her pere would continue to love and care about her wellbeing, just as she did his, until they took their last breath. The thought warmed her insides and brought a smile to her face.

"You're most welcome. Safe Travels. Au revoir."

She waved farewell and turned to retrace her steps back to the tunnels, not to come out at the hospital but back at home.

Chapter 12

Dominique removed her hat and retrieved the skirt she'd hidden in the cellar. Dressed and looking feminine again, she left the cellar via the steps into the back garden, rather than open the door in the entrance way. She sighed with relief; her mission had been a success.

Balls of tiny blue petals covered in drew drops catching the first rays of the morning sun, paraded along the edge of the garden. Dominique stopped to admire the hydrangeas in full bloom. She bent to sniff at the closest flower, not expecting much of an aroma, but the tiniest scent of nature at its most beautiful.

It was the acrid smell of tobacco that filled her nostrils. She froze, realising she wasn't alone in the garden. Her mind raced. None of her family smoked. It had to be one of the German soldiers. She'd never seen Hans with a smoke. It was Wolfgang. The German she'd tried to avoid more than any other was in the garden.

She dared not turn around until she concocted an excuse for her presence. It was certain to be needed. She considered saying she couldn't sleep but that wouldn't suffice if he'd seen her coming from the cellar. Perhaps she could head to the woodshed and say she was getting more wood for the fires. He'd know that was Marie's job not hers.

Wolfgang couldn't understand her French anyway. Her alibi needed to be something visual. Her chest tightened and a painful throb at her temples inhibited her ability to think. *Stop! Breathe!* The seconds she took to calm herself worked; she knew what to do.

She walked slowly back down the steps, retrieved her mother's secateurs and a wicker basket from the cellar. Wolfgang would see the flowers, think it totally innocent and pay her no attention. She hoped a bunch of hydrangea heads would save her own head.

As calmly as her trembling legs and shaky hands would allow, she worked her way along the row of hydrangeas snipping a collection of the prettiest flowers. She collected more flowers than needed to fill her mother's favourite vase, stalling for time, calming her nerves, hoping he'd disappear before she had to interact with him.

By the time she reached the end of the row, she was deep in the garden and another thought set her heart pounding again. What if he came into the garden after her? Dominique remembered the Belgian refugees, the stories they told, or worse the stories they implied but couldn't tell.

She glanced up at her parents' bedroom. Their window shutters were firmly closed against the sights and sounds of the garden. No-one would know if he chose to take from her what wasn't his. She didn't imagine he'd care. The evil glint in his eye, his look of disdain; he would have no respect for an innocent child.

Dominique scoffed at herself. *You can't demand to be treated like an adult but retreat into childhood when the moment serves you.* She shook her head, stopped her thoughts from wandering and focussed on the task of getting back into the house.

The basket could carry no more so she hooked it in the crook of her elbow and concealed the secateurs in the deep pocket of her skirt, hoping she wouldn't need them for anything more than snipping flower heads.

Wolfgang sat at the small cast iron table, sheltered between the wings of the building, blowing smoke into the morning air. The closer she got the more his presence riled her. How dare he sit there like he owned the place, polluting the fresh air.

This setting was where her parents often sat on a Sunday afternoon, chatting away, enjoying a glass of pinot noir while birds flitted about the trees, their chorus an accompaniment to the couple's tête-à-tête. Dominique yearned for those pleasant times to return.

"Guten Morgen." Wolfgang lifted his tobacco-stained fingers in what Dominique interpreted as a greeting.

Instead of blowing the smoke directly at her, he tilted his head back and blew it vertical. Stretched out in the seat, his long legs crossed at his ankles, he seemed so relaxed, as if he was on holiday and not in the middle of a war. Dominique's fingers tightened over the secateur handle. She clenched her teeth to curb the urge to plunge the pointed blades deep into his heart.

She replied with the smallest of nods, not wanting to acknowledge him at all but knowing it was safer to do so. She was almost past him when his hand reached out. His fingers wrapped around her wrist like a handcuff. She was captured. Her heart thudded. She held her breath. Did he know she had the secateurs? Had he read her thoughts?

Her arm hairs stood on end, but she couldn't let him see her fear. She held her head high and eyed him with disdain.

"Blumen." He released her arm and took one of the hydrangea heads from the basket.

Dominique sighed with relief as she translated his German, matching his words with his actions. *Blumen, bloom, flower.* He only wanted a flower. Not her.

"Oui, une fleur." Free of his hand, she seized the opportunity to move away, out of his reach. "I'd better put them in a vase, make sure they have fresh water. I'll put it on the breakfast table for all to see."

Dominique knew she was babbling, that Wolfgang wouldn't understand a word she'd said but she couldn't stop herself until she was back inside. She leaned back on the wall and closed her eyes until her limbs stopped trembling.

"Let me take those for you." Marie took the basket of hydrangea heads from Dominique. "You head on up to bed and get some sleep. I'll tell your mere you've got a headache. I'll come and wake you for lunch. That should be enough to make up for last night."

The offer of help was nearly Dominique's undoing. Relief flooded through her, weakening her knees.

"Merci beaucoup, Marie. Merci beaucoup." Dominique clung to the banister as she pulled herself up the stairs.

It wasn't until she lay down, cocooned by her soft mattress that Marie's words, or more the knowledge they conveyed fully registered. Marie seemed to have an innate knowing of all that went on, in the Favier house and beyond. How would she know Dominique hadn't been in her bed all night unless she'd seen or heard her leave? Or she had a secret web of spies?

Dominique was fast asleep before the notion had time to be dismissed as nonsense.

Mid-afternoon, when Dominique finally rubbed the sleep from her eyes, the sandwich she found on her bedside table signalled she'd slept through lunch. Ravenous, she gorged herself. Thick junks of jambon and cheese wedged between equally thick slices of white bread satisfied her hunger. She was grateful Marie had been generous in making the sandwich, forgetting that they'd been rationing their food to make it last.

Dominique pulled the drapes back, opened the window just enough to be able to tilt the slats on the shutters and peer into the garden. She pressed her palm to her heart when she saw Wolfgang was no longer invading the space.

She'd already decided to visit Clemence and Alphonse today, to be reassured that he'd made it safely to the Foret de Mormal with the escaped soldiers and back home again without rousing the attention of the Germans. She dressed and headed downstairs.

Returning the plate to the kitchen she found Marie bent over a large pot stirring its steaming contents.

"Salut, Marie. Merci beaucoup for the sandwich."

"Salut, Dominique." Marie drew a spoonful from the pot and blew on it until it was cool enough to taste. "Good to see you are rested."

Dominique inhaled the spicy aromas. "It smells delicious. What are you cooking?"

Marie's chin dipped and her gaze lowered to the floor as if guilt sat heavily on her shoulders.

"What's wrong? What's happened?" Dominique gasped. Had Wolfgang done something to Marie when Dominique had gone upstairs?

"It's chicken broth." Marie reached the spoon out for Dominique to taste. "I had to slaughter a chicken so we could eat."

It was Dominique who was now consumed with guilt. Her hands clasped her stomach, where the sandwich sat heavily.

"My sandwich ..."

Marie cut her off. "You missed breakfast. It was two meals in one."

"But ..."

"You deserved it after your efforts." Marie licked the spoon clean and turned back to the pot, dismissing any further conversation on the matter. "It needs more salt."

She knows. But how? I'm sure I never told her of the escape plans. Marie wouldn't betray them and inform the Germans of their actions so how she found out was irrelevant.

"I thought I'd visit Clemence and Alphonse today," Dominique said.

"Be sure to be back before eight," Marie warned.

"You sound like Maman, demanding I'm home for dinner."

"It is not me nor your mere demanding." Marie stopped stirring the pot and turned to face Dominique ensuring she had her full attention. "The Germans have put a curfew on. Anyone on the streets after eight o'clock risks punishment."

"What? When did that happen?" Dominique felt stifled by yet another restriction.

Le Quesnoy was becoming a giant prison and the townsfolk prisoners of the enemy.

"They posted the notice this morning, effective immediately."

"What about the bread dist …?" Dominique caught herself and glanced around to ensure no-one was lingering nearby to hear her.

"With winter nearly here, the sun sets much earlier." Marie lowered her voice to a whisper. "You should be able to get there and back under the cover of darkness and still meet the curfew."

"I hope you're right." Dominique bit the inside of her lip. "So many people are dependent on it."

"Worry about that later. Go and enjoy your visit with Clemence and Alphonse."

"Sacrebleu! Damn the Boche!"

Dominique heard Alphonse's cursing from the end of the road that led to the brewery. Her heart see-sawed. It was wonderful to see him alive and free, but something had obviously gone wrong.

Had his mission been discovered? Had some local who wanted special treatment dobbed him in? Him or them?

Dread sat in the pit of her stomach.

Her brother-in-law stood at the doorway to the brewery, raking his hands through his hair, his face with a look of utter despair. Clemence stood nearby, her eyes red from crying, her shoulders rising and falling with each sob.

Sensing her approach, Alphonse turned suddenly, adopting a stance that said he was ready to fight. His left eye was swollen shut, deep purple bruises covered his eye socket, dried blood clung to his bent nose. The injuries churned Dominique's insides. The Germans had hurt her brother-in-law.

"What has happened?" Dominique dismissed the usual greeting.

"We are ruined!" Alphonse thumped his fist against the brewery wall. "The damn Boche have destroyed everything."

"They beat you. What for?"

The couple's focus remained on the interior of the brewery. Dominique stepped in front of them to investigate. The lock that would normally have held the door shut against intruders was smashed, splintered wood spiked like the prickles of a porcupine. She slid carefully past them into the dim interior.

Dominique gasped. Her eyes widened as she stood, numb at the sight before her. Alphonse's pride and joy was no longer. The vats, copper pipes and tubes through which he brewed his beer were missing. The bolts that held them in place, wrenched and strewn about like the discarded shells of bullets. The wooden stands on which they were mounted lay in ruins on the floor. The stash of empty kegs into which he poured the beer were smashed in a pile in the corner. The full ones stolen. The only thing that remained was the aroma of the beer the enemy had spilled on the floor.

"Oh, Alphonse. I'm so sorry."

"It is not your fault," Alphonse replied. "The bastards think they own everything. They don't care about our livelihoods."

"Did they find out about last night?"

"Non!" Alphonse shook his head.

"Thank goodness." If the Germans didn't know about last night's mission, the escapees should be safe and so should she. "Why did they beat you?"

"I tried to stop them. The butt of a rifle soon put paid to that." Alphonse winced as he touched his forehead.

"But why did they pick on your brewery?"

"It's not just me. They have done this in every brewery. Every factory."

Dominique struggled to see the connection. The German soldiers enjoyed drinking the beer. It seemed to be all they did.

"Why? Why would they destroy the industry that provides them with what they want?"

"They think only of winning the war." Alphonse shook his head, his shoulders slumped. "They've stolen the metal to melt it down to make weapons. They might as well line us all up and shoot us now. I don't know how we are going to survive without any money coming in."

Clemence stepped forward. "We have my wages from the hospital. It's not much but it will be enough to keep us fed. Perhaps you could work as a medic as well, there is plenty of work at the hospital."

"Oui, mon amour." Alphonse wrapped his arm around Clemence's shoulder, pulled her into his side and kissed her forehead. "And we have each other."

Their obvious love for one another enveloped Dominique as well. The Germans could take everything else, but they couldn't steal that.

"And you have lots of firewood now," Dominique joked to lighten the mood. "At least you'll be nice and warm when the snowfall arrives."

The trio laughed. Alphonse pulled Dominique into a group hug, and they stood huddled together, their backs creating a barrier to the atrocities of the war.

"Right, we'd better stack the firewood then." Alphonse let them go and began picking up the pieces of wood that were unable to be salvaged for anything but burning.

"I thought something must have happened last night." Dominique added another piece of timber to the pile cradled in her arm. "Did everyone make it to their destination safely?"

"Oui," Alphonse nodded. "The rendezvous went according to plan."

"Just as well you didn't leave it any longer," Clemence said.

"Why?"

"The dam Boche didn't just ransack my brewery." Alphonse's voice rose with anger. "They stole my horse and wagon to cart away their plunder."

"Oh, non, how are you going to get about now?" Dominique asked.

"The way everyone else has to, shank's pony." Alphonse's laugh was half-hearted. "The men we helped have further to walk than me."

"I hope they'll be alright, that they'll manage to get home before winter truly sets in."

"I believe they've joined the British already there. They've got a camp set up, but they must keep moving to avoid the German patrols."

"Lucky it's a big forest."

The lean-to woodshed beside the cottage was filled to overflowing by the time the sun was dipping towards the horizon.

"Merci beaucoup, Dominique." Clemence took the last few sticks from Dominique. "I'll take those ones inside. Would you like a cup of tea?"

"Do you still have tea? Marie has only been able to find a meagre amount which Wolfgang and Hans insist she keep for them. Maman is furious."

"Well, it's a tea of sorts, as good as you can get with walnut leaves and licorice." Clemence sighed. "Calling it tea helps me drink it and if you add some boiled beetroot to sweeten it, it's even better."

"That's what Marie's been doing too." Dominique pictured her mother's grimace when she first tasted the alternative brew. "Maman is slowly warming to it, but it doesn't have the same calming effect on her nerves."

"I don't think anything is capable of smoothing your mere's frayed edges," Clemence smiled.

"Apart from Pere."

"Oui, apart from Pere." Clemence turned to head inside. "Are you coming in, or not?"

"I'd better be going." Dominique readied to leave. "It's a long walk home, and I need to see Nathalie on the way and be home before the eight o'clock curfew."

"Eight o'clock curfew?" Clemence frowned. "Another restriction. Another rule. It feels like we are prisoners. Perhaps we'd better escape to the forest too."

"I'd offer you a lift, if I could." With his eye swollen shut, Alphonse looked as if he winked at them.

They all knew escape wasn't an option for the Quercitains. They were reliant on the French and their allies overpowering the Germans and reclaiming their homeland. It was all supposed to be over by Christmas.

Chapter 13

"You're spending a lot of time stuck in here." Dominique found Nathalie in her bedroom. "Almost like you are a prisoner in your own home."

"It feels like it." Nathalie sighed. She leaned against the window frame and stared longingly outside.

"We should go down, hide in the storeroom again and listen through the wall." Dominique wanted to re-ignite the spark in her friend.

"What's the point. They speak in German." Nathalie shook her head. "I can't understand what they're saying except when that ogre Lubbert is yelling orders at Pere, repeated in French by his offsider just to be certain they are understood."

"Your poor pere." Dominique saw the glassiness in Nathalie's eyes as she hugged her. "How is he holding up? His heart?"

"Maman and I are worried about him, but he is putting on a brave front."

"What are the Boche demanding now?

"Thirteen hundred eggs a week for the soldiers."

"That's a lot of eggs. There won't be any left for us."

"Exactly what Pere argued," Nathalie replied. "He told Lubbert they demanded too many, that the children and the sick would be deprived of the food they desperately needed."

Dominique thought of the chicken stewing in the pot at home, one less chicken to lay the eggs demanded. Perhaps Marie should have left it alive.

"I'm guessing the Kommandantur isn't worried." Dominique had never seen him show leniency any other time, why would he now? "His order is to be followed no matter what."

"He literally said 'I don't care'. He was so malevolent it is hard to believe he is human." Nathalie wrapped her arms around her torso. "He's a monster, Dominique. He told Pere the town would suffer if they didn't get the right number of eggs."

"Yet they destroyed the crops. The grains to feed the chickens that lay the eggs they want." Dominique saw a pattern emerging. "They ransacked all the metal from Alphonse's brewery too; made it impossible for him to brew the beer they like to drink. Alphonse said they did the same in all the breweries and the factories too. No more shoes can be manufactured. They'll be walking around with holes in their boots, and they'll likely blame us."

Nathalie's eyes went wide. "It's going to get worse, Dominique."

"Don't lose faith, Nathalie. We'll be alright. We've got to stick together. We're all we've got."

Unfortunately, Nathalie was right, as winter wrapped its frozen fingers around Le Quesnoy, the German grip also tightened.

With games of peloto prevented by both the weather and the occupation, Dominique returned home with Louis and Victor as soon as the school bell rang. The boys hurried inside, dumped their satchels in the entrance way and rushed through to the kitchen. There was nothing unusual about them thinking of their stomachs, hunger was becoming a constant in everyone's lives.

Dominique paused at the door; she had to look twice to ensure her eyes weren't deceiving her. The brass plaque, her pere's name was no longer proudly displayed on the wall. Four holes and a square of bricks, brighter and cleaner than those around them were the only evidence that the plaque existed.

"Pere, Pere." Dominique found her father in the ground floor room he used to see patients. "Your plaque is gone."

"Oui, I know." Henri looked despondent sitting at his desk with an ink pen in hand instead of a stethoscope. "The Boche requisitioned it."

"You mean stole it."

"Oui, but they insist on calling it requisitioning." Henri shook his head. "Theft by another name in an attempt to make it sound legitimate."

"You should demand it back." Dominique huffed, her hands on her hips. "Tell them you're a doctor and patients need to know where to find you."

She was clutching at straws, the townsfolk already knew where the doctor lived.

"They will." Henri waved his hand over the piece of paper he'd been writing. "We are required to post a notice on the outside of the house, listing everyone who lives here, their ages and occupations."

Dominique saw her name, in between her parents and her brothers. At the bottom of the list, Henri had also written Marie Roux, servant, seventeen years.

"Why do they want to know all that information?"

"They've been taking an inventory of everything else. We're just another resource they want to keep track of. I'm sure they'll find a use for us ..." Henri looked up at Dominique and shook his head. "I mean ... it ... the list."

Dark shadows under his eyes reflected the many hours he'd spent at the hospital. The German demands were wearing Henri down. He looked much older than the sixty-seven years he'd written beside his name.

Henri may have changed his words for Dominique's benefit, but she knew he was worried.

"I won't be a student for much longer, Pere." Although school wasn't her favourite place, apart from collecting milk, the Germans had so far left the schoolchildren alone. "The baccalaureat exams are coming up. What will happen after that?"

"You should just concentrate on the exams, Dominique. Don't worry about what follows."

Dominique knew Nathalie would pass but she wasn't so sure about herself.

"Everyone expects the war to be over by Christmas," Henri continued. "Make sure you do your best to keep your options open."

He finished his list and went to pin it to the outside of the house as required.

In the following days and weeks, Kommandantur Lubbert's reasons for the lists became obvious. His demands were made known by the posting of notices about the town. One large poster displayed on a board in the square declared that all French, British and Belgian soldiers hiding in the care of local inhabitants must give themselves up as prisoners of war. The ultimatum given that if they hadn't done so by 4 December, they would be regarded as spies and shot. Thank goodness the British soldiers they'd helped were well beyond the walls of the city and this fate hopefully wouldn't befall them.

With only a family of six and the two German soldiers living in the largest home on Rue Brancion the soldiers turned up regularly demanding to search the house, convinced that the Favier family must be harbouring some fugitives. Each time their searches were unsuccessful, but they never went away empty handed, helping themselves to a bottle of wine, some food Marie had planned for dinner, or an ornament cast from brass or copper.

At the beginning of November, Lubbert demanded the presence of all men aged between eighteen and fifty at the town hall. They hadn't been old enough or fit enough to fight for their country, what would the enemy require of them now?

The French tricolour no longer adorned the brick building's flag post, torn down by the enemy when Mayor Carlier refused to remove it in favour of the German flag. Previously the location for many of the town's celebrations, the hall now served more as a control centre, no one ever emerged happier than when they entered.

Louis and Victor were too young and her pere too old but at forty years old Alphonse received his summons. Dominique joined the other worried women gathering on the sidewalk opposite the hall's double doors. They watched the men herded inside like cattle in the yards of an abattoir, unsure of the reason for their presence but with a sense of foreboding. Alphonse's bruises had finally faded, but his anger towards the enemy had not. Dominique hoped he wasn't about to incite another beating.

When the doors were slammed shut, the woman beside Dominique broke down, her shoulders shuddering as she sobbed loudly. It was the first time Dominique was grateful Gabriel was away fighting. She wanted to console the woman, to tell her everything would be alright, but nobody could guarantee that outcome. The French army that should be overpowering the enemy and rescuing them was out there, but their whereabouts was unknown.

Dominique crossed the road, seeking a view of the proceedings but the sills on the row of windows running along the side of the hall were above her head. Only the tips of her fingers reached the brick ledge beneath the panes of glass, not enough to haul herself up. She could hear but not see the goings on.

"Climb on my shoulders." Nathalie appeared at her side and crouched down. "I'll lift you up."

It felt like the days before everything changed, two friends up to mischief, spying on proceedings they had no right to. Dominique didn't have to think twice about it. She hooked a leg over each of Nathalie's shoulders.

"Ready," she said, tapping Nathalie lightly on the head. "Can you lift me?"

Last time they'd attempted this, Dominique had been too heavy, and they'd collapsed in a fit of giggles on the ground. This was too serious an issue for that to recur.

"You've lost weight, Dominique," Nathalie observed. "You're a featherweight compared to before."

Despite Marie's ability to cook something out of nothing, they had been eating less, and the waistband of Dominique's skirt sat loosely around her middle.

"Oui. Lift me up then."

Some of the other women crossed the road to help, supporting Nathalie as she stood back up.

"What are they saying?"

"Are they hurting my sons?"

"What are they doing?"

"Is my husband alright?"

"Ssh! I can't hear what they're saying when you're all talking. Everyone is alright." Dominique wanted to add 'at the moment' but didn't.

Armed German soldiers patrolled each end of the rows of men. With rifles over their shoulders, they looked ready to shoot anyone who tried to escape. Lubbert commandeered Mayor

Carlier's podium at the front of the hall. He thumped his fist onto the rostrum, demanding the attention of all present. He had Dominique's, her stomach churned, her mind raced, trying to guess the fate of the gathering.

She recognised boys from school, the few that had turned eighteen since the war had begun. A little older than her, but now unable to enlist. Some huddled beside the older men as if appearing younger, weaker or feebler would protect them. Others wore a defiant look, their backs straight, their shoulders back.

The sneer that seemed to be a permanent feature of Lubbert's face looked out over the men with disdain. What did he have planned for them? Whatever it was, would the same fate befall her and Nathalie when they turned eighteen?

Lubbert launched into a propaganda speech, relayed by the French speaking officer who was so often at the Kommandantur's side. He promoted the German way as the best way, the only way and the sooner the people of the town realised that the better it would be for them.

"What is he saying?" The women demanded in unison.

"He's spouting lies, saying they are superior to the French," Dominique replied.

"Non! Sacrebleu!"

Chair legs scraping across the wooden floor drew Dominique's attention from Lubbert.

"He's making the men stand up."

The Quercitain men were made to break into groups according to their skills. The Germans wanted to make use of their labour.

Builders, bakers, brewers, vintners, plumbers, bricklayers and bank tellers all had to record the contribution they could make going forward. The teenage boys with no skillset were deemed forestry or road workers. They were to report for duty each morning, either to be sent to Foret de Mormal to mill the trees or out on the roads to repair the holes left by artillery fire.

"They've been sorted into work groups," Dominique relayed what she saw.

"Merci, merci, merci," one of the women looked skyward and raised her hands to her chest as if praying. "They are alive."

They were, but for how long? The Germans seemed to destroy the equipment and resources they needed to survive. Would they work these men to an early grave? Would Alphonse show his defiance and be beaten again?

"Let me down, please, Nathalie." Dominique had seen all she needed.

The mention of the Foret de Mormal raised another concern. If they were milling trees, the British and French soldiers they'd helped escape would be in danger. If the soldiers were recaptured, their efforts had all been for nothing. Dominique felt as if the energy had been sucked from her.

When the men were finally released from the confines of the hall the women rushed to their husbands and sons, filled with relief they showered them in kisses and hugs. Alphonse emerged with an angry scowl and with Clemence working at the hospital, he had no-one to placate him.

"I'll never work for the enemy." He shook his raised fist defiantly. "No matter what wages they promise to pay."

"Alphonse," Dominique rushed to her brother-in-law. "Don't you need the money? Isn't any job better than none?"

"They say it is for our benefit," Alphonse complained. "But it is only to fill their greedy stomachs, to help them win the war. I am French. I cannot and will not help the enemy against my own country."

"Oui, Alphonse, you are right but please don't put yourself in danger and get beaten again."

Alphonse stormed off and Dominique couldn't be certain he would heed her plea to stay safe. She shook her head and returned to Nathalie.

"We should finally go on that picnic we planned in the Foret de Mormal," Dominique suggested.

"What?" Nathalie looked puzzled. "Have you gone crazy? It's no longer summer, Dominique."

"We'll just dress warmer," Dominique reasoned. "A little chill has never stopped us before."

"We're not allowed to leave town without a permit," Nathalie frowned, "and I hardly think we'd get issued one for a picnic."

"We could say we need to collect firewood." Dominique wasn't going to give up. She was desperate to get to the forest, the British soldiers had to be warned. "Pere tried to get more coal last week, there's none left."

"Non, the Boche have kept the supplies to ensure they keep warm through winter. Never mind us." Nathalie sagged against the wall and sighed heavily.

"We could go and apply for the permit now."

"What is it you're not telling me, Dominique?" Nathalie eyed her suspiciously. "I've never seen you so keen to walk the eight miles to the forest."

Dominique hesitated. The less people that knew about the soldiers the better, but Nathalie could be trusted, she would never dob in the men hiding in the forest. She cupped her hand and leaned over to whisper in Nathalie's ear like they were two giggly girls sharing a secret.

"There's a camp of British soldiers hiding in the forest. With teams being sent to the forest to mill the trees, they're in even more danger of being found. We've got to warn them."

Nathalie leaned back and stared wide eyed at Dominique. "*We've* got to do it?"

"Nobody will suspect us. We're just girls." Dominique smiled when she realised being a 'girl' had its advantages.

"Well, I'm not going to ask how you know all of this." Nathalie shook her head slowly. "But if you can get a permit issued, it will be nice to leave the confines of the city walls for a while. Florent and Leo have a little wagon their dog can tow. I could ask if we can borrow it. At least we could get some wood."

Dominique hugged her friend. "I'll go straight away and apply. We can go to the forest in the morning."

Applying for a permit was harder than Dominique expected. No matter which reason or excuse she offered, the German officer wouldn't budge. It was almost like he took pleasure from denying her request. Hopeful for a better response or perhaps a different, more kind, officer the next morning, she tried again.

"Nein," came the response with a dismissive hand waving her away. "Citizens may walk in the woods on Thursdays and Sundays between 3pm and 7pm. No other times."

She left the building despondent. It would likely be too late by Thursday to help the hiding soldiers. She was powerless.

The horn and hiss of a train pulling into the Gare du Quesnoy drew her attention. Like a curious cat she hurried along the road eager to see who was arriving, more Germans or perhaps the French army en masse, a whole train full to overpower the Germans and free the city, save them all from this oppression.

"Don't be silly, Dominique, you're letting your imagination get away on you." Dominique glanced over her shoulder, imagining her mother was there. She was alone, she'd just been talking aloud to herself. She chuckled at the irony.

The men who dismounted from the train weren't soldiers of any country. They wore civilian clothes, and their gaunt, downcast faces said they weren't arriving voluntarily. Their murmurings were French, fellow countrymen captured and at the mercy of the enemy. German soldiers jabbed their bayonets at any who dallied, gazing at their new surroundings, wondering where they were now.

The men were herded along the street. The thwack of leather kept the group moving as soldiers at the rear cracked their whips.

The captives shuffled past Dominique, reluctantly dragging their feet. She silently counted as they passed. Mathematics was never her strongest suit and having run out of fingers to help her keep tally, she gave up when she reached one hundred. The lines went on and on, at least four times what she'd counted.

When the group was beyond the station it was split into two. Half of the men had to walk behind a wagon loaded with shovels and pick axes; they headed out of town to repair the roads damaged in the fighting. The other half went in the opposite direction. Dominique swallowed the lump sitting heavily in her throat. The wagon they were forced to follow was full of axes and saws, all the equipment needed to fell trees. The group must be on their way to the Foret de Mormal. It was too late to warn the British soldiers.

Feeling as downcast as the prisoners, Dominique headed to Nathalie's.

Chapter 14

Dominique found Nathalie at the back of the house with the borrowed wagon. The rickety homemade cart was hitched to a great Dane, still with his grand stature but protruding ribs and a brindle coat that lacked its normal sheen.

"It's alright big fellow." Dominique patted the dog's head. "We won't make you work today."

"Are we not going?" Nathalie asked.

"Non, there is no point." Dominique sighed and shook her head, imagining the fate of the men. "A train load of workers arrived and half of them are on their way to the forest with axes and saws."

"Oh, non, je suis désolé."

Dominique was sorry too but there was nothing else they could do.

"We might as well collect the sticks and branches from the orchard, while we've got the wagon," Nathalie suggested.

They were gathering the fallen branches of an old apple tree bereft of any leaves when vehicle engines revved at the front of the building. The vehicles screeched to a halt; doors slammed, and Germans yelled commands.

Dominique and Nathalie abandoned the wagon and hurried to the side of the building to investigate.

"Sacrebleu!" Dominique sagged against the cold brickwork when she recognised some of the men. "They've been found already."

They were skinnier than when she'd last seen them. Life camping outdoors as winter cast its chilling grip had taken its toll. Black shadows beneath sunken eyes, dirty clothes that hung loosely as if pegged at the shoulders on a clothesline almost made them unrecognisable, but Dominique would never forget the young soldier with his hands amputated. He was instantly identifiable by his missing features. Her chest tightened as she watched him being jostled into a line. She wanted to yell out, demand that the enemy be kind to him, but she knew it was pointless, they didn't seem to have a gentle bone in their bodies.

He and nineteen others were presented for inspection to Lubbert who stood smugly on the front steps. Mayor Carlier was summoned to watch the proceedings.

"You cannot hide the enemy from us," Lubbert proclaimed. "We will find them wherever they are, and they and you will be punished accordingly."

"They're not the enemy, you are," Dominique muttered under her breath, careful to ensure only Nathalie could hear her.

"You shall disclose the whereabouts of all other French and British now." Lubbert glared at Mayor Carlier as his threat was issued. "Or your actions of treason shall see you imprisoned with them."

"I have no knowledge of any more soldiers." Mayor Carlier's face gave nothing away.

"Take them all," Lubbert yelled, his face flushed with anger. "To the prison. Now!"

Nathalie shuddered as a German soldier manhandled her pere, dragging him down the steps towards the British prisoners. The group was marched at gunpoint from the compound.

"I must go after them." Nathalie was almost in tears. "Make sure Pere is treated well."

Dominique clutched Nathalie's forearm. "You can't. It's not safe. They'll be taking them to the barracks. That's where they imprison everyone."

"But his bad health. What if ... what if his heart gives out?"

"They've done it before, used him as a pawn to demonstrate their might. It'll just be overnight. They'll let him go tomorrow." Dominique tried to sound more certain than she was.

"I hope you're right, Dominique."

"Go tell your mere," Dominique suggested. "She can demand they allow her to see him. She is his wife, they cannot deny that."

Mayor Carlier was released the following day, a little worse for wear but maintaining his vow of silence as to the whereabouts of any French or British soldiers still in Le Quesnoy. He became the least of Dominique and Nathalie's worries as all women in the town received their summons to the town hall.

They'd enjoyed many fun times in the hall, watching pantomimes and plays, concerts and choirs. Sitting on the hard wooden seats now, surrounded by armed soldiers with Lubbert standing at the front, a lecherous look on his face, made Dominique's stomach churn.

Her mere, indignant at being summonsed at all, sat beside Dominique. She refused to look at Lubbert and gazed out the window as if she'd mentally transported herself elsewhere.

What fate would befall them?

They didn't have to wait long. The murmuring crowd went quiet when Lubbert's words were repeated for their understanding.

"We are experiencing a shortage of food supplies. We must eliminate all useless mouths."

A mother sitting along the row from Dominique gasped and hugged her small children protectively. They were too young to work, too young to be at school so she could work. Were they all to be considered 'useless mouths'?'

"Dogs and cats, that serve no purpose should be disposed of," the heartless Lubbert continued. "The soldiers will inspect at the end of the week and ensure this is done."

The mother sighed with relief and relaxed her hold. The 'useless mouth' term only referred to animals.

"You will be assigned to work. You must perform the tasks assigned to you."

"I don't have to do anything." Lucie raised her chin defiantly.

She'd spoken quietly but not so quiet that the soldier at the end of the row didn't hear. He raised his rifle and eyed her. Whether or not she saw his threatening look, or the rifle aimed at her head, Dominique couldn't tell. Her mere remained as still as a statue, her back straight, her chin high. Dominique's heart was pounding in her chest, but her mother appeared more calm and serene than she'd ever seen her.

"Those of you who are unwilling or unable to contribute to the workload can volunteer to be evacuated."

Is that what her mere wanted? To be evacuated? Evacuated to where? Somewhere better like Paris, so they could see Eugenie. Or would it be to somewhere worse? Could they end up in a camp starved like the men who'd arrived on the train?

Dominique needed to read her mere's mind, but her face gave nothing away.

"All willing evacuees go to the table at the back of the hall."

The instruction came but nobody moved from their seats unless it was to gaze around the hall to see and judge the actions of others. Dominique had never been so grateful for her mother's aloofness. Lucie sat perfectly still. They weren't evacuating. It wasn't an option for Nathalie and her mere either. They would never abandon Mayor Carlier as he battled for the rights of the citizens.

Dominique spotted Marie sitting on one of the last rows of seats closest to the table. It would be easy for her to simply turn and offer her name to the soldier, but she didn't move. Their eyes met and they nodded at one another, sharing a comforting look that tried to convey everything would be alright.

Lubbert shook his head. "You may regret your choices. If you are not prepared to leave, then you must be prepared to work. All those aged between twelve and twenty-five will sweep the streets each morning. Inspection will be at seven o'clock. Ensure they are clean before then and you will not be punished."

That didn't seem too onerous. With the chill of winter, hardly anyone would venture out. Most of the horses were off fighting and the excrement of those that did walk the streets, was soon scooped up as manure for the garden. Dominique would have to get out of bed a little earlier but if that was all she had to do, she'd manage.

"Stand up all those aged between seventeen and fifty," Lubbert demanded.

Lucie ignored the command and continued to gaze out the window. Dominique, certain her mother was within this age group, bit the inside of her cheek as she pretended to study the floor, silently urging her mother not to do anything to incite the enemy's wrath.

The armed soldiers marched up and down the rows, stopping to point their rifles at women who appeared to be in the age category.

"Your age?" a soldier demanded, the head of his rifle pointed at Lucie.

They'd celebrated Lucie's fiftieth birthday back in May. Knowing her mere should be standing, Dominique froze. The hairs on her arms stood on end, she held her breath, waiting, waiting for her mother's response. The rifle's barrel looked like it could blast a hole in them both.

Was her mere's defiance going to get her imprisoned? Or worse still, with the barrel aimed at her head, killed? Perhaps she hadn't heard the instruction. Should she nudge her mother, encourage her to comply? What if she was aware of what she was doing? Dominique's lips curled into a knowing smile.

Damn the Boche she thought as her emotions flip flopped from fear to anger. Why should they work for the enemy? Alphonse refused to and he needed the money. Her pere always seemed to have money when needed. It was lack of supplies, not lack of money that affected the Favier family's lifestyle so far. Her mere was right to refuse to work for the enemy.

It seemed Lucie took forever to answer but it was only a few seconds before she turned and looked directly at the soldier.

"Fifty-one years," she said before turning to face the front of the hall.

Dominique clasped her hands in her lap. It was the only way to stop herself from raising them in a triumphant fist. She waited until the soldier moved on before she whispered to her mere.

"Fifty-one?"

"Oui, I am in my fifty-first year, Dominique. I am not between seventeen and fifty."

The tremor in Lucie's wrist when she squeezed her daughter's hand was the only outward sign that her boldness had taken more courage than Dominique thought she possessed.

"Bravo, Maman, bravo!"

Those that did stand were ordered to report to the hospital laundry. Not only would they be required to wash and dry the hospital linens, but also launder the clothes, uniforms and linen of all German soldiers stationed in Le Quesnoy.

"Those over fifty will be employed in filling sandbags." It appeared Lubbert was leaving no-one idle. "You will report to the train station at eight o'clock tomorrow morning. That is eight o'clock German time. You live in German territory now; we live by German time."

Lucie looked down at her neatly manicured fingernails and huffed as if she had no intention of damaging her nails by filling sandbags.

The next morning, when the grandfather clock chimed eight, Lucie was still seated at the table finishing her breakfast. She was dressed but not suitably attired for filling sandbags. Dominique waited until Hans and Wolfgang had left before she broached the subject.

"You're not going to fill sandbags, Maman?"

"Non! Never! Your pere helps them more than any family should have to." Lucie huffed. "Sandbags are for the trenches. They cannot demand we help them with their war effort. It is against the Hague Convention."

"The Hague Convention?" Dominique had never heard of it.

"Get yourself off to school and ask your teacher." Lucie refilled her cup from the coffee pot. "Louis and Victor, go with your sister."

"Oui, Maman," Louis replied.

"Where is Marie?" Lucie stared at the kitchen door as if Marie would appear. "Tell her the table can be cleared now."

"She's gone to the hospital."

"Is she ill? Has she gone to help your pere?"

It was difficult to tell if Lucie was worried about Marie or annoyed her servant wasn't around to clean up.

"Non ..." Dominique hesitated, unsure how her mother would react. "She's working in the laundry."

"Sacrebleu! She's given in to their demands."

"She had no choice, Maman." Dominique relayed the conversation she'd had with Marie after the meeting. "They've heard her pere has been captured and taken to a prisoner of war camp in Germany. Her Grand-mere and Grand-pere are too old and frail to work, her mere is already struggling to feed everyone. Marie must do whatever she can to save them from starving to death."

"But what about us?" Lucie looked incredulous.

"Marie will do what she can when she's not at the laundry." Dominique gathered the plates and cutlery into a pile. "I can help too."

"Non." Lucie raised her palm, signalling for Dominique to stop. "You have your baccalaureat exams coming up. The examiners will be arriving soon. Your pere insists you focus on that, although how an exam is going to help you get a good husband I'll never know."

"I'll just take this pile." Dominique carried a stack of dirty crockery to the kitchen before her mother could protest further.

She'd been trying to forget the end of year examinations. They filled her with dread. Nathalie would pass, of course, but Dominique's doubt about her own ability to pass lingered. The examinations were necessary to anyone who wished to further their education at university. What chance was there of furthering her education if the war continued?

"The permit applications for the baccalaureat examiners to travel to Le Quesnoy have been refused," the teacher announced to the small group of senior students she'd assembled at lunch time.

"Why would they do that?" Nathalie sounded panicky. "Our futures depend on passing those exams."

Dominique hoped her future depended upon a lot more than one exam or she was doomed for certain. She might have to resort to her mother's plan to find her a good husband. *Come home safe, Gabriel, please.*

"They will not allow them to travel from school to school when there is the opportunity for them to relay information," Mademoiselle Forestier explained.

"They're not spies," Nathalie protested. "They're examiners. What are we going to do? How will we sit the exams?"

"You may have to travel to Lille." The teacher frowned. "I've applied for travel permits for you to go by train, sit the exams and return home. It's not ideal but it is all I can think to try."

Travel to Lille was all Dominique heard as her mind raced with the implications, both positive and negative. An opportunity to leave the confines of Le Quesnoy. A chance to get much needed supplies that would surely still be available in the big city. Perhaps they could look around, go to the movies, after the exam of course. Maybe she could convince Maman to give her some money for new clothes. Despite losing weight, her blouse was tight across her chest and was no longer a crisp white.

However, getting to Lille on a train controlled by Germans could be a ploy to remove the 'useless mouths' from the town, send them to the city to work in the factories? What if there was no intention to let them sit the exams at all, they were a work team to be sent wherever the Germans wanted without parents around to object? Dominique tried to shake the negative thoughts away, but a heavy lump sat in the pit of her stomach. Was she old enough to look after herself or should she get her parents to intervene?

There was no sense worrying her mother with details of the planned trip until the permits were issued, but Dominique needed to tell someone. She wanted reassurance so she headed to Clemence and Alphonse's.

"Do you think I should go?" she asked when she'd finished relaying the travel plans.

Alphonse glanced around the room before responding, as if he was checking no-one was listening, despite them being in the privacy of their home.

"Oui, oui, it is the perfect opportunity." His weather-beaten face lit up as he lent closer to Dominique and whispered. "You can visit a friend of mine. I have a very important message for them."

"Why are you whispering, Alphonse?" Dominique's brow furrowed.

"It is a special friend, not a friend of the Boche." Alphonse tapped the side of his nose and nodded knowingly. "You will be able to visit her on the pretence of getting help with your exams, deliver the message and be gone without raising any suspicion."

Dominique sat back and digested Alphonse's suggestion. She was intrigued but at the same time apprehensive. Who was this woman in Lille that Alphonse knew? Dominique looked to Clemence for reassurance.

"Don't look at me, Dominique." Clemence shrugged her shoulders. "I know nothing of Alphonse's *other* business. He insists it is safer that way. What I don't know can't hurt me."

"Take some time to think about it," Alphonse suggested. "If you decide to help the cause then come back the day before you leave for Lille and Clemence will sew the message into the hem of your skirt."

A spy. Alphonse was offering her the chance to be a spy. Dominique's heart skipped a beat. Her eyes took on a gleam, their sparkle radiating the excitement she felt. She sat up straight, pulled her shoulders back and proudly announced her decision.

"I don't need time to think. I'll do it."

Chapter 15

The permits were issued; the day arrived with a thick blanket of snow. Dominique was a bundle of nerves as she huddled together with Nathalie and the other students on the platform waiting for the train to arrive. Normally adolescents wouldn't have been allowed to venture so far without their teacher or a parent chaperone, today it was an armed German soldier that verified their permits and watched over them like they were prisoners rather than students.

Dominique's stomach churned, threatened to rise and make her lose the meagre breakfast Lucie had insisted she eat. Her nerves couldn't be attributed to any one thing: the ride on a German train, a visit to a city she'd never seen the likes of before, the examination, the message carefully sewn into her hem, the visit she agreed to make to a woman she'd never met – all were intertwined to create an uneasiness beyond any Dominique had felt before.

"The train is late." Nathalie eyed the large clock on the station wall.

"Perhaps the snow has blocked the line, and it can't get through," another student added.

"We won't make it to the exam in time," a student with teary eyes said. "They'll fail us."

Not being the only bundle of nerves buoyed Dominique. She broke away from the group, wrapped her coat tight against the cold and went closer to the tracks to get a better look. In the distance she could make out the train, a black engine grew larger as it approached, the smoke from its stack indiscernible from the falling snow but the familiar clickety clack of its wheels on the tracks was now audible.

"It's coming," she announced, returning to the group, ignoring the German soldier's threatening glare.

The train hissed and screeched as it drew to a stop alongside the Gare du Quesnoy. Clouds of smoke shrouding the engine dissipated to slowly reveal a carriage of passengers wearing the familiar grey uniform of the enemy. These were battle weary, wounded soldiers with bloodied bandages and makeshift crutches. Emerging through the smoke, they looked more like zombies surfacing from the graveyard.

"Not more Germans," Nathalie groaned.

"More patients for the hospital." Dominique sighed knowing their arrival meant more work for her pere, Alice and Clemence who were already exhausted. "Why do they have to come here to recover? Why don't they just go home?"

They were questions Dominique knew no-one would give her an answer to.

A truck pulled into the station with a load of soldiers who'd been nursed back to good health. The injured soldiers were helped into the truck; the fit and able soldiers boarded the train. Nobody gave a second thought to the students standing out in the cold. They were shivering by the time the Germans settled in their seats and the students assigned guard waved them forward with the barrel of his rifle.

"Sich setzen," he commanded, pointing to two rows of wooden slatted seats.

Dominique made certain she sat by the window. She wanted to take in everything beyond the walls of the city. She'd only ever travelled south as far as Foret du Mormal, never north, not even to Valenciennes and Lille was four times farther away. It was the adventure of a lifetime. A niggling doubt she couldn't suppress, made her hope it wasn't the last trip she'd ever make. She braced her feet firmly on the floor and squeezed her knees together to halt their trembling.

Nathalie sat next to Dominique. They held hands and stared out the window as the train left the station and gained momentum along the tracks.

Whatever Dominique had imagined the vista would be; it wasn't. There was no beautiful French countryside as conveyed by poets in their prose. Blackened tree stumps jutted from the snow, their branches bereft of green foliage, not from a winter shedding of leaves but burned beyond recovery.

"Sacrebleu!" she cursed and pointed, drawing Nathalie's attention to the carcase of a horse, an innocent victim of a battle, left to rot where it fell.

Dominique had to turn away. What if there were dead soldiers as well? It was one thing to see the hide and bones of an animal, but a person, a skeleton and shreds of clothing all that remained of a man who gave his life fighting for his country, for a freedom none of the Quercitains were experiencing. She couldn't bear to witness that; the stories that filtered through were more than enough.

Gabriel. What if it was Gabriel lying out in the cold? Learning of his demise would break her heart, but she'd want to know, to give him a proper burial. She took a deep breath and turned back to the view.

The train passed a farm located close to the tracks for ease of transporting its produce to the market. All that remained were the unliveable charred frameworks of buildings that used to house families and animals. Dominique hoped they'd manage to escape before the blast of artillery fire destroyed their homestead and their livelihood.

Closer to Valenciennes they saw the first farm with cattle, heads hung low, bony ribs protruding. The barns that should have been overflowing with hay and straw supplements to get the animals through until the new spring growth were empty bar a few raggedy bales.

"Looks like the Boche have been requisitioning here too," Dominique observed.

A group of women boarded at Valenciennes, but they were made to sit at the opposite end of the carriage as if any contact would allow them to collude against the enemy. Dominique studied them as they passed, wondering what their German escorts had planned for them. They were a mixture of ages, some as young as Dominique, others older, more Clemence's age. Seeing several of them smile and giggle with the German soldiers riled Dominique. She silently vowed to never get so desperate. Her heart went out to the others, those who cowered away from the soldiers and were obviously unwilling travellers.

The snowfall stopped, revealing a city damaged almost beyond repair. Streets strewn with bricks and debris from buildings blasted in the battle were being picked over by those desperate for scraps and morsels. Smoke drifted skyward from buildings still smouldering in the aftermath. Parts of the city looked abandoned: churches without spires, window frames missing glass panes, doorways minus the doors that could be closed against the weather, roofs lacking the tiles or iron to render them waterproof, houses bereft of the people that made them homes.

"Perhaps we are fortunate to live in Le Quesnoy." Dominique gave Nathalie's hand a comforting squeeze.

"Oui, I think so." Nathalie rested her head on Dominique's shoulder as if the war had worn her out.

Their predicament was bittersweet. Living with the Germans brought tension and uncertainty to their everyday lives but at least they still had the roofs over their heads. Dominique slept in her own bed not on the streets or seeking shelter in ramshackle buildings. Her family still had food on the table three times a day, rationed and not of the same quality they enjoyed before the war, but they weren't scavenging for food.

Their spirits lifted slightly when the train left the city behind, and the images of destruction faded to a memory. Snowflakes were replaced by raindrops which spattered on the carriage windows and ran down the pane like tears wept for the fallen.

The students chatted amongst themselves, swapping notes and asking questions to revise for the exams. Dominique knew she should listen more attentively; the last-minute revision might be the difference between her passing or failing but she struggled to focus.

A row of crosses in the field caught her eye. They sat beside the remnants of a trench, coils of barbed wire, twisted sheets of iron and shards of timber which were intended to protect the soldiers who crouched within their walls. She caught a glimpse of the water pooling in the bottom and imagined the soldiers' wet boots and cold feet.

Lille came into view, a replica of Valenciennnes except on a much larger scale, the damage multiplied beyond anything Dominique could comprehend. When the students stepped from the train, it was to the sound of distant gunfire. It had been three months since Dominique had heard the distinctive noises of a nearby battle, but it quickened her pulse the same as it had then. She turned, tilting her head, trying to discern the direction and proximity of the fighting. Was it coming closer or moving away? She swallowed. Were they in danger of being embroiled at the frontline of the battle? Was this the end of the line for them in more ways than she expected?

Dominique lifted the hem of her skirt, dodging a puddle as the students were led away from the station. She remembered the message hidden in her hem and the sound of gunfire heightened her fear. Did someone know she had the message? Had she not been careful enough to keep her secret? Did she look like a spy? Were the enemy coming to get her? Was she to be arrested as a spy and shot before she'd even accomplished her first mission? Had she endangered not only herself but the rest of the students? Was she foolish to accept Alphonse's request? Her thoughts raced as fast as the adrenaline coursing through her veins.

"Are you alright, Dominique?" Nathalie took her hand and gave it an encouraging squeeze. "Don't worry about the exam. You'll be fine."

Dominique doubted her examination results would be anywhere near as good as Nathalie's but realising her friend was oblivious to the letter that weighed heavy in her hem, allowed her to breathe easier.

"Oui, I just want this trip over and done with." She didn't lie; she gave away nothing she shouldn't. The sooner the missions had been completed, and they were back on the train going home, the better.

The group of women alighted the train and were led away. A young girl who should have been with the students, sitting exams, dragged her feet at the back of the line. Tears streaked her face, and her pleading eyes begged silently for help. Where were they being taken? What would they be made to do? If only, Dominique could help her. The girl looked helpless, and Dominique felt just as powerless. She couldn't save her. She could only mouth 'stay strong' and hope that would be enough.

"I wish we could help those women," Dominique murmured to Nathalie.

"Why?" Nathalie looked askance at Dominique. "I think they've found a way to take care of themselves. I heard Pere say the Germans had recruited prostitutes to keep the soldiers happy."

"I don't think all of them are willing participants." Dominique swallowed the lump of dread wedged in her throat.

"We need to focus on our examination, Dominique or we could end up in the same desperate situation, willingly or not."

"Oui, you are right, as always." Dominique had no choice but to push the image of the girl from her mind.

She smelt the remnants of gunpowder in the air, the rain soaking it into the earth. Parts of the city appeared untouched, life continuing as normal, people bustling about completing their business. The guard led them along the footpath to the school where they were to sit the examination. They walked close to the buildings, sheltering in the lee to avoid as much of the rain as possible.

Peering down the side streets revealed segments of the cityscape not so fortunate. Buildings reduced to rubble, women skirting around the strewn piles of bricks or the large craters bisecting the road, children clambering over or through, finding fun in the mayhem.

They had to go around a long straggly line of people on the footpath. Hunched elderly men and women, mothers carrying babies with toddlers clinging to their skirts, all dirty faced, and clad in clothing that had long since been laundered or patched. Some clutched bowls, ready to beg for any morsel of food, all had a look of hunger and desperation, gaunt cheeks and lank hair. The front of the line revealed a soup kitchen – the aroma of onions filled the expansive room and wafted into the street, steam rose from the large pot from which a stout woman ladled the soup, one portion per person. Dominique's stomach rumbled but the students weren't permitted to stop and satisfy their hunger.

Eventually, they reached the school, a brick building much the same as their own, as if all schools had to be built strictly to a syllabus, much like the subjects required to be taught within their confines. Before being ushered inside, Dominique scanned her surroundings, taking in the street names, the signs and numbers on buildings, wondering how she was supposed to meet up with her contact in this unfamiliar city.

"Beeil dich." The German escort hurried them inside.

The thud of the door closing behind them sent a chill down Dominique's spine. She gulped, feeling as if she'd already failed her mission.

"This way children." An elegantly dressed woman led them into the classroom. "Put your things down and take a seat at a desk."

Dominique had no choice but to follow the instructions. If she failed in delivering the message, she needed to ensure she gave the exam her best effort, so everything was not lost.

A wood burner in the corner took the chill off the room, the basket of wood being used as sparingly as the soup in the kitchen. While each desk was built to seat two students, they were requested to separate for the exam. There was to be no copying of answers nor sharing of information.

Dominique had expected a tough examiner but the delicate lace collars on the woman's dress reflected the softness in her voice and demeanour. Her hair was styled in a bun at the nape of her neck but wasn't pulled harshly away from her face, rather wavy brown locks framed a motherly look Dominique immediately felt comfortable with.

"Bonjour, je m'appelle Mademoiselle Thuliez," she announced when all the students had settled.

Thuliez. Dominique's eyes went wide as she sat up straighter to study the woman. Did she say 'Thuliez' or had Dominique merely imagined she'd heard the name Alphonse had told her to seek out? Was this lady the contact she was supposed to pass the message to? The coincidence was too much.

Dominique took deep breaths trying to slow her heartbeat. The code word Alphonse had whispered in her ear, the word she had silently recited to imprint it in her memory, vanished as if she'd never heard it spoken before.

How could she be a spy when she couldn't even remember the code word? Dominique shook her head. She felt the blood drain from her face replaced by a clammy, nauseous feeling. Was her contribution to the war effort to be thwarted at the first hurdle?

"Are you feeling alright, my dear?" Mme Thuliez stood beside Dominique and placed a comforting hand on her shoulder. "We have a little time before the examination will begin, would you like a drink of water to calm your nerves."

"Oui ... non ... oui." Dominique couldn't string a coherent reply together.

"Come, follow me."

Dominique stood on wobbly legs and followed the woman from the classroom, down a passage to the back of the building and into a small basic kitchen.

"Merci beaucoup." Dominique drank from the glass of water Mme Thuliez poured for her, gulping down the liquid as if it was the courage she needed.

"Slow down, child, you don't want to choke."

Dominique paused and took a deep breath. "I should give you something in return."

"You have something for me?" Mme Thuliez raised a questioning eyebrow.

"Oui." Dominique lowered her eyes to the hem of her skirt.

"Oh, your hem, you've got it wet in the rain. Let me dry that for you. We don't want you catching a chill."

Mme Thuliez took a tea towel from the bench and knelt beside Dominique. She fidgeted with the hem of Dominique's skirt. If anyone entered the room, their ruse would appear wholly plausible. Even Dominique couldn't see what she was doing and stood in awe of the intelligent and quick-thinking Mme Thuliez.

"There you are, dear." Mme Thuliez stood back up. "All better now, ready to rejoin the others."

Unsure whether it was a question or a suggestion, Dominique hesitated. She couldn't see Alphonse's note and was uncertain whether the message had been delivered or not.

"All you need to do now is pass your exam." Mme Thuliez must have seen Dominique's confused look and patted the side of her skirt where a deep pocket would be sewn into the seam. "I will take care of everything else."

The tension in Dominique's shoulders eased slightly, replaced by a sense of pride. She followed Mme Thuliez back to the classroom with a gleam in her eye. The mission had been accomplished with relative ease. If she could carry out secret missions during a war, then surely, she could pass an examination.

Despite alternating from cheek to cheek on the hard wooden seat, Dominique's bottom was numb by the time she replaced the lid on her ink pen. She'd given the exam her all. The questions were hard, she'd had to pause and ponder her answers, trying not to look across at Nathalie whose head was down as her ink pen charged across the page.

"Merci beaucoup, for *all* your efforts," Mme Thuliez said as she collected Dominique's exam paper and added it to the pile to be marked.

"Merci beaucoup, Mme Thuliez, for *all* your help."

The pair shared a subtle conspiratory smile, undetectable to anyone else in the room as anything more than relief the examination was over.

"Safe travels children." Mme Thuliez led them out of the classroom, depositing them back under the supervision of the German guard. "Au revoir."

"Au revoir." Dominique hoped she'd see Mme Thuliez again.

Back on a train, heading in the opposite direction, the landscape blurred as Dominique lost herself in thoughts of the ways she had already helped the war effort: the distribution of the secretly baked bread, guiding the escaping British and French soldiers through the tunnels, delivering the message to Mme Thuliez. While Gabriel was off fighting, she was stifling the enemy from within. Her grin conveyed her satisfaction and filled her with a radiating warmth.

"You're looking happy with yourself," Nathalie interrupted her musing. "Do you think you've done well?"

Dominique knew Nathalie was referring only to the examination, but she answered in relation to everything that had occurred and all she was yet to do.

"Oui, I have done well."

She planned to visit Alphonse as soon as possible to see what else she could do to help the cause.

Chapter 16

23 December 1914

"What are you cooking, Marie?" Dominique found their servant at the kitchen bench stirring the floury contents of a mixing bowl.

"Lubbert has *gifted* us extra rations of flour, one hundred grams per person." Sarcasm laced Marie's reply.

"And you are not saving it?"

"Non, your mere doesn't want Christmas to be any different than before and she insisted I bake a Christmas cake." Marie put the bowl down and licked the end of the spoon to taste the mixture. She grimaced. "There's not enough sugar or fruit and it needs sweetening."

Despite knowing Hans and Wolfgang had already left for the day, Dominique leaned in and whispered to Marie.

"I know where Pere has his brandy hidden. Would a dash of brandy help?"

Marie grinned. "Oui! Oui!"

Dominique crept over to her pere's office. She kept looking over her shoulder, expecting the enemy to be watching her. They had raided their house so often, 'requisitioning' anything they felt like taking for themselves. The wine cellar had been looted, every bottle of merlot and pinot noir gone, champagne opened and drunk on the spot or sprayed around the cellar as if they were celebrating a win.

Nobody was winning the war, supposed to last six weeks, it was now four months and ruining a Christmas. When families should be reuniting, they were stranded on opposite sides of the battle front unable to even send best wishes to their loved ones.

Henri had a secret panel in the back of the bookcase where he kept his medical texts and journals. Dominique only knew about it because she'd snuck down one night and seen her father enjoying a drink at the end of a long tiring day. She found the books that hid the panel and piled them on her pere's desk before sliding the panel out.

She paused, the bottle in mid-air as the ramifications of her actions dawned on her. The Christmas cake might taste better but her pere would know someone had found his hidden alcohol. If they had to share the cake with Hans and Wolfgang, they too might taste the alcohol and know something was amiss. She bit her lip, weighing up her options.

The Christmas tree in the sitting room made the decision for her. It could barely be called a tree, merely a meagre branch, all that could be spared. The Germans demanded the wood too. The trees were milled into timber to line the walls of the trenches; the offcuts were burned in the fires to ensure they were warm. Without a second thought all they left the Quercitains were twigs.

Last Christmas and all the Christmas days before, for as long as Dominique could remember, the tree that sat in the corner of their sitting room, adorned with decorations, both handmade and passed down through generations, had an angel on top, her wings nearly touching the ornate ceiling. That same angel was now downcast on the thin branch unable to support her weight only two feet from the floor. Dominique had tried to prop her up numerous times. Perhaps she too was as disappointed as Louis and Victor with the lack of presents under the tree.

"If the angel can't look over us and keep us safe." Dominique poured two capfuls of brandy into a cup, and restored everything back to the way it was. "Then let the cake at least cheer us."

Clutching the precious liquid Dominique left her father's office feeling triumphant. A thud at the entrance way door stopped her in her tracks. She froze, fearing she'd been caught already. The noise was familiar but not a sound she'd heard recently. She watched the door, listened for more noises, expecting the door to open. Seconds ticked by. Nothing.

Mail! That's what the noise was. The sound of letters being dropped into the letterbox. It had been so long since they'd had mail, she'd forgotten. The thrill of receiving anything quickened her heartbeat. Had the Germans allowed the post to come through because it was Christmas? That would be the best gift ever.

Dominique held the cup in one hand, retrieved the letters with the other and hurried back to the kitchen.

"Marie, Marie, quick, take this!" Dominique passed her the cup and held up the envelopes. "Look there's mail."

There were two letters addressed to Dominique, the remainder to her father. Her heart skipped a beat when she recognised what they were; her examination results and a letter she was certain was from Gabriel. She felt giddy and slumped onto a stool at Marie's workbench.

"Are you alright, Dominique?" Marie abandoned the cake and hurried to her side. "Do you need a drink of water?"

"Mail? Did I hear you say mail, Dominique?" Lucie strode into the kitchen. "Is there a letter from Eugenie? Have the Germans found a heart at Christmas and let the mail through?"

Dominique stuffed the letters addressed to her inside her cardigan, grateful for the extra layer of clothing she'd worn to ward off the cold.

"Non, Maman." She handed over the other letters. "Just bills for Pere, I think."

"Oh, sacrebleu." Lucie lost interest in the mail and put the bills on the sideboard. "I am so tired of having to work for them when they do nothing in return for us. Marie, please bring me a hot drink in the sitting room."

"Oui, ma'am," Marie replied, already preparing a cup and saucer on a tray as if nothing was amiss until Lucie left the room. "Who are your letters from?" she whispered.

"My exam results." Dominique wanted to keep the letter from Gabriel to herself.

"Well open them up then. Keeping them hidden won't change what they say."

"I'm not expecting to pass." Dominique was happier she'd got the secret message to Mme Thuliez than finishing the last question in the exam. "I think I'll go up to my bedroom and open them."

"Off you go then. I've got to get this cake in the oven," Marie said. "I expect to hear your squeal of delight from here."

Dominique took the stairs two at a time and hurried along the passage to her bedroom, closing the door behind her. She sat on her bed, curling her slippered feet underneath her and pulling the eiderdown over her knees for warmth. She held the envelopes one in each hand.

"Which one should I open first?" She looked from envelope to envelope expecting them to answer her.

She opted for the exam results, deciding they would be quick, a pass or a fail, which, in the midst of the war, meant nothing. Before the war, a pass would have qualified her to go to university, to study for a career that could take her places, other than the marriage bed of the wealthy husband her mother intended to find her. Now, going away to university, in Paris or England wasn't an option, the Germans would never grant a travel permit for that. Fortunately, a wealthy husband wasn't an option either, there were none left that weren't involved in the war in some way and no social occasions to meet them.

That left Gabriel and he had written to her. Whether or not he'd written to Nathalie as well didn't matter. She could linger over whatever he had to say.

She hooked her thumb under the official envelope's flap and edged it along until she could retrieve the paper inside. Her fingers trembled as she unfolded the results.

"Pass!" Dominique squealed with delight; not loud enough for Marie to hear but Remy must have because he scratched at the door to be let in. "Do you want to celebrate with me Remy? A double celebration: my exam results and you still being alive. I don't know what Pere did to save you but I'm glad." She picked Remy up and twirled around the room while the dog licked her chin excitedly.

The second letter beckoned.

"Now, let's hope Gabriel has good news for me too." Dominique put Remy on the end of the bed.

She lifted the envelope to her face and inhaled but there was no scent that was reminiscent of Gabriel. The letter looked well-travelled but the details of where it began its journey and how it got to Le Quesnoy were not evident. It was obvious though, when Dominique turned the envelope over, that someone had already read its contents. She wouldn't let this ruin her delight. She savoured the moment, holding the envelope in her hands as if she was holding Gabriel himself. He had written to her. In the midst of a war, the young man who made her heart soar, had taken the time to write. Where was he? How had he gotten a letter through when correspondence between those on either side of the battle front wasn't allowed?

Dominique swallowed as the realisation Gabriel might not be beyond the German trenches occurred to her. Desperate to know she ripped the envelope open, snatched the note and pored over its contents.

Dearest Dominique. Tears welled in the corners of her eyes.

I hope this letter finds you well and Le Quesnoy's winter isn't too harsh this year. Dominique blinked the tears away and huffed, she didn't want pleasantries and polite conversation about the weather. She wanted Gabriel to declare his love; to say he missed her as much as she longed to be with him.

I hope you don't mind me writing to you rather than my family. Please relay the parts of my letter that you think they will want to hear about and be able to cope with.

Dominique gasped. What was so bad that Gabriel's family wouldn't be able to deal with? He clearly had no idea what they were living with, the harshness of the Germans that Mayor Carlier had to try and counter daily to protect not just his family but the entire town.

I was injured and captured by the Germans. I am now in a prisoner of war camp at XXXXXXXXX. Gabriel's location had been obliterated with black ink. It made no difference. Dominique had no chance of rescuing him.

Instead of the walls of the city to keep the enemy out we have fences of barbed wire to keep us in. I haven't counted but I reckon there are 250 of us in the shed they call our barracks and I'm not yet mobile enough to see how many sheds there are.

"Oh, Gabriel." Images of Gabriel injured and broken blurred the letters on the page. "What have they done to you? Please get better. Please stay alive until the French beat the enemy and free you."

Each hut has a fire but there is little to burn so it is just as well there are so many of us to keep each other warm. We aren't always successful. A few have been lost. Those who are well enough, and some who aren't are put to work each day. We are fed but XXXXXXXXXXXXXXXXXXXXXXXXXXXXXXXXXXXX.

"They're not feeding you well are they, Gabriel? Perhaps I can get a food parcel sent to you." Dominique sighed. "Not that we have much to spare ourselves."

Anyway, I am not writing to be morbid. I need you to be the shining light you always have been, to write back and tell me all the good things you are up to, the mischief you and Nathalie get into, to give me hope that this is not forever.

I remember the secret notes you and Nathalie used to write and hope you will find just as much treasure in this one.

Please write back soon with all the news of Le Quesnoy and more, Gabriel.

There was no declaration of love, but Gabriel needed her, and Dominique would help him in whatever way she could. She folded her arms across her chest, holding the letter against her heart.

"I'll shine as bright as I can for you, Gabriel. I promise."

An inkling there was more to the letter made Dominique read it again, line by line, word by word. She paused and reread about the childhood secret notes. Was there more to this sentence than just the memory? Gabriel used to tease them about the notes, why would he recall them now? Dominique's desire to investigate quickened her pulse. There was only one way to find out.

"What's he trying to tell us, Remy?" Dominique discarded the eiderdown, flipping it over Remy who whined but stayed hidden beneath the blanket.

She grabbed the candle kept beside her bed and rushed back down the stairs to light it with a taper from the fire.

"Why do you need a candle, Dominique?" Marie asked. "Did you pass your examination?"

"Oui, I did." Dominique ignored Marie's first question and disappeared again before she could ask further. "I'll be back soon."

Back in her room, with the door securely shut and a chair wedged under the handle as an extra precaution, Dominique held Gabriel's letter over the candle. Not close enough to burn but just as she and Nathalie did as children to reveal their messages written in lemon juice.

She squeezed her eyes shut, silently urging a secret message to appear. What would Gabriel write? A declaration of love for her eyes only. The thought enveloped her with a heat she'd only felt when he was near.

"What do you want to tell me, Gabriel?" Dominique slowly opened her eyes and made out the words emerging beneath the inked writing.

I knew you would understand, Dominique. Let me know in the same manner anything that might help the cause. I'll get it to those who can make a difference. Together we'll win.

Gabriel hadn't told her what she wanted to hear but his message made adrenaline course through her veins.

"Merci beaucoup, mon amour." Dominique's eyes sparkled as she smiled. "You've given me the best Christmas present ever."

She snuffed out the candle, folded the letter back into the envelope and stowed it under her pillow. She'd read it for a third time later just to be sure it wasn't her imagination getting carried away as her mother kept telling her it was prone to do.

"Where are you going?" Dominique asked Louis and Victor who were in the entrance way, heads adorned with woollen hats, hands gloved, and scarves wrapped around their necks.

"Christmas Carols in the square," the boys chimed together as if they were already singing. "It's Christmas Eve. We always go to the square on Christmas Eve remember."

Dominique smiled. Carols in the square, when all the town turned out, candles glowing, voices in harmony celebrating the festive season until the church bells were rung at midnight, was a highlight of her childhood.

"But it is nearly eight o'clock," she replied, remembering the newly imposed rule that no-one was allowed on the streets after eight.

Apart from having to make the secret bread distribution from the hospital courtyard earlier, the curfew hadn't impacted much else, not with the plummeting temperatures keeping everyone inside.

"But it's Christmas Eve," Louis countered.

"We've got to go." Victor moved to open the door.

"Wait." Dominique raised her palm to stop them. "I'll get my coat, hat and gloves and go with you."

Henri, Lucie and Marie also turned up ready to enjoy the celebration as if the war too had stopped for a Christmas break. Dressed for the winter weather, the group left the house. Henri and Lucie walked arm in arm, Dominique and Marie held hands for the short distance to the square. Louis and Victor weren't to be contained, they ran about scuffing the snow with their boots, making and tossing snowballs like they were cannon fire.

A thick blanket of snow was like a bride's veil, a symbol of innocence.

"Have you found out anything useful yet?" Dominique whispered to Marie.

Last night, Dominique revealed to Marie just enough to gain her assistance but not sufficient to get her in trouble should the messages to be sent to Gabriel be intercepted.

"Apparently Lubbert is leaving," Marie replied.

"Oh, that is the best Christmas present he could give the Quercitains." Dominique smiled as they entered the town square.

The paved area in front of the church had been cleared of snow, and the Favier family joined the townsfolk already gathered. The flickering flames of the candles they carried lit up the square like a starry night sky.

Friends and neighbours greeted one another, cheeks were kissed, hands shaken. United they stood, their backs turned against the weather and the German sentries posted at each corner of the square. A local man had brought his piano accordion and began to play *Douce Nuit, Sainte Nuit.*

As she sung, Dominique almost believed the words were true, that all was calm and bright. Snowflakes fell gently on the group, glistening in the candlelight, like a blessing from the skies.

"Stopp es jetzt!" An unfamiliar wiry German officer stood on the church steps and yelled at the group.

The townsfolk continued singing, raising their voices to block out the intrusion.

"Stopp es jetzt!"

Gunshots fired into the air brought the singing to an abrupt halt.

"I am Major Vierordt. I am in control now." The waxed sides of his moustache flapped like wings as he spat at the crowd. "You will obey my command. You will return home now. Gatherings of more than four people are not permitted."

Heads turned, townsfolk looked at one another, deciding whether to protest or comply. Another gunshot into the still air made the decision for them, and they slowly dispersed. The accordion player decided he would not cower, he walked with a straight back, his fingers danced over the keys and buttons, as his arms caressed a melody from the bellows. The crowd laughed when they recognised the tune and broke into song. *Entre le boeuf et L'âne gris*, the oldest French carol about the baby Jesus between an ox and a grey donkey, rang out through the streets of Le Quesnoy as its people returned home.

"Lubbert may have been an Ox, but his replacement appears to be more of an ass," Henri observed as they reached their home. "Hopefully we won't feel the brunt of his kick too badly."

Chapter 17

January 1915

Vierordt proved to be worse than an ass, he was a tyrant who put so many townsfolk in the civilian prison for petty misdemeanours they had to commandeer the schoolhouse to keep them captive. The alternative to long days and nights imprisoned without food and heating was to pay a fine. Most opted for captivity, either as a protest at funding the German coffers or because they were without the means to make any payment. Many Quercitains were now reliant on the town council or the Commission for Relief in Belgium for sustenance. Shelter in the schoolhouse was preferable to wandering the streets begging for food.

Without a building from which classes could be taught, Vierordt seized the opportunity to put the children to work.

"We're off to the Foret de Mormal today," Louis sounded excited. "To collect blackberries."

"Non, we have to gather nettles." Victor was the listener of the two so was more likely to have heard correctly.

"Well, I'm going to eat as many blackberries as I can." Louis licked his lips and rubbed his stomach.

"Sorry to disappoint you, Louis." Dominique ruffled his hair. "But there won't be any blackberries left at this time of the year."

Louis pouted and pushed her hand away. "Oui, there will be, and I will find them!"

Dominique wrote about Vierordt in her first letter to Gabriel. She detailed his tyranny in plain ink but before she could finish the letter and send it on its way, she needed the information to be encoded, something, anything that Gabriel could relay to help the French war efforts.

Without school, she'd been assigned to work at the hospital laundry. There was no waiting until she turned seventeen to make use of her. As prepared as she'd ever be for a day washing dirty linen, Dominique left the house, pondering what she could relay to Gabriel as she walked.

"Salut, Nathalie," she greeted her friend as they took their places at the tubs of water in which the hospital sheets soaked.

"Salut, Dominique," Nathalie replied wearily.

"Are you alright? You look tired." Dominique hauled a wet sheet onto the washboard and began scrubbing.

"I didn't sleep well." Nathalie sighed and shook her head. She took the clean sheet from Dominique, rinsed it and wrung the water out. "I kept thinking of Gabriel injured in a prisoner of war camp, imagining what those brutes would be doing to him, a soldier who fought against them. They treat us bad enough, making us wash their dirty laundry. Uggh!"

"We need to help the French soldiers win the war."

"How can we do that from here? We have no weapons. We barely have enough to eat."

Dominique lowered her voice to a murmur as she scrubbed the next sheet. "Information. Anything we can find out about the German's plans we can relay to the French. Like a game of hide and seek, if you know where they are, it's easier to win."

"How are we going to let the French army know when we can't write letters?"

"We can write to Gabriel, and he can write to others."

"I don't want to get him into any more trouble."

"Nobody will know. It's all by code." Dominique discreetly tapped the side of her nose. "I just need your help to get the information. Have you heard Vierordt discussing anything with your pere?"

"They're calling for volunteers to leave Le Quesnoy, promising to transport them to safety." Nathalie wiped her already red and wrinkled hands on her skirt. "They're demanding he promote it as a good option for the townsfolk, but I don't think Pere trusts them."

"Why are they offering to do that? They won't have anyone left to do all their dirty laundry." Dominique passed another sheet to Nathalie.

"Useless mouths."

"Useless mouths? I thought they were just the cats and dogs."

"Women whose husbands are away fighting, and they can't work because they're busy taking care of their children. Old people who are too frail to work. Anyone who can't provide for themselves is deemed useless."

Dominique pictured the townsfolk who came each evening to the hospital courtyard for bread. They looked desperate as if it was the only food they had, even now when flour was scarce and the bread baked by Francois was half wheat, half rye, hard crusted and black. If everyone who needed help was transported there'd hardly be anyone left.

"Have many people volunteered?"

"Non, not yet."

They carried the heavy basket of wet sheets to the line strung from one side of the room to the other and pegged them out. While Dominique was physically tired from the effort, her mind raced with possibilities. Perhaps the Boche were running out of food and would have to abandon the war and retreat to Germany. It was the best-case scenario but unlikely to be true. Maybe the French could surround them, not allowing any food supplies to get through and starve them into submission. It was the tactic the Germans were applying to the Quercitains, it would be nice to turn the tables. Whatever the reason, Dominique itched to hurry home, complete the reply to Gabriel and send it on its way.

Realisation that only one letter per month was allowed tempered Dominique's eagerness to put her note to Gabriel in the post. She needed to make the most of the opportunity and decided Alphonse would likely have something to add that could be of use.

When her duties at the laundry were finally finished Dominique buttoned her jacket against the weather, pushed her hands deep into her pockets to keep them warm and hurried to the cottage where her half-sister and husband lived. It looked abandoned, the shutters closed against the weather, no candlelight seeping under the front door.

"Clemence, Alphonse." She knocked on the front door as she called out.

She turned the door handle when there was no response and poked her head inside. No flames flickered or hot embers glowed in the hearth, the house almost colder than outside. It was clear no one was about, and they hadn't been home for some time.

"Where are you?" Dominique scratched her head. "I hope nothing bad has happened."

It dawned on her that Clemence was likely still at the hospital. Dominique could have saved herself the walk, avoided saturating the hem of her skirt and getting wet stockings and boots. Afraid her toes had frozen she wriggled them to keep the blood circulating before she set off again.

The hood of her jacket kept the rain from pelting her face, but she had to hold it in place. She alternated hands, plunging her cold hand back into her pocket. By the time she reached the hospital, her fingers were icy and red. She struggled to unbutton her jacket and walked into the ward with water dripping from her clothes.

"Dominique!" Alice abandoned the patient she'd been tending to and strode over. "What are you doing, dripping water all over our clean floor?"

"Salut, Alice." Dominique looked down at the puddle of water forming at her feet. "Pardon. I was looking for Clemence."

"Wait in the courtyard, where you can't make any more mess." Alice's words were spoken to Dominique, but her focus was on the patient she been tending to. "I will send her to you."

Thinking it was likely Clemence who'd have to mop the floor, Dominique hurried toward the courtyard before guilt sent her from the hospital altogether. She paused at the door, feeling there was something more to Alice's abruptness. Her half-sister was a stickler for the rules, but etiquette was equally important to her, and she hadn't even greeted Dominique or shown any concern for her wellbeing.

Alice had returned to the patient she'd been tending and sat on the edge of his cot. They appeared to be chatting as if they were old friends. Studying the man's features, Dominique decided that wasn't possible. He was blonde haired and blue eyed. She'd seen enough men of that colouring in the last few months to know he was German.

He must have sensed her watching, he turned her way, and his piercing ice-blue eyes looked directly at her. A shiver ran down her spine and it wasn't from the chill that was biting into her toes. She blinked away the image and left the ward, sheltering under the veranda out of the rain while her heartbeat slowed.

"Salut, Dominque." Clemence sat on the bench beside her as if she had to snatch every opportunity to rest. "What brings you out in this horrid weather?"

Dominique was so concerned about everyone she shook her head to clear her thoughts. Who should she ask about first?

"Salut, Clemence. How are you? You look tired."

"I am tired, Dominique. There is a constant stream of injured German soldiers coming through, so we are having to work long hours." Clemence tilted her head and looked askance at Dominique. "But you didn't come here to ask how I am."

"Non." Dominique wrung her hands together. "I went to your house and neither of you were there. I was worried something had happened."

"You were right to be concerned." Clemence placed her warm hand on Dominique's and sighed. "Alphonse has got himself thrown into the civilian prison for refusing to work for the Boche."

"Oh, non, Clemence." Dominique was proud of Alphonse for taking his stance but afraid for him at the same time. "When will they let him out?"

"It was a three-day sentence and he's been there two already."

"Have you been allowed to see him? Is he doing alright?"

"He's moaning about the coffee," Clemence replied.

Dominique chuckled. "Excusez-moi? Alphonse is in prison and all he's worried about is the coffee!"

"Oui. Vierordt has decided coffee is too expensive, even though they were watering it down, so now it's just a mixture of water and flour."

"Oh, yuck, no wonder Alphonse is complaining." Dominique swallowed, imagining the taste, or lack thereof.

"Did you come to see us just for a catch up, or is there something else?"

"A catch up." Dominique stopped herself from adding more. She hadn't lied; she just hadn't told the entire truth. She would have to hold off sending the note to Gabriel until Alphonse was released. "What is Alice doing with that German soldier?" she asked to change the subject.

Clemence squeezed Dominique's hand and sighed. "Not much gets past you, does it?"

Knowing Clemence didn't expect an answer, Dominique stayed quiet, waiting for the silence to be filled.

Clemence glanced back at the door to the ward and lowered her voice. "She's fallen in love with him."

"What?" Dominique squealed. That wasn't the answer she'd expected.

Alice was in her late thirties. Dominique had never seen her with a man, thought that she was so dedicated to nursing, she didn't have time for one.

"She is a woman, Dominique. It will happen to you too one day."

"I know." Dominique didn't clarify her response. Revealing her growing love for Gabriel, even to Clemence, was a step too far. "But ... he's a German. How can she fall in love with the enemy?"

"She never intended to," Clemence defended her sister.

"You sound like you think it is alright."

"It's not something I would do but I know what it's like to be in love." Clemence smiled as if she was daydreaming of her and

Alphonse. "You're blinded, you don't see a person's faults, you only see the good parts."

"Good parts?" Gabriel had lots of good parts but a German, they were heartless brutes. "What is she going to do about it? Surely, she can't be going to marry him or anything silly like that."

"His injuries aren't too serious; he'll be discharged from hospital soon."

"Good, they'll send him home or back to fight." It wasn't fair; Gabriel was injured but he couldn't be sent home. If this German went back to fight, he could shoot another French soldier. Either way, no one would win.

"He'll likely have a couple more weeks in Le Quesnoy to recuperate first," Clemence added.

"Alice needs to stay away from him," Dominique warned.

"She is." Clemence looked sad. "She's going to volunteer to be transported to 'free' France."

"What?" Dominique's eyes went wide. She wanted the problem solved but not by Alice leaving Le Quesnoy. "That's just for 'useless mouths.' Alice isn't useless, she can look after herself, she has a job, a house, family. They won't let her go."

"They want someone to volunteer, as an example, so others will follow."

"And she trusts them? What if it's all a lie? A trick to ship them out to labour camps to work for them somewhere else?"

"It's a risk she's prepared to take." Clemence stood, pulled her shoulders back and arched her spine to stretch her weary body.

"I'd better get back to work and you should get home out of the weather."

Dominique went straight home and hurried to the kitchen to make a real cup of coffee for Alphonse.

"It'll hurt less if you stay still, Louis." Marie held tight to stop his fingers from flinching as she worked to remove the tiny prickles embedded in his palm.

"It's not fair," Louis groaned. "Why did they make us go to the forest anyway, we're only children."

"I thought you were going to eat blackberries." Dominique knew she shouldn't tease her brother, but she couldn't resist the opportunity.

"There weren't any." Louis poked his tongue at her. "And now my feet have blisters from walking so far."

"Lucky you're not a soldier having to walk from here to Paris."

Dominique left them to it. With her hand over the cup to keep the heat in and the rain out she headed to the schoolhouse. Her brother-in-law was staring out the window, a bored look on his face. She raised the cup so Alphonse could see it. He nodded his head vigorously, licked his lips and gave her the thumbs up.

"Coffee for Alphonse," she explained to the German soldier on guard so he could see she was unarmed.

"Eintritt verboten," the sentry barred her entry with his rifle but must have smelled the coffee's aroma. "Kaffee?" He too licked his lips.

Dominique looked from the soldier to Alphonse, wishing she'd brought two cups, one to bribe the sentry and one for Alphonse. She hesitated, debating what to do, before deciding it was more important to talk to Alphonse, the coffee was only the pretence for doing so.

"You have coffee, I talk to Alphonse." Dominique pointed from the soldier to the coffee and then from herself to Alphonse hoping the language barrier wasn't too great.

The soldier nodded as if he understood, hooked his rifle back over his shoulder and took the coffee cup before Dominique could object and demand entry to the schoolhouse. She had no choice but to stand in the cold rain and wait while he drank the brew, hoping he would keep his side of the bargain she thought they'd made.

It was as if the clouds chose that moment to punish her for colluding with the enemy. The sky darkened, the laden clouds released a deluge that splattered against the windowpanes blurring the image of Alphonse's ruddy face, his evident rage at the German drinking the coffee meant for him. Raindrops fell from the brim of Dominique's hood and rolled off the hem of her jacket to form a puddle at her feet. She silently urged the soldier to finish before she froze.

Eventually he passed the empty cup back without a thank you or any sign of appreciation.

"Entrée?" Dominique pointed again from herself to the schoolhouse, trying to look as demure and innocent as she could.

The soldier looked up and down the street as if he had to ensure no-one saw his leniency. Dominique sighed with relief; grateful the rain kept both soldiers and civilians inside. He stepped to the side, allowing her entry to the porch while he unlocked the door and summonsed Alphonse. The other prisoners were pushed back inside, and the door relocked.

"Zwei minuten." The soldier held up two fingers.

"Dominique, merci beaucoup for my coffee." Alphonse maintained his sense of humour despite his predicament.

"I'll bring two next time," she replied. "One for him and one for you."

"Oui, always thinking, merci." Alphonse became serious. "What brings you here? It must be important for you to venture out in this weather."

The soldier turned his back to them, and Dominique was sure his limited understanding of French made it safe for her and Alphonse to talk.

"I have a way to get information out of the city," she still lowered her voice as an extra precaution. "I was hoping you may have something I could share that would help."

"Ah, Dominique. I think you must have a sixth sense, you always show up when I need you." Alphonse leaned closer and murmured. "On Sunday, after mass, there will be a group of men ready to leave. I will still be in here. You can guide them to the last farm on the road before Potelle."

It wasn't the information she sought to share with Gabriel, but the new mission sent her stomach into a flutter, like a kaleidoscope of butterflies was released inside her.

"Oui! Oui! I'll do it." She grinned from ear to ear. "How will I know who they are?"

"They will find you." Alphonse enclosed Dominique's delicate hand in his. "Be careful, mon amie, be careful."

"Zeit abgelaufen!" The soldier turned, ushered Dominique out of the porch and nudged Alphonse with the butt of his rifle back towards the schoolhouse door.

Dominique skipped all the way home, not caring if the rain splashed, oblivious to anyone who saw and thought her crazy. She had a secret, a purpose that sent the adrenaline coursing through her veins. She was getting another opportunity to do something that would help win the war.

Chapter 18

Major Vierordt made a big fuss about Alice volunteering to leave. He demanded the townsfolk come to the townhall to witness her name being added to the list. She stood on the stage, a seeming picture of happiness while he expounded about the benefits of transportation and encouraged more to volunteer. Mayor Carlier sat on the stage too. Vierordt demanded he show his support for the initiative, but Mayor Carlier's scowl looked far from supportive.

A few Quercitains followed Alice's lead; mainly widows with young families unable to support themselves and for whom the contributions of food and clothing from the CRB were inadequate. Their reasons for leaving, far different from Alice's.

A young man who'd recently turned eighteen but was unable to enlist and fight for his country stepped up. Vierordt took one look at him and laughed. A flick of the Major's wrist signalled for a soldier to push the man back into the crowd. Knowing his fate, his eyes glassed over, dreading the hard labour he'd be forced into.

The townsfolk left the hall more despondent than when they arrived, wasting their precious energy to allow Vierordt to lord over them was exasperating.

Later in the week, the German commander made another demand; everyone must attend church. Attending mass was something Dominique did because she was made to, usually by her parents but today by Vierordt. It wasn't because of any sense of calling, except for today, although the excitement that had her bouncing from foot to foot and humming the tune to 'La Marseillaise', the French national anthem, had nothing to do with religion.

"What is wrong with you, Dominique?" Lucie frowned. "You're all over the place like a monkey in a circus."

Dominique stopped momentarily while she thought of an answer that would satisfy her mere.

"I'm just excited the rain has finally stopped."

"Oui, that is très bien but please behave like the young lady you are supposed to be." Lucie fussed with the bow on her bonnet then turned her attention to Louis and Victor. "Boys, pull your socks up."

Dominique could never understand why her mother always insisted on propriety. It wasn't like there was going to be a prospective husband to be found this afternoon. The church would be full of Germans who insisted their priest take the service and all the prayers recited, and hymns sung in their native tongue.

There were no bells chiming to summon them to the service. They too had fallen victim to the war, removed lest they be used to communicate to the allies, sent away to be melted down for weapons. The wind whistled through the empty belfry, chilling the church's bones just as it did to Dominique.

When the Favier family arrived, the Germans had already filled the front pews leaving the rear to the townsfolk. In the very last row sat a group of *les Brassards rouge*, identifiable by their red armbands. Dominique recognised some of their faces from the train, the young men who had been forced to work on the roads or milling trees in Foret de Mormal. Their gaunt faces and baggy clothing indicated they'd been worked from dawn to dusk with little food to sustain them. Mental images of a German soldier flailing his whip at the men lagging as they trudged out of town, another poking the men with his bayonet to prod them into action made Dominique feel weak at the knees. It was likely these were the only ones still fit and able despite their mistreatment.

The Favier family took their seats in the row in front of the men. Lucie held her head high and eyes forward, but Dominique was curious, were these the men she was meant to escort? She leaned back and turned to look along the row. She'd never been this close to them, able to see that they were young men, probably the same age as her or only two or three years older. Their characteristic curly dark hair and chocolate brown eyes reminded her of Gabriel and deepened her resolve. If these were the men she was to help, then she would do everything she could to set them free from their persecutors.

The man at the end of the row sat taller than the others as if he was their natural leader assuming control. He caught her eye, his solemn look ensured he had her attention before he discreetly nodded then tilted his head towards the door. Dominique swallowed, her excitement vanished, replaced by self-doubt and uncertainty. What if she failed them? What if they were all caught? What if she was caught? Death. Execution by firing squad. Fear gripped her momentarily. She bit the inside of her lip. *You can do it.* The voice inside her head could have been Alphonse trusting in her ability, it could have been Gabriel admiring her tenacity or it could have been her, knowing she would do whatever was required to help win the war. What she did was nothing compared to those at the frontline under attack, day in and day out.

She mirrored the man's actions, confirming her understanding of the plan.

The mission had to wait until the end of the service which seemed interminable. The priest's sermon in a foreign language droned on. When everyone's heads were bent in prayer, Dominique dared to peek at *les Brassards rouge*. Some of them bowed their heads, steepled their fingers and prayed like their life depended on it. Others looked straight ahead as if it was a protest, a refusal to worship a God that the enemy also worshipped. She herself struggled to understand how any God could permit the atrocities of war. Why didn't he step in to stop all the needless deaths? Did he want them in heaven for some purpose beyond the understanding of mere mortals?

The congregation standing to exit the church drew Dominique's attention back to the present. Her chest tightened; the moment had arrived.

"I'm going to visit Alphonse, Maman," she told her mother as they shuffled from the church. "I'll be back before supper."

She'd planned to walk with the escapees past the schoolhouse as if they were casually returning to the barracks where they were housed. Alphonse would see them and know all was well.

"Alphonse? He is Clemence's responsibility." A furrow formed above Lucie's neatly shaped eyebrows and made Dominique want to point out to her mother, she would end up with a permanent wrinkle if she kept frowning. "You should come home and practice your embroidery."

"Clemence is busy at the hospital. She asked me to check in on him."

"Busy, just like your father." Lucie sighed. "That hospital, this war, is demanding too much of them. Too much of everyone."

Did her mother know what Dominique was about to do? Non, she barely left the house, she'd have no knowledge of the underground efforts being made. Besides, Dominique was volunteering, no-one had demanded she help the men.

"I'll come home via the hospital and collect Pere for supper," Dominique offered, knowing it would cheer her mother.

"Very well, don't be late." Lucie turned her attention to the neighbours who had seized the opportunity to chat before the Germans made them disband.

Les Brassards rouge peeled away from the group. Dominique sought out the man who appeared to be their leader. Her eye contact was momentary, a flick of her hand as she walked past was the signal for them to follow her, albeit a couple of steps behind so it appeared it was merely coincidence they headed in the same direction.

They left the square, walking into the wind that funnelled down the street. Its chill ensured Dominique remained on high alert, her head clear, focussed on the route she had to take the men. As expected, Alphonse was sitting at the window of the schoolhouse. A different guard was on sentry duty, and he stood, alert, rifle ready, eyeing them suspiciously.

Dominique dipped her head to Alphonse and his face lit up with delight. She couldn't help but smile back. The fear that had her heartbeat racing and stomach churning abated, her courage buoyed by her brother-in-law's joy.

She turned at the next corner, like rats following the Pied Piper the forced labourers followed. A short distance further, a narrow alley ducked off to the left. Dominique glanced up and down the street to ensure there were no Boche about. Out of the corner of her eye she saw movement across the street, someone peeking around lace curtains in a window. Hopefully they were merely curious, not desperate enough to nark on her and her entourage.

The temperature seemed to drop ten degrees in the shade between the buildings that fronted either side of the alley. Washing, rinsed again by the rain, drooped sadly on the rope line hitched between the buildings, the wind unable to stretch its tentacles into the void. The air felt dense; a mustiness cloaked the alley. Dominique wrapped her arms around her body, unsure if her trembling was from fear or cold.

She jumped in fright when a grey tabby cat leapt down from the top of a brick fence and scooted across her feet to squeeze through a drain and disappear on the opposite side.

"Sacrebleu!" she cursed, her hand on her chest to still her thundering heart.

Finally, they reached the gate that would lead the men to their freedom. A tunnel in the ramparts the Germans hadn't bothered to patrol. It wasn't big enough for vehicles or horses so can't have been deemed a threat on a Sunday afternoon. The gravel floor crunched beneath her shoes as she stepped from the street cobbles, the noise amplified in the stillness. She raised her hand, indicated the men should stop and wait while she investigated the tunnel. If there was a German patrol outside the ramparts it would be easier to pretend, she was hungry and out looking for wild mushrooms or walnuts that had fallen from the trees.

She tiptoed the length of the tunnel, stopped and caught her breath, inhaling and exhaling long and slow to at least appear calm and casual even if her insides were a jumble of nerves. A spider had chosen the arch of the tunnel to weave its web and sat at the centre of the intricate net, waiting.

"Nobody has disturbed you recently, have they, Mr Spider?" Dominique whispered before she peeked around the last bricks that formed the tunnel's archway. "It's now or never."

Leaves rustled in the wind as she stepped from the tunnel; a falcon's *kack-kack-kack-kack* alarm startled her. Was it alerting fellow birds of an eminent threat or warning her of danger? Either way she took notice, the hairs on her arms stood to attention too.

She looked up and down the rampart's high walls, visually scoured the bush line on the other side of the moat and when she was finally certain the coast was clear, she waved the men on.

They had to walk single file across the narrow bridge that spanned the moat. They would be easy pickings if a soldier saw them now. Dominique dared to look down, the muddy waters swirled beneath her, a watery grave that her body may never be retrieved from. She shook her head, disbanded the treacherous thoughts, she needed to be positive and picture the successful outcome she desired.

When safely across she sighed with relief, stood to the side of the narrow path obscured by the limbs of an oak tree, and counted *les Brassards rouge* as they passed her. She clapped her hands as the twentieth man moved to stand under the cover of the trees. They'd escaped Le Quesnoy, the most difficult but only the first part of their journey. It would be days if not weeks before they were safely back in free France.

They stopped to regather, catch their breath and rip the red armbands that identified them as forced labour from their sleeves. Several men threw their armbands into the air like confetti in a celebration and others joined in as if the action released them from their shackles. Floating to the ground they covered the path, still muddy from the rain, and looked more like red flags to a bull.

"Non, non." Dominique gathered them up, screwed them into a ball and hid them under the brambles of a blackberry. "We don't want to leave a trail."

Walking single file, they continued through the bush until it opened onto a field. In the distance was the road they needed to follow. The day's light was already beginning to fade, if Dominique was to make it home by supper she had to start back now. She couldn't lead them any further.

She turned to the leader of the group who'd been in the line behind her.

"Over there," she pointed to the hedge running alongside the road. "Stay behind the hedge, out of sight from any troops or patrols on the road. Follow the road all the way to Potelle, stop at the last farm before the village."

The man nodded his understanding. "Oui, we know the village, we've been working on the roads."

Dominique hoped he was smart enough to stay away from where they'd been working. That would be like walking straight into the wolves' lair. They'd be recaptured for certain, likely shot or treated even worse than before.

"Stay hidden," she added not wanting it all to be a wasted effort even though the war had left a barren land bereft of buildings and bush to conceal them. "The last men were re-captured. Don't talk to anyone you aren't one hundred percent sure you can trust."

"Oui, oui. Getting caught is the last thing we want."

"Your contact will have a code." Dominique leaned over and whispered the code to the leader. "They'll take you on the next stage."

"Merci beaucoup, mademoiselle. We will be forever grateful." His solemn look suggested he wanted to add 'if we ever make it out of occupied France alive' but he inhaled deeply and turned to his men. "Come on, let's go, our families await."

Each man relayed his heartfelt thanks to Dominique before they crept from the shelter of the trees. She stood at the edge of the bush, unable to move until she saw the last of them reach the lee of the hedge. Her breath caught in her throat as each man crossed the field, nothing to hide behind, within firing range should any sentry be posted to the top of the ramparts. She imagined she heard the *rat-a-tat-tat* of a gun, but it was just her own heartbeat thundering in her ears.

Dominique turned for home, hurrying back the way she'd came, stopping only to check the armbands were safely hidden. A mishmash of footprints in the mud were printed like the clues in a puzzle, a sure giveaway should the Boche discover there were men missing and send out a search party. She grabbed a branch and tried unsuccessfully to brush them away, the slender limb broke under the pressure. She stomped her feet, backwards and forwards across the track, imprinting the mud with her identity, obliterating the men's.

"It's not safe to leave you here, is it?" She reached down to grab the armbands from under the brambles. The red cloth bundle came free, but thorns snagged her skin and drew blood. She ignored the pain and the drops of blood dotting her hand, divided the bundle in two and stuffed her skirt pockets.

Dominique smoothed down the folds of her full skirt, hoping her pockets would be hidden but she imagined she looked more like a mother with childbearing hips. She'd thought her mission over but now, with pockets bulging with evidence, she had to make it back through the streets to home where the armbands could be burned in the fire.

Her pulse quickened, she scanned the track, one final check before leaving the cover of the bush and recrossing the moat. A few acorns at the edge of the track caught her eye. It was out of season for the fruit of the oak; they must have lain undiscovered under the bramble and come free with the armbands. She eagerly gathered them up, their protective husks now soft bristles. Not only would they be a treat to eat but they also provided the pretence, should it be needed, for her presence beyond the ramparts.

With hands and pockets full, Dominique crossed the moat. At the tunnel entry the spider was busy recreating its web. Some of the men must have broken it on their way through.

"Je suis désolé," she apologised. "Don't you tell anyone we were here, will you?"

The spider stopped; its multiple eyes appeared to look warily at Dominique. It waved its pincers, a warning to stay away. She skirted around the spider and hurried on.

When Dominique exited the alley, she remembered the promise she'd made to her mother and turned in the opposite direction towards the hospital.

There weren't many people in the streets but those that were, seemed to look at Dominique strangely, or was it merely her imagination or guilt making her see things?

Henri Favier wasn't to be found in the ward, but Dominique noticed Alice at the bedside of the German soldier who'd captured not just the town but her half-sister's heart. Dominique glared at him, silently conveying her annoyance. Why did he have to come into their lives and force Alice to leave?

"You're bleeding, Dominique." Clemence bustled over, a concerned look on her face. "Whatever have you done?"

"Oh, nothing." Dominique turned her hands over to reveal the acorns. "Just caught my hand on a blackberry while I was collecting these."

"Acorns?" Clemence frowned. "Wherever did you find them? They're way out of season."

Clemence was asking far too many questions. Dominique didn't want to lie to her.

"I just went for a walk after mass." That much was true. "I needed to clear my head."

"Well, you need to be careful. It's not safe out there with all those soldiers."

Dominique looked around the ward. "You've got just as many in here. I hope you're being careful, not like Alice."

"Dominique!" Clemence growled. "Come over by the fire and I'll clean your wounds and make sure you have no thorns that will fester."

Clemence's tone was like an echo of Dominique's mother, but she had to admit her hand was stinging so she followed her half-sister across the ward.

"I've come to collect Pere," she said as she sat on a stool beside the fire. "I promised Mere I'd bring him home in time for supper."

"He's finishing up in surgery so should be ready to go when you are." Clemence reached out for Dominique's hand. "Put the acorns in your pocket so I can tend to your hand."

"Ah ... umm." Dominique gulped. She glanced around the ward; guilt coloured her cheeks as red as the armbands weighing down her pockets. "I can't. They're full."

"Where did you find that many acorns? I'll have to send Alphonse when he gets released."

Lost for a reply, Dominique stared wide-eyed and speechless.

Clemence looked back at the injured German soldiers propped up in their beds and then moved herself, so she sat like a protective barrier between them and Dominique.

"What do you have in your pockets, Dominique?" she murmured.

Seconds ticked by as Dominique contemplated her options – tell Clemence and thereby endanger her or keep everything secret, the less people implicated, the safer for all. She sat mesmerised by the flames until they revealed the answer. What better way to hide the evidence than right under the enemy's nose.

"I have fuel for the fire." Proud of her ingenuity, Dominique smiled. "Open the door, will you."

Clemence frowned at Dominique as she unhooked the wood burner's door. Warmth and an orange glow spilled from the fire, adding to the heat Dominique already felt. She pulled a bundle of armbands from one pocket and quickly threw them into the flames. Embers and sparks flew; the fire crackled with delight as the armbands ignited. Buoyed by success, Dominique retrieved the second bundle and tossed them into the fire.

"Quick, close the door," she ordered. "Don't let the heat out."

"The heat? That's all you're worried about." Clemence shook her head and sighed. "You'll end up in prison with Alphonse if you're not careful."

Chapter 19

The atmosphere at the breakfast table felt jovial and carefree, how it used to be before the war. Even the watered-down porridge couldn't dampen Dominique's triumphant smile. She'd slept well, both from exhaustion and knowing her mission had been a success. She ate with a lightness in her limbs as if a weight had been lifted. She laughed at her brothers' sword fighting with their knives, pretending to be knights.

The absence of Hans and Wolfgang also lifted the mood, but her natural curiosity had her wondering why.

"Hans and Wolfgang have left early," she remarked as if it was of no consequence.

"There's a big search on." Louis sounded excited as he stabbed his knife at Victor.

"A search for what?" Dominique gasped.

Could they be looking for the forced labourers? Could they be after the person who helped them escape? A quiver, ever so slight, started in her fingers. Her spoon shook as fear seeped into her bones, replacing the lightness with a suffocating grey. She lowered her arm, pressed her elbow into the table but she couldn't stop the shaking. Beneath the table her knees trembled.

"Are you alright, Dominique?" Lucie asked. "You've gone as white as a ghost."

Dominique squeezed her eyes shut and inhaled deeply. This couldn't be happening. She needed to remain calm, or she would give herself away for certain. Several deep breaths slowed her heartbeat.

"I think I must be getting my monthly," she offered as an excuse.

"Very well." Lucie pursed her lips. "We don't need to speak of such matters at the table. Perhaps you should retire to your bedroom. I'll have Marie bring you up a hot drink."

"I have to work at the laundry today." Today and every day. Dominique needed to continue doing what was demanded of her as if she was an obedient citizen, keep up the pretence so she appeared beyond suspicion.

"When will we ever get out lives back?" Lucie huffed. "You'd better eat your porridge then, keep your strength up. Boys, will you stop that fighting and eat your breakfast before it gets cold."

The meal continued in silence except for the clanging of spoons on crockery and the boys' slurping. Dominique's need to get beyond the walls of the house to discover the status of the search made her gulp down her porridge.

"I'd best be going." She stood from the table and took her empty plate to the kitchen, not waiting for any more admonition from her mere.

"You need to keep your strength up, Dominique." Marie handed her a small package wrapped in a napkin. "You can't continue to burn your candle at both ends. I've made you a sandwich. The bread is not that nice, but the honey should sweeten it and give you energy to get through."

Get through what? Her monthly, a day working at the laundry, an interrogation by the Germans? Was there a hidden message in Marie's words or was Dominique merely overthinking everything? Did Marie, once again, know what Dominique had done yesterday? Should she confide in her? Non, it was too risky, the less people that knew the better.

"Merci beaucoup, Marie." Dominique's fingers trembled as she took the sandwich.

"Merci beaucoup to you, Dominique." Marie turned to stir a pot boiling on the stove.

"What are you thanking me for?" Dominique frowned and rubbed her temple to ease the tightness in her head.

"The acorns. I assume it was you who left them on the bench."

"Oui, it was me."

Marie pointed to the pot. "I'm just boiling them to get rid of the bitterness, then I'll grind them into flour. We can have some bread that tastes like bread and not straw."

Marie's resourcefulness in the kitchen was a skill Dominique could never imagine herself possessing.

"That'll be nice," she replied. "I'd better be going."

It felt like she was running away, keeping busy to hold her fear at bay. She hurried from the kitchen, grabbed her jacket from the entrance way and left the house. Rue Brancion seemed eerily quiet and empty. Shutters and doors were firmly closed. Whether it was against the weather or the Boche, Dominique couldn't tell.

She turned at the corner and came face to face with a soldier.

"Where you go in such hurry?" This one could speak some French but that didn't make him any friendlier.

The secret Dominique was hiding made every question feel like an accusation.

"Off ... off to work ... at the laundry," she stumbled over her words.

"And what you have there?" The soldier pointed to Marie's package.

"Just a sandwich for my lunch." Dominique clutched the bundle to her chest.

The soldier licked his lips. "I have sandwich."

"Non!" Dominique protested before she thought of the consequences.

"You want to give me something else instead." The soldier's eyes dropped to her chest and his mouth curved into a lecherous grin.

Dominique's chest rose and fell beneath her jacket, not from any mutual wanting but from panic about how to save herself. She looked up and down the street, hopeful for the presence of someone else but no-one was about. She glanced through the windows of Francois's patisserie, praying his familiar white hat would be bobbing away at his workbench but the bakery was empty.

Resigned she was alone, Dominique knew she'd never pawn herself. Her choice was an easy one.

"Have it." She pushed the sandwich at the soldier and skirted around him.

"Not so fast."

"I have to get to work." Dominique kept walking, her head down, long determined strides taking her as far away from the soldier as possible. She listened for his footsteps, the determined sound of a German boot following her. There was only the distant squawk of a bird.

She looked at no-one and nothing but the cobbles until she reached the laundry and closed the door behind her. She leaned back on the shut door until her heartbeat slowed and the sick feeling in her stomach dissipated. Perhaps she was taking too many risks. Non, she should be able to walk the streets of Le Quesnoy without fear for her personal wellbeing. It was something she'd always done as a child. Was it now not safe; because of the war or because she was no longer a child?

"Did you hear?" Nathalie's question made Dominique shudder, she'd been so deep in her thoughts she hadn't heard nor seen her friend.

"Did I hear what?" Dominique moved away from the door, grabbed the first bundle of dirty washing and submerged it beneath the water as if nothing was amiss.

"Twenty men from *les Brassards rouge* disappeared."

"Really?" Dominique tried to sound surprised.

Again, she didn't want to lie, not to her best friend, but it was best to keep the mayor's daughter unaware of Dominique's part in the escape.

"Oui, after mass yesterday. Major Vierordt is furious. He wouldn't stop yelling orders at Pere, or at his own soldiers. He's demanded a search of every building in the town."

"Well, they won't find them at our home."

"Non, ours neither. The soldiers searched all through the night. There's not a trace so far. They think they might have left Le Quesnoy already."

"But all the gates are guarded, aren't they?"

"They are now. That little one, off the end of the alley, you know the one I mean?"

Dominique's mouth curved into a knowing smile. "Oui, I know the one. They must have left on foot if they went through that gate."

"Apparently, there were footprints in the mud but no trace beyond the bush."

Dominique's cockiness was rinsed away like the stains in the laundry. Her heartbeat quickened yet again. What if the Germans matched the footprints to her boots? Her feet had always been smaller. Surely the Boche would realise the prints weren't those of a man.

"Pere told Major Vierordt he shouldn't have ordered the destruction of the dogs," Nathalie continued. "He could have used them to sniff out the escapees."

"Did your Pere want them caught?" Dominique couldn't imagine Mayor Carlier not protecting the people.

"Non, he just wanted to make a point about the stupidity of the Major's orders."

Dominique nodded. "It's just as well he couldn't set the dogs on them. They deserve to escape the forced labour, return home to their families, especially after the way they were being treated."

The way all Quercitains were being treated. What if the entire town escaped? Abandon their homes and businesses and leave the town to the Germans. Non, that would never happen. The French were too patriotic. They just had to sit it out until the Allies conquered the Germans. The sooner the better.

Inside the brick walls of the laundry, there was little awareness of the outside world with only one small window to let light in. Even the German commands yelled beyond the walls were muted to a point where they almost sounded civilised.

The end of the day couldn't roll around fast enough, not knowing what was happening outside made Dominique feel like the washing she rolled through the wringer. Her head continued to throb, as if her scalp had shrunk and was now too tight.

"Au revoir, Nathalie." Dominique farewelled her friend. "I look forward to hearing all about Major Vierordt's next moves."

"He yells at Pere so loud; I can't help but hear. I'll tell you all tomorrow. Au revoir."

Dominique hoped there would be some intelligence she could relay to Gabriel, anything that could help the allies triumph over the Germans.

She hesitated at the laundry door, knowing she should walk directly home. The urge to walk via the tunnel was stronger and she headed off in the opposite direction. She could almost hear her mother saying, 'curiosity killed the cat.' Dominique had never listened to the warning before, and she wasn't about to now.

The tunnel entrance was a hive of activity. German soldiers stood in a semi-circle, some with rifles at the ready, others yelling commands and flailing whips at a group of men working with shovels, wheelbarrows, and bricks. Slashes of red on the arms of those toiling away made Dominique's heart skip a beat. Had the men she'd helped been re-captured? Surely, they weren't foolish enough to come back to Le Quesnoy. It took a few seconds for her to realise her nerves were making her leap to conclusions that were impossible. She'd burned the evidence; the red armbands that identified *les Brassards rouge* were ashes at the bottom of the hospital fire.

A soldier flicked the end of his rifle, indicating she should move on. She did but slowed her pace until she could see the faces of the labourers, determine that these were different men, no less unfortunate and mistreated but at least not the men she'd helped. She also noted that if these members of *les Brassards rouge* were to be aided in their escape, it wouldn't be via the tunnel. A wall of bricks was being built to block the exit. The spider was about to lose his home and the people another means to leave the town.

The presence of German soldiers about the town seemed to have multiplied, as if Major Vierordt had called them back from the front. They were on every corner, positioned strategically around the square. The numbers patrolling the city gates had doubled. When Dominique reached Rue Brancion she saw they were also inside people's houses, thrashing about and then exiting with a bounty: anything and everything made of copper, brass, and leather. Bottles of wine, if there were any left to be found, were also amongst their hauls.

The Favier house was not exempted, its doors opened wide to the weather, an invitation to all that hadn't been issued willingly. The thumping of boots echoed down the stairwell.

"Non!" Lucie wailed from her bedroom. "Not my great-grandmother's vase."

Dominique stood and peered up the spiral staircase, picturing the delicately shaped and ornately etched brass vase that sat on her mere's dressing table, most days with a flower fresh from the garden. The *Ali Baba brigade* as the German loiters had become known believed nothing was sacred. What they wanted, they took, without question or sympathy.

The scuffing of boots resounded from the top floor. Dominique imagined them rifling through her room, finding the letter she'd half written to Gabriel. What news had she told him? Had she incriminated herself? Should she bound up the stairs and retrieve it before it was found? Her legs threatened to buckle beneath her. She grabbed the balustrade for support, unable to take the first step, let alone flights of stairs.

She retreated to the sitting room, took comfort in her father's armchair, feeling the warmth as if he was there and she was a little girl, sitting on his lap, giggling as he tickled her. She curled her legs up beneath her and closed her eyes, shutting out the war, taking herself back to a time when life was simpler. Physical and emotional exhaustion took her into a deep sleep, oblivious to the soldiers upstairs.

They'd gone by the time she awoke to her mother's voice.

"Where is your Pere when I need him? He should have been home to ensure those awful soldiers didn't take my grandmother's vase."

Dominique shook her head to wake herself up fully.

"Of course he should," Lucie growled. "Why are you shaking your head?"

"I was just waking up, Maman. I don't think Pere would have been able to stop them. They seem intent on doing whatever they want and will hurt or imprison anyone who tries to stop them. You wouldn't want Pere in prison, would you?"

"Non, non, of course not." Lucie went to the writing bureau, folded down its lid and took a sheet of paper. She sat down; fountain pen poised ready to write. "Take your feet off the furniture and sit like a lady, please."

Dominique stood, appearing to obey but more curious about her mother putting pen to paper when no letters could be posted.

"What are you doing, Maman?"

"I'm writing to Eugenie." Lucie began to write, ink flowing gracefully across the page.

"But ... but no letters can be posted to free France."

Lucie lowered her voice. "Alice is going to take them when she leaves on the train tomorrow."

"Alice is leaving tomorrow!"

Dominique was torn. She seesawed from relishing her departure, the separation from the German soldier before anything untoward was to happen, to regretting her decision to leave behind her family, friends, her career, going somewhere unknown for who knows how long. Although Alice was always telling her what to do and not to do, she knew she was coming from a place of love and caring. Dominique would miss her.

"Oui," Lucie nodded but continued writing, hurrying to relay all the news of the past few months. "You should write to your sister too."

"Does Alice think the Germans will simply allow her to take a bundle of letters? Surely, they'll search her and destroy them."

Eugenie was the only one Dominique would reveal her secrets to. Whispered revelations after the bedroom candle had been snuffed out, had always been their way. The relief of unburdening herself in a letter to Eugenie would be wonderful but the secrets she carried now were not the innocent ones of childhood, the consequences of them being discovered by the wrong party weighed heavy.

"Your Pere says they'll be sewn in the hem of her skirt or tucked into her corset." Lucie huffed. "The Boche wouldn't dare search there. A pity I couldn't have hidden my vase on my person."

After this morning's interaction, Dominique wasn't so certain the Germans wouldn't welcome the chance to look under a woman's skirt, but she wasn't going to miss the opportunity to share her news with Eugenie.

"I shall go and write then. I have so much I want to tell her."

Chapter 20

27 January 1915

Alice, Clemence and Alphonse, released from prison, came for dinner on the eve of Alice's departure. All the Favier family, except for Eugenie, gathered at the dining table to enjoy the feast Marie had managed to magically create from the meagre ingredients left on the kitchen shelves and gathered from the garden.

Unlike other meals when Hans and Wolfgang had been present, Marie ignored the letter recommending, for the sake of economy, that potatoes no longer be peeled before cooking. She used the acorn flour to make a cake which she decorated with the last of the walnuts. The walnut tree had stood in the back garden for decades but was destined to become another victim of the war. The timber was perfect for crafting rifle-butts, so another demand had been posted – all walnut trees with trunks a foot or more in diameter had to be felled by the end of the month. Henri, and all other walnut tree owners, were to be compensated through the issue of vouchers but he held off as long as possible as a silent protest.

The meal was a bittersweet celebration after which the letters were folded, over and over until they would fit in the seam of Alice's skirt. Lucie insisted Dominique, needing to practice her needlework, be the one to unpick the hem and re-stitch it once the pages had been evenly spaced around the skirt.

"You will make sure they get to Eugenie," Lucie pleaded as Dominique tied off the last stitch.

"I will, but you need to appreciate it may take a while." Alice stood and walked around ensuring her skirt sat and moved normally. "I don't know where I'm going or how long I'll be travelling and then I'll have to enquire as to Eugenie's location. If she's near the front, it may take some time for mail to reach her."

"You are very brave, my dear." Henri rested his hand gently on Alice's shoulder. "I will worry about you constantly until I hear you are safe."

Dominique wanted to tell her pere, he'd be worrying more if he knew how close she'd gotten to a German but a stern look from Clemence warned her to stay quiet. She had to chew the inside of her mouth to do so.

The day of departure arrived, the middle of the week, a Wednesday, not that the Quercitains paid particular attention to the days of the week anymore. The Germans insisted they work every day but Sunday. Thursday used to be market day, but with no produce being harvested from barren fields, or left over after the Germans had taken their requisitions, none of the surrounding farmers brought their wares to the square.

Market days had been a social occasion as well, where everyone gathered in the square for a chin wag, to catch up on the news, who'd had a baby, who was marrying who, whose cattle were the fattest and whose cheese was the tangiest.

Expecting an empty square, Dominique was surprised by the cacophony of sounds coming from the town centre as they walked to the train station to farewell Alice. There was a band playing music, soldiers sung, yelled, cheered, and danced on the cobbles. Even from a distance, she recognised the soldier whose lecherous leer had sent a shiver down her spine. He was laughing and joking as if he hadn't a care in the world. Dominique recoiled in disgust and refused to look at him.

The black, white, and red tricolour flag was being waved about vigorously. Soldiers, uniforms unbuttoned and rifles askew on their shoulders, swigged from bottles, staggering about, even though it was not yet eleven in the morning.

"What are they celebrating now?" Lucie asked. "Have we been defeated, Henri?"

"Non, it's the Kaiser's birthday."

Lucie scoffed. "We'll never celebrate that horrid man."

"Careful, my dear," Henri turned the group in the opposite direction.

"What? You do not agree with me?" Lucie sounded offended.

"I agree wholeheartedly with you, my dear, but your voice is best lowered for the expression of such opinions." Henri spoke quietly as he patted her hand. "We don't want you incarcerated in the prison."

The warning was enough to silence Lucie for the rest of the walk. Dominique was happy to wander along lost in her own thoughts, her feelings about Alice's departure still a jumble, unsure whether to feel sorry for her or be angry, especially after seeing the soldier in the square. How Alice could feel attracted to any of them, let alone fall in love was beyond Dominique's comprehension.

Alice, Clemence and Alphonse were already on the station platform when the group reached the Gare du Quesnoy. The three of them were huddled together in a bear hug that looked inseparable. When they finally broke apart, Alphonse emerged glassy eyed, the two women clasped each other's hand and let their tears run freely, streaming down ruddy cheeks.

"Come here, my darling daughters." Henri opened his arms to enfold the pair. "This is au revoir, not a final farewell. We will be together again. We must hope that it is soon."

"Oui, mon pere." Alice withdrew a handkerchief from her purse, wiped her eyes and blew her nose.

The train hissed; steam billowed from its stack as the other passengers boarded, their meagre possessions firmly gripped in tatty bags and worn suitcases. At least Alice looked like she was merely going on holiday. Pere had given her his leather bag. It had been neatly stowed at the back of the wardrobe and had escaped the Ali Baba brigade or perhaps they'd shown a little leniency for all his work at the hospital operating on German soldiers. Either way, Alice was about to board the train with enough leather to make a dozen rifle straps, another silent protest against the enemy's requisitions.

"I want a hug from each of you." Alice moved towards the twins. "Starting with you, Louis."

"I'm too old for hugs," he protested and ducked out of Alice's arms, not out of reach though, before she ruffled his hair and pinched his cheek. "Ouch!"

"I'll hug you." Victor stepped forward and wrapped his arms around Alice.

"Merci beaucoup, Victor."

The Favier family had lined up according to their age, so Dominique was next. Any harbouring resentment vanished the moment Alice pressed her heart against Dominique's.

"Keep yourself safe, Dominique," Alice whispered. "I'll pray your Gabriel comes home to you and you get to live a long and happy life together."

Dominique squeezed her eyes shut. She had no idea how to respond and was unsure if any sound could breach the lump in her throat and leave her parched mouth. All she absorbed from Alice's message was love and caring, none of the admonition or chastising of the past, as if they were equals in this moment, both in love with a man they couldn't be with.

Alice broke away, continued to hug the rest of the family, leaving Dominique glassy eyed and reaching for her handkerchief.

There was a collective holding of breaths when Alice took her bag and stepped up into the train. She paused in the doorway and turned back. She waved but wasn't looking at her family as she smiled, a glow lighting up her face. Dominique turned to look where Alice appeared to gaze and there he was, a blonde-haired man blowing a kiss to Alice, his eyes reflecting the same adoration ... and love.

Dominique couldn't despise him. She longed for Gabriel to gaze at her with the same depth of feeling. Was Alice's German not so different than them, tired of the war and the hatred, clinging to whatever goodness he could find?

The stationmaster blew his whistle, a loud and piercing shrill that broke the magic of the moment. Alice was pushed into the train and the door closed. She hurried to a seat, pressed her palms and face against the window and kissed the glass. The train moved off, slowly taking the image of a broken heart with it, a love lost in the futility of a war, another victim with wounds that might never heal.

Come home to me, Gabriel. Please come home.

The German celebrations continued long into the night. Commotion in the street below Dominique's window kept her awake, off-key singing, glass shattering, yelling, and swearing punctuated by the retches of those who'd over imbibed. The morning clean of the cobbles, the Kommandantur insisted upon, would be a more arduous task than usual. Dominique tossed and turned, eventually folding her pillow around her ears to dampen the noise.

When she finally awoke and went downstairs for breakfast the grandfather clock was chiming ten.

"Ten o'clock already." Dominique shook her head. "I know I didn't sleep well but I didn't think I'd slept that late."

"You didn't," Marie said. "Wolfgang put the clock forward to German time this morning."

"Why? We should put it back, it's our clock, we're in France now, not Germany."

"That's not what they think. We're occupied, supposedly that makes us part of Germany, so we must live by their time."

"Oh, what next?" It wasn't a question Dominique wanted answered, especially on an empty stomach but the sound of people in the garden drew her attention away from the table.

"They're here to chop down the walnut tree."

Dominique moved to the kitchen to peer out the window. Two soldiers stood guard, their rifles pointed at several of the forced labourers, two of whom were either-end of a two-man saw, another had brought in a wheelbarrow.

"I wish they'd requisitioned and melted down the saw." Dominique stood, hands on hips, annoyed but helpless. "What can we do to stop them?"

"Louis and Victor have stalled them so far." Marie pointed to branches near the top of the tree and smiled.

"Sacrebleu!" Dominique saw her brothers, straddling branches, riding them like horses galloping into battle.

"What are you cussing about now, Dominique?" Lucie made a rare visit to the kitchen. "A lady doesn't speak like that."

"Louis and Victor are trying to save the walnut tree." Dominique pointed to her brothers.

Lucie gasped. "Sacrebleu! They'll fall and get hurt."

Lucie strode from the kitchen before Dominique could protest at her mother making rules that she herself didn't follow. Her arrival on the scene startled the Germans who turned their guns on her.

"Put those down," she ordered waving her arms to reinforce the command, oblivious to any threat to her personal wellbeing, the danger to her children overpowering all else. "Louis and Victor, get down now, before you fall."

"But Maman, they want to cut down our tree," Louis yelled from above, cupping his hands around his mouth to carry his voice.

Lucie brushed a hand across her face as if she was about to faint.

"We'd better go help," Dominique suggested. "We can't have her fainting."

Dominique and Marie rushed outside and stood either side of Lucie. The boys' position looked even more precarious from directly underneath. The top limbs of the walnut swayed in the breeze.

"The view is grand from up here; we can nearly see all the way to Potelle." Louis's reasoning wasn't helping their cause, being able to see and therefore communicate with those beyond the walls of the city was exactly what the enemy sought to prevent.

The Boche ordered the labourers to take up position. They looked apologetic but had no choice and stepped either side at the base of the trunk, the saw blade resting on the rough and fissured bark.

"Come! Down! Now!" Lucie yelled an order that wasn't to be disobeyed.

Slowly the boys began the climb down. Victor, ever the thinker, sized up the stronger branches and made sure he had his footing before lowering himself to the next limb. Louis, of course, wasn't so careful. A spindly branch snapped beneath his weight, and he fell several feet before a thick, strong limb stopped his fall and he managed to hold on.

Lucie swooned and slumped against Dominique.

"Quick, fetch a seat for her to sit on."

The soldiers found humour in the predicament and laughed, a gentlemanly offer of assistance the furthest from their minds. Marie had to run back up to the house, she returned struggling with the weight of a cast iron seat. Together they lowered Lucie onto the seat and fanned her face with their hands until her eyes fluttered open.

"What? Where? Why?" Lucie glanced all around, a puzzled look on her face.

"You fainted, Maman."

Reality dawned on Lucie, and she looked skyward, her hand splayed across her chest as if protecting her heart.

"You nearly fell down like me, Maman." Louis reached the ground and strode proudly over. "Lucky you had Dominique to catch you, and I had a branch."

As soon as Louis stepped away from the walnut tree, the labourers were forced to commence their task. The saw bit into the bark, which groaned with each cut. Slowly the labourers settled into a rhythm as sweat beaded their brows. The walnut tree wasn't going to give up its fight easily. The men moved the saw and made another cut to create a wedge before moving to the other side of the trunk to begin the final cut.

"Au revoir, walnut tree," Louis chimed.

Unlike Alice's departure, this wasn't a temporary farewell. Decades of growth were about to end, another gift of nature stolen by the enemy without a thought for the loss of a precious food source.

"We'd better move," Lucie suggested. "Or we'll be crushed like the rest of my garden."

From the safety of the patio, they watched the tree meet its demise, its last splinters fracturing with a loud crack, leaves whooshing towards the earth, twigs snapping on the garden's outer brick wall before the trunk landed with a thud.

Tears welled in the corners of Dominique's eyes. She blinked to stem them. Telling herself it was just a tree didn't uncoil the painful knot inside her. It may not have been human, but the tree's felling was symbolic of everything the enemy and the war the Quercitains involuntarily found themselves in, was stealing from their lives. How much more could the Germans destroy? How much more would the French tolerate?

The only consolation was the branches and twigs they could collect for the fire.

Chapter 21

29 June 2015

If the Quercitains thought Kommandantur Lubbert was horrid, his replacement was the devil himself. Perhaps Major Vierordt despised being posted away from the front or maybe he hated everything French, whatever drove the man, he acted without heart.

On Major Vierordt's orders Mayor Carlier and Doctor Flament, were arrested and incarcerated. The doctor had been in the middle of surgery with Henri when the soldiers arrived to apprehend him. He'd been allowed to complete the operation only because the patient was German.

Dominique had a sense of déjà vu. So much had changed since the Germans occupied Le Quesnoy, but Mayor Carlier's arrest was one event that kept repeating. This time he'd refused, yet again but rightly so, to provide the German authorities with a list of French and British soldiers still in the city. He'd seen the consequences of soldiers being found, those whose presence had been revealed by locals who wanted favours from the Germans or were too fearful to stay silent. The men were shackled, piled into trains, not in seated carriages like passengers but jammed into freight wagons, like livestock off to slaughter, the trained hissing as they faded from sight.

There were four remaining soldiers – three French and one British, those with injuries so serious they were unable to be moved when the others were evacuated. They were being cared for in a separate ward at the hospital. Away from the German patients. They should have been safe, but someone revealed their presence and speculation as to who could be the culprit was rife. Rumour said it was a woman who'd found favour with the Major, a refugee from St Quentin. She'd sought shelter and protection in Le Quesnoy, been taken in by the Quercitains but now, if the gossipers were correct, she'd betrayed them in the bed of Vierordt.

Henri knew about the soldiers too but fortunately wasn't arrested. The enemy couldn't take both surgeons, the only doctors available to operate on their own wounded.

The mayor and Doctor Flament were marched at gunpoint, not to the schoolhouse serving as a prison for the civilians deemed to have committed a crime, but to the barracks where they were separated and locked in cells. Their only connection to the outside world was a small opening with thick cast iron bars to prevent their escape.

When Nathalie arrived in tears, banging frantically on the Favier front door, Dominique had already heard from her father what had happened.

"Pere's been arrested," Nathalie sobbed as she collapsed into Dominique's arms.

"He's been arrested before, Nathalie, Vierordt is just flexing his power again." Dominique attempted to downplay the situation. "They'll let him go tomorrow. He'll be back home, you'll see."

"Vierordt is furious this time." Nathalie shuddered as she tried to stem her tears. "He threatened Pere with a court martial for treason. There's to be a trial tomorrow."

"You and your mere could visit him. I'm sure the guards would permit that." Dominique knew it was foolish to make promises about what the Boche would or wouldn't allow the Quercitains to do but she needed to give Nathalie a sense of hope. "I was able to visit Alphonse."

"Mere already tried." Nathalie's shoulders slumped with defeat. "She couldn't get past the front door."

Buoyed by an idea, Dominique stepped away and tucked her hand under Nathalie's chin to ensure she had her attention.

"We could do what we did when we were children," Dominique grinned at the memory and the opportunity it provided.

"What? I don't understand." Nathalie's eyebrows drew together in a puzzled look.

"Remember when we used to sneak around behind the barracks and peek into the cells," Dominique's eyes sparkled with the memories. "We would drop stones and nuts through the bars, listen for the clunk when they hit the stone floor, have races to see whose was the quickest."

"Oui, oui, I remember." Nathalie rubbed her tears away with the back of her hand. Her smile started to form but quickly vanished. "We're not children anymore, Dominique, and there'll be soldiers everywhere. We won't be able to sneak around without being caught. We'll end up in prison with Pere instead and I don't think my mere could cope with that."

"You don't know that." Dominique gave her friend's hands a reassuring squeeze. "We must try. For your pere's sake."

The outside of the barracks was surprisingly free of guards. Perhaps because there were soldiers housed within; the Germans saw no need to add a further layer of protection. Dominique and Nathalie walked casually past, appearing as carefree as their nerves would allow.

A lawn, now green and lush with the summer warmth, sloped away at the side of the barracks providing a path to the rear of the building.

"We'd better duck when we pass the window," Nathalie whispered even though there was nobody about.

There was only one window in the end of the building and the murmur of soldiers' voices indicated they were close to it, so Dominique followed Nathalie's lead and ducked, hugging the wall as she passed by.

The rear of the barracks ran parallel to the rampart walls, and the sun was unable to breathe warmth into the space. Dominique shivered. She told herself it was just the drop in temperature, but she knew it was a lie. Her stomach churned with the now familiar nerves of a mission she knew came with risks. At the same time adrenaline coursed through her veins, the desire to help, to succeed and to triumph over the enemy was stronger than the fear.

"Which cell is he in?" she asked Nathalie as she counted the narrow openings just above ground level running the length of the building.

"I don't know." Nathalie knelt at the first. "Pere, are you in there?"

No reply came so Nathalie crawled to the next one, not caring that her skirt dragged along the grass.

"Pere, are you there?" She pinched her nose and waited, still and quiet.

"What's wrong?" Dominique asked.

"Nobody's in there but it stinks of urine and ..." Nathalie turned to take a breath of fresh air before she crawled to the next opening.

Dominique went to the fourth opening. "Mayor Carlier, are you in there?"

"Non, je suis Docteur Flament. Who are you?"

Unwilling to reveal her name, Dominique gave a tempered reply. "Just a friend looking for Mayor Carlier."

"I believe he's next door," the Doctor replied. "But I don't think you can help him ... us."

Dominique and Nathalie crouched beside the next opening. Peering between the bars they could see Mayor Carlier lying prostrate on a narrow cot.

Nathalie gasped. "We're too late! They've killed him!"

Dominique turned her head, pushed her cheek against the cold bar to get a better look. She strained to see in the semi-darkness of the cell but felt certain she saw the mayor's torso rise and fall.

"He's still breathing."

"Are you certain? Pere! Pere! Wake up."

Mayor Carlier stirred. He groaned as he rolled over, realising he was not alone. He must have thought it was the Boche coming to persecute him again.

"Pere, it's me, Nathalie. At the window."

The mayor's face lit up when he saw his daughter, but a frown quickly formed.

"What are you doing here?" His voice was croaky from lack of use. He kept one eye on his daughter and one on the door to his cell. "It is not safe."

"We've brought you some food, Pere." Nathalie took a wedge of cheese and a thick chunk of bread from the napkin she had stowed in her pocket and passed it through the bars.

"Merci ma fille, merci beaucoup." Mayor Carlier snatched the food and ate as if it was the first sustenance he'd had in days.

"Have they not fed you?" Dominique was surprised by his manners, or lack thereof.

"Non," he mumbled through a mouthful. "They seek to weaken me. They think I will admit to what they want." He managed a feeble smile. "But I will never reveal the whereabouts of any man who doesn't want to be found."

"Bravo, Mayor Carlier." Dominique admired his loyalty and patriotism.

"But Pere, if it means you can come home, you must tell them something."

"There is a trial tomorrow. Well, I think it's tomorrow, it is difficult to tell the time in here." Mayor Carlier yawned and raked his fingers through his beard. "Justice will prevail. They will see I am not guilty of anything that harms their war effort. They will have to let me go. It will be alright, Nathalie, you'll see."

"I hope so, Pere, I hope so."

"Tell your mere not to worry." Mayor Carlier ate the last of the food.

"Should you save some of that for later?" Nathalie asked.

"No point. There is a rat that scurries under the door. He'd be sure to sniff it out. I'd rather eat it than do battle with the vermin."

The German were vermin as well, Dominique wanted to say but didn't. Mayor Carlier's life, along with the rest of the Quercitains, had become a constant battle with them for nearly a year now. When would it end?

"You'd better leave. I couldn't bear it if you were imprisoned too." The mayor stepped back from the bars.

"Au revoir, Pere," Nathalie's voice quivered, and Dominique had to help her stand.

"Stay strong, Mayor Carlier," Dominique bid him farewell as she led Nathalie away.

The townhall was packed for the trial. Mayor Carlier, Doctor Flament and the four soldiers faced a row of German officers,

Major Vierordt in the middle, presiding over the proceedings. It was announced as a trial but there were no lawyers present for the defendants.

Dominique sat in the front row, her pere on one side and Nathalie on the other beside Madam Carlier. She felt protected, tucked in beside her father and held tightly onto Nathalie's hand hoping to transfer some of Henri's calmness to her friend.

"Stille!" Major Vierordt demanded silence so the charges could be read.

"Achille Constant Francois Charles Carlier, you are charged with treason for knowingly harbouring soldiers of the enemy."

Mayor Carlier held his head high despite the black shadows under his eyes and the slight tremble in his handcuffed hands.

"Gastin Flament, you are charged with treason for knowingly harbouring soldiers of the enemy."

The soldier reading the charges continued with the names of the wounded prisoners who were dressed in civilian clothes, their army uniforms distant memories. Two stood with the aid of crutches, the other two with bandaged arms and torsos, solemn looks on bowed heads, fresh bruises coloured their cheeks, split and swollen lips revealed their interrogation had not been gentle.

A summary of the facts was read – they couldn't be disputed, because no opportunity to do so was provided nor was it possible to deny the men were arrested in the hospital. The defendants weren't asked how they pleaded. Vierordt's smirk signalled they'd already been found guilty, and he would take pleasure in the moment he could announce their fate.

Dominique squeezed her knees together and bit the inside of her cheek. It was all she could do to stop herself from leaping up to defend Mayor Carlier. The urge to yell out, to demand how they knew he was involved, just because he was mayor didn't make him responsible. He should be spared from whatever punishment Vierordt was about to deal out.

She felt Nathalie stiffen beside her, an attempt to stem the sobs that shook her body and the tears flowing down her cheeks. Mirroring her friend's distress, Dominique's chest tightened. She looked from Mayor Carlier to her father and sighed with gratitude that it wasn't him standing in front of Vierordt.

The German stood, puffed his chest out as he clasped his hands behind his back. His stance demanded the murmurs which crept about the hall be hushed and slowly everyone heeded the warning. All heads turned toward the stage, a collective breath held, waiting.

"Schuldig!" Vierordt pointed to each of the soldiers and repeated his guilty verdict.

His evil eyes settled on Mayor Carlier. No-one dared make a sound. Time seemed to linger, hesitating to move forward as if the future would be unwelcome. Vierordt paused. He closed his eyes. Perhaps he was reconsidering. Maybe he would act out of character and show leniency.

He opened his eyes, glared at Mayor Carlier and raised his hand, his index finger pointing like a gun to the defendant's forehead.

"Schuldig!"

Madam Carlier's scream pierced the air.

"Non! Pere!" Nathalie cried out.

Vierordt ignored their distress, moved his attention to Doctor Flament and repeated the guilty verdict a sixth time.

"Todesurteil!" Vierordt sat down, his job complete, his mouth drew into a triumphant sneer.

"What does that mean?"

"Say it in French?"

"What is their fate?"

The hall erupted, the Quercitains despising the German language that held them captive as much as the army themselves.

The soldier who'd read the charges stood and stepped forward. A nervous tic flickered his eye. It almost looked like he carried out his duties with some remorse, but Dominique couldn't imagine that to be true.

"The prisoners are all sentenced to ...." The soldier hesitated. "Death."

Dominique gasped. Realisation that it could well have been her pere, settled a heavy lump of dread in the pit of her stomach. Clemence. Alphonse. Alice. Sister Jeanne. They'd all helped, assisted in some way to free those whose lives were in danger. Dominique added her own name to the list. Could a death sentence be hers?

While such thoughts paralysed her, the crowd erupted, their anger filled the hall.

"Sacrebleu! It cannot be!"

"This is not a trial! This is a farce!"

"You're nothing but monsters!"

"Unjust. Against the Geneva Convention!'

"We demand a fair trial!"

The protests fell on deaf ears. Vierordt conversed with the Germans beside him as if it was a casual afternoon chat. When he finally turned back to the crowd it was only to order that the prisoners be escorted back to the cells where they would be held overnight. They were to face the firing squad tomorrow.

With an armed German soldier either side of each man, they were led from the hall. Mayor Carlier's eyes were glassy when he looked at his wife and daughter and mouthed.

"Stay strong. Je t'aime."

Madam Carlier blew her husband a kiss. "We will get you out, Achille. I promise. Do not lose hope."

Her promise set Dominique's mind racing.

"What can we do, Pere?" Dominique tugged on her father's sleeve. "This could have been you. We cannot let this happen."

"Non, we cannot." Henri shook his head. "I will meet with the other councillors. We will request an audience with Vierordt to demand the release of the men."

It didn't seem enough. Dominique wanted to storm the barracks, steal the German's rifles and arm the townsfolk to fight back. They could take revenge, assassinate Vierordt and imprison the rest of the Germans.

"We must do more, Pere," she implored. "Rescue them from the cells, kill the Boche, put Vierordt in front of our own firing squad."

"Ah, ma fille." Henri patted Dominique's hand. "The passion of the French runs deeply in your veins. We need to save six men, not get the rest of us killed. Let us try the voice of reason first."

Henri stood and went to Madam Carlier's side to escort her from the hall, relaying his intentions as they went. Dominique followed her father's lead and helped Nathalie.

"Don't worry, Nathalie. Pere is going to save your father." Dominique hoped the faith she had in her father would be rewarded.

"Oh, Dominique, I hope you are right."

Older women in the dispersing crowd reached out to Madam Carlier, offering comforting words or a gentle touch; their facial expressions telling her they shared her pain. The younger ones, those with more fight than resignation, offered to protest by refusing to work for the enemy.

"Let them wash their own clothes."

"We'll refuse to nurse their injured soldiers."

"No more eggs for them. We'll ignore their requisitions."

"I will not bake for monsters," Francois added his opinion. "Let them starve."

They were all valid forms of protest, but they would take time to have an impact, time that Mayor Carlier and the others didn't have if Vierordt was to follow through with the planned execution.

Once outside, Henri scanned the crowd and sought out the deputy mayors, Monsieurs Croix and Deleporte.

"There is no time for delay," Henri said to the men. "We must demand a meeting with Vierordt. You are the Deputy Mayors; you have authority to do so."

"Oui, we will go now."

The walk from the townhall seemed to take forever, each step like a wasted moment, a clock ticking down the time until fate had its way. Vierordt's car drove by with German flags fluttering from the front mudguards as if in a celebratory parade. The Major sat in the back; his stony face held no glimmer of hope that the group would be able to change his mind, but they had to try.

Chapter 22

30 June 1915

Dominique and Nathalie huddled in the storeroom, their ears against the wall, listening to the pleas of Henri and the deputy mayors. Madam Carlier, a mere woman without a worthy opinion in the eyes of Vierordt, had been denied entry to the meeting and stormed up the stairs, refusing the hot drink presented on a tray by Madam Cacheux.

Madam Carlier's determined footsteps could be heard overhead, along with slamming doors, scraping drawers and vows of refusal to live under the same roof as her husband's murderer.

"She's packing to leave," Nathalie murmured.

"I don't blame her."

The only advantage of sharing a house with Vierordt was the gathering of information but neither Madam Carlier nor Nathalie could speak German, and they wouldn't be given the time of day by the Boche unless it was for unsavoury purposes. They'd be better off elsewhere.

"But where will we go?" Nathalie frowned.

"You can come and stay with us." Dominique wrapped her arm around Nathalie's shoulder and gave her a reassuring squeeze. "We have plenty of room."

"Merci beaucoup." Nathalie's smile was feeble but at least it showed a glimmer of hope. "I'm not sure Mere will be willing to accept charity though."

"Let's just listen for now. The men may be successful in getting your pere freed. You mightn't have to move anywhere."

The odds of success were slim, but Dominique clung to the possibility like it was a life buoy saving her from drowning. Beside her, Nathalie's desperate gasps for air sounded as if she was already submerged.

"Article 12 of the Geneva Convention mandates that wounded and sick soldiers who are out of the battle should be humanely treated." Henri's voice took on an authoritative tone. "And, in particular should not be killed, injured, or tortured."

"I am in command here," Vierordt replied. "I decide what happens."

Henri ignored the rebuttal, which had been relayed in French, and continued his recital. "The Kingdom of Prussia signed the convention, along with France, Belgium and other countries. There is an obligation to respect medical units and establishments."

"We have respected your hospital. We have sent our own soldiers there," Vierordt countered.

"That obligation extends to the personnel entrusted with the care of the wounded," Monsieur Croix added to the argument. "If you wish to continue to send your soldiers to be treated at the hospital, then it would be foolish to sentence to death the doctor who has been treating them."

Dominique's eyes went wide, and she sucked in a breath as she waited for Vierordt's response to the implication he was foolish. The silence was unbearable. She wished she could see through the wall, to watch the Major's face, discern his reaction. Did the pause mean he was taking heed or was he busy thinking of a punishment for Monsieur Croix's insolence?

"Verlassen!" the German yelled.

Dominique wished she understood the language. What did he order? It wasn't the same word he'd used at the town hall. Through the wall they heard footsteps, Henri and the deputy mayors had been spared the death penalty but were leaving. Had their pleas been for nothing?

"We'd better get out of here," Dominique nudged Nathalie. "If we're caught eavesdropping, we might be punished too."

She edged the door open and peeked out to ensure it was safe before she took Nathalie's hand and left the storeroom.

"That was a waste of time," Monsieur Deleporte shook his head with dismay. "I'll have to take on the mayoral duties. Le Quesnoy cannot function without a leader."

"Oui, that is true," Monsieur Croix said. "But you cannot assume the leadership. That is for the council to decide."

"Gentlemen, gentlemen, please." Henri raised his palms to stop the men. "Monsieur Carlier is still the mayor until he is not. You are acting as if he has already been executed when we must continue to do all in our power to ensure that is not his fate."

"You saw Vierordt," Monsieur Delaporte countered. "He didn't look like he was about to change his mind."

"The man listened." Henri waited until he was outside before he continued. "He knows we are right. He just needs to make it look like it's his decision, that he's not caving to our demands."

"He's never shown leniency to anyone else."

"He's never had both the mayor and the hospital's senior doctor in his cells." Henri shook the deputy mayors' hands. "His job will be harder without their services; his own men will suffer. I suggest you go home; spend the night thinking of any arguments we can use to get the sentences overturned. We'll demand another audience in the morning."

Dominique hurried to her father's side as soon as the men left.

"Pere, you save Nathalie's father, can't you?" Despite the desperate situation, Dominique held onto the unwavering faith she had in her father.

"I haven't given up hope yet." Henri placed his hands on Nathalie's shoulders. "And neither should you."

"Madam Carlier and Nathalie don't want to stay here." Dominique clutched her father's arm. "Not under the same roof as Vierordt. They can come and stay with us, can't they? We have plenty of room."

"Oui, we have room, but I think it is best they stay here until ..." Henri hesitated as if he was choosing his words carefully. "If they leave before they have to, it is unlikely they will be allowed back in."

Nathalie's face drained of colour. She too had heard everything Henri didn't say. The situation was grim.

"Go now and be with your mother," Henri continued. "She will need your support to stay positive. Dominique, you come with me, we'll go to the hospital. I want to try to get a message out to someone with some influence."

Dominique hugged Nathalie and whispered. "Don't worry, Pere will fix it."

Nathalie looked unconvinced. She only managed a feeble nod before she turned and trudged with heavy feet back to the house. Dominique hurried to catch up with her father who'd strode on ahead. She paused at the gateway where a woman stood, half concealed behind the brick pillar. She didn't recognise the woman who was elegantly dressed, her high cheek bones highlighted with rouge, her lips defined with red lipstick. Dominique gave a fake smile as she eyed her from head to toe. Who was she? Why was she dressed and made up the way she was, not at all like a Quercitain going about their daily business? And most importantly, why was she lingering outside the mayor's office?

"Are you coming, Dominique?" Henri called out as he reached the corner, drawing Dominique from her scrutiny.

The shiver down her spine signalled the woman was up to no good but there was no time to do anything about it now.

"Oui, Pere, oui," Dominique hurried to join her father. "Did you see that woman?"

"Oui, I did." Henri continued walking as if he had more important things on his mind.

"Who was she? What was she doing there, dressed like she was going to a party?"

"She may well be the woman at the centre of the rumours."

"Which rumours?"

"The gossips say that it was a woman seeking the favours of the major who told him about the soldiers at the hospital."

Dominique's suspicions were confirmed. She wanted to turn back, to accuse and berate the woman, tell her she should be the one tried for treason, point out the heartache and damage she had caused, seek an apology or at least a show of remorse.

"We should go back and confront her." Dominique's cheeks reddened with rage.

"Non, the damage is done." Henri's manner remained calm despite his daughter's agitated state. "We need to focus on freeing the prisoners. Her time will come."

Dominique had no choice but to follow her father. With hands tightly balled into fists, she stomped along the cobbles, venting her anger with every step.

While Henri put through calls to the various committees Achille was the representative of, seeking help for his predicament, Dominique caught up with Clemence and Alphonse.

"What are you doing here, Alphonse?" She was surprised to see him dressed in a uniform of sorts. "He's working as a medic," Clemence replied on her husband's behalf. "That way I can keep an eye on him and ensure he stays out of trouble."

"The hospital is the centre of the trouble." Alphonse winked at Dominique. "That's why Dominique is here too."

"Pere is trying to get the sentences reversed."

"I hope he is successful." Clemence sighed. "We worked so hard to keep those soldiers safe."

"We should have tried to get them out with the rest," Alphonse added.

"It was too dangerous. You might have ended up in court with them too." Clemence's pained expression indicated that would have been more than she could bear.

Rays of sunshine stirred Dominique on the first day of July. She didn't dally under the covers but cast them aside, leapt out of bed with purpose and hurriedly dressed so she could see her father before he left for the hospital.

Henri was at the table attempting to rally support for the prisoners from Hans and Wolfgang. With the language barrier it was a difficult task; Henri's hands and arms talked as much as his mouth, his gestures signalling a gun to the head was wrong. There was a hint he had the support of Hanz, a slight nod of acknowledgement and eyes reflecting the pain of loss, but Wolfgang's look was hard, as impenetrable as his stoney heart.

The German soldiers were enjoying poached eggs on toast. There weren't enough eggs for Dominique to do the same. She had to be satisfied with a watery hot drink and a wedge of cheese on a slice of bread. Each day her ration seemed to get smaller, Marie making the meagre supplies last.

Watching the Germans sit at their table, eating food she no longer got to eat, fuelled Dominique's anger. They might not be willing to share but she was. She wrapped half of her breakfast in a napkin and stowed it in her skirt pocket.

Unable to sit a moment longer at the same table, she rose with her father and followed him from the room. "Were your phone calls successful, Pere?"

"I don't know." Henri pulled his jacket on. "I'll head over to Vierordt's office now and find out. Hopefully he has had an overnight change of heart."

I don't think he has a heart.

Dominique kept her thoughts to herself. "I hope so."

They opened the door to find Nathalie about to knock. Dark hollows under her eyes reflected her anguish.

"I ... um .... Can ...." Nathalie broke down, sobs wracked her shoulders as she collapsed into Dominique's arms.

Dominique embraced Nathalie as if her life depended upon it. It didn't seem enough, that all she could offer was a hug to ease her pain, but Dominique continued to hold her tight, feeling her tension gradually seep away, her breathing slow and deepen.

Henri had gone off on his mission before the two edged apart. Dominique offered her handkerchief to wipe the tears that left rivulets down Nathalie's cheeks and dripped from her chin.

"I have some food for your pere." Dominique pulled the napkin from her pocket. "Shall we go visit him?"

"Oui! Oui! Merci beaucoup." Nathalie blew her nose loudly. "I knew you would know what to do."

Usually, it was Nathalie who came up with solutions, appearing older and wiser than her years. Dominique felt taller, bigger and stronger.

"Come on, let's go." She took Nathalie's hand, closed the door and turned down the street toward the barracks.

By the time they reached the prison cells, some of her courage had dissipated. It was difficult to remain positive for Nathalie when there was a possibility, they may already be too late. What if the prisoners had been taken at dawn, moved beyond the walls of the town to meet their fate away from the eyes of their loved ones?

Dominique shook herself. *Stay strong. Hold on to hope.* She didn't want the next letter she wrote to Gabriel to be delivering the news of his father's death. That might destroy him too.

She pushed aside her doubt and went straight to the middle cell.

"Pere, Pere, are you there?" Nathalie dropped to all fours to see into the cell where her father was pacing back and forward.

He stopped with a jolt, but his face lit up when he recognised the familiar voice.

"Oui, ma fille." He reached for Nathalie's hands. They clasped one another and the bars as if trying to cling to something solid. "I am still here. News has just come through that our sentences have been commuted."

"They have!" Dominique clapped with joy. "Oh, that's wonderful news."

Merci beaucoup, Pere. Je t'aime.

Dominique had no certainty her father's reasoned pleas had been successful, but she gave him credit for the outcome anyway.

"Oui, but we are to be sent to a prisoner of war camp." Mayor Carlier tried to look cheerful, but his forehead furrowed into a worrying frown and the glimmer of hope faded from his eyes.

When were they to leave? How long was their sentence? Where would they be sent? Dominique sat on the grass, her back against the wall while questions raced through her mind. With his poor health would Mayor Carlier survive the camp conditions? Was the prison camp a death sentence with another name?

Dominique's chest tightened and her temples throbbed as she looked at Nathalie and her father. She couldn't surrender to the dread sitting in the pit of her stomach. She had to be strong for all the Carlier family. She tried desperately to think of the positive aspects of this sentence.

"You'll be able to write." Dominique voiced the only plus she could think of. "Prisoners of war can write a letter every month. You can write to your wife and daughter. You can write to your son." Dominique leaned over closer to the bars and whispered. "Do you know about the code, Mayor Carlier?"

"You must stop calling me Mayor Carlier. I am no longer the head of the council." Mayor Carlier glanced over his shoulder at the cell door. "What code are you talking about? This is no time for childish games."

Dominique huffed. She was momentarily offended. She wasn't a child playing games. She knew the seriousness of using the codes to share information.

"It's not a game," she said with a solemn tone and look. "It's the way we share information to help with the war effort."

"We, who is we? I hope you haven't got yourself involved in some dangerous espionage."

"Gabriel and Dominique have been writing to one another, Pere, letters of hope every month," Nathalie came to Dominique's defence.

"That's all very well, but ..." Mayor Carlier checked the cell door again. "What is the code?"

"If Gabriel overhears anything about the German army's plans," Dominique whispered. "He'll write them in lemon juice under his ordinary letter, and I can read them."

Mayor Carlier perked up. "What has he told you so far?"

"Nothing to change the course of the war, but the tetchiness of the German soldiers who want everything to be over and done with, as much as us."

"Oui, there are murmurings of unrest among the men here too." Mayor Carlier, deep in thought, raked his fingers through his beard. "Perhaps it is their own men who will commit treason and refuse to fight."

"Oui, let them surrender. Then you won't be sent away, Pere." The tension in Nathalie's face appeared to ease with the thought her father wouldn't be imprisoned. "Our soldiers can come home. Everything can go back to normal."

Dominique wanted to share Nathalie's positivity but felt it was tinged with naivety. *What was normal?* Dominique was certain she'd never be the same as she was before the war. How could anyone be? There'd been so much destruction of lives and property that it would take a very long time to recover and rebuild.

The stomp of boots drew Mayor Carlier's attention to his cell door.

"Quick, the soldiers are coming, you'd better not be seen here," he warned. "They'd likely arrest you too, for fraternising with the enemy."

"But Pere, surely not, we're just children."

"With access to secret codes." Mayor Carlier arched an eyebrow. "I don't think you could claim that defence anymore."

"Au revoir, Pere." Nathalie blew her father a kiss. "I'll let Mere know the good news. We'll visit again soon."

"Au revoir, Mayor ... Monsieur Carlier." Dominique waved. "Stay strong."

Chapter 23

3 July 1915

Each time Dominique walked anxiously with Nathalie to the barracks, she half expected to see an empty cell, believing Vierordt to be so evil, he'd likely reverse his decision and order the men's execution. Fortunately, her misgivings proved false, but another three days passed before the captive men were finally loaded into a truck and shipped out through the gates of the city for the half day journey to Werden sur-Ruhr. The prisoner of war camp near Essen was to be their home for the foreseeable future, ten years of hard labour their dismal prospect.

Nathalie and her mother clung to each other as they watched the truck disappear. Their tears flowed freely. Ten years seemed like an eternity. Was this the last time they would see their beloved husband and father? How would his weakened heart cope with the camp conditions; the hard labour demanded of him?

It was going to be a long wait for his first letter to arrive.

As soon as the details of the prisoners' destination was known, Dominique put pen to paper to let Gabriel know his father's location. She suggested they write to one another, to buoy each other's spirits and keep hope alive.

Now, she needed to instil some hope into Nathalie and Madam Carlier.

"Come now." She waited until the truck had gone from sight before she beckoned them. "Let us move your things into Madam Severin's house. It might need a bit of a clean before it is liveable."

The Carlier women had been staying with the Favier family, but Madam Carlier insisted she wouldn't impinge on their hospitality any longer than necessary. Madam Severin's abandoned house became the perfect solution. Across the road, it was close enough if Nathalie and her mere required assistance but afforded them their privacy and independence.

The windows would have to remain battened shut; there was no glass available to replace the panes broken when the Boche ransacked the building all those months ago.

"It'll be like closing the shutters against the summer heat," Dominique tried to sound positive as they opened the front door.

Eight months of emptiness greeted them with a musty smell and the distinct aroma of the mice droppings that littered the floor. The vermin scurried from the rays of light flooding in from the open door, hiding in the dark corners.

"Mmm," Madam Carlier hesitated before shrugging her shoulders in resignation. "We'd best get to it, Nathalie, there's a lot of cleaning to be done."

"And Alphonse will be here soon to bring some furniture from home." Dominique remembered Madam Severin's splintered tables and chairs that she'd retrieved for firewood.

The trio went to work. Nathalie swept the dust, mice droppings and dead insects into a pile. Madam Carlier tied an apron around her middle and took a rag to wipe the kitchen shelves and the bench down. Meanwhile, Dominique trekked backwards and forwards across the road, bringing, first an armful of firewood to get the stove going so they could have hot water. Another trip delivered crockery, cutlery, pots and pans, anything that Marie could spare from the kitchen. Alphonse arrived and made several trips with his arms laden: two chairs, a wooden dining table, an armchair. Dominique helped him with a settee. Its threadbare arms were disguised with lace doilies and the back corner with a missing castor propped up with a piece of wood.

By the time the kettle whistled, they had the room looking liveable.

"It's not quite what we've been used to, Nathalie." Madam Carlier stood back with her hands on her hips and looked around. "But we'll make do. I imagine it is far more comfortable than your pere is having to endure."

Endure. Everyone was having to cope with the consequences of the German occupation. From prisoners suffering horrendous conditions in camps, farmers labouring away in unproductive fields to the townsfolk rationed, requisitioned and forced to work for the enemy. They all had to make do, clinging to the hope that France would one day be French again.

Each day their ability to endure was tested. New notices from the German Kommandantur were posted daily. Dominique and Nathalie always stopped to read them on their way to the laundry. Today there was a small crowd gathered at the town hall's noticeboard.

"Look, Nathalie." Dominique pointed to the latest posting. "They're introducing a dog tax, ten to twenty marcs depending on the dog. Oh no, Remy! We're going to have to pay a tax on Remy."

"I can't afford to pay that," a woman beside them complained. "I'm going to have to get rid of my dog."

"I've already killed mine," an elderly man admitted.

Gasps of horror rippled through the group.

"I'll not pay those bastards," he shook his fist. "Never a franc nor a damn marc."

Dominique understood his unwillingness to finance the enemy war effort but killing Remy? Her parents had already argued against him being classified a 'useless mouth'; she hoped they would spare him again and find other avenues to voice their objections.

"You could find other ways to protest the war," she suggested.

"They seek to fine us for even talking about the damn war," the man groaned. "Ten francs, just for talking, it is absurd."

"Did you not hear?" another man added. "One woman was overheard asking when we would be rid of these pigs, and she was fined 3,000 francs. Three thousand francs, how ridiculous. Who has that sort of money to pay a fine for speaking?"

He was right. The rules and restrictions placed on them seemed to get more ridiculous with every passing month. Was it just a demonstration of power? Vierordt trying to impose his authority on a population who had few choices available to them?

After a long hot day in the laundry, Dominique hurried home.

"Remy! Remy!" she called to the dog as soon as she opened the front door. "Where are you, boy?"

Remy barked and came running in from the garden, his tail wagging.

"Oh, merci, you're alright." Dominique ruffled his ears. She tried to pick him up, to stop the barking which would draw the attention of any nearby Germans, but he continued to bark, darting between her and the door to the backyard. "What is it, Remy? What do you want to show me?"

She followed the dog as he sprinted back outside. The sight that greeted her, stopped her in her tracks. The backyard, her Mere's precious garden, the lawn where her brothers played, were being trampled by soldiers. Each held a long pole, some taller than themselves. The ends were being poked into the ground.

"What are they doing now?" Dominique stood beside Marie who looked just as puzzled by the men's actions.

"Supposedly, we have buried wine and other treasures in the backyard," Marie replied. "They're probing for them."

Dominique leaned closer to Marie and whispered. "Will they find anything?"

Marie smiled and pretended to rub her nose. "I have much safer places to hide our precious reserves."

"Merci!"

As expected, the probes found nothing, but the Germans were determined not to leave empty handed. One of the soldiers whacked the weathervane attached to the roof of the woodshed. The brass rooster and his east, west, north and south arms fell from their perch, landing with a thud, the rooster's beak poking into the ground.

"You were ordered to deliver all copper, brass and nickel to the town hall." The soldier shook the weathervane at Dominique and Marie as he passed. "You should be fined for your defiance."

"I didn't know what it was made of," Marie pleaded ignorance.

The men left with their bounty, a trail of destruction behind them.

"Maman will be devastated when she sees what they've done to her garden."

Broken branches, snapped stems, and trampled plants littered the backyard.

"She's already seen." Marie looked back at the house where Lucie stood in the upstairs bedroom window. "She had to stay inside to control her temper. She was afraid of what she might do to them."

Lucie's face was red with rage. Despite the men having left, she continued to pace backwards and forwards across the bedroom, her hands balled into tight fists.

"Perhaps we'd better retrieve one of the bottles of wine from the reserves to console her," Dominique suggested.

"Oui, that would be a good idea except Hans and Wolfgang will know."

A month passed before the first letter arrived from Monsieur Carlier. It was obvious it had been censored, black ink blotted out portions of the note. He wrote he was being fed three meals a day and had not been made to cut stones like some of the prisoners but was assigned the easier task of making baskets to hold artillery shells. He wished his family well and sent his love.

"That doesn't seem too onerous," Nathalie observed. "Pere will be alright."

"Oui," Madam Carlier nodded. "Sometimes our own rations are such that we don't get three meals a day."

"I wonder if he used the code," Dominique asked.

"What code?"

Dominique took the letter and held it by a lamp, waiting for words to reveal themselves as the paper warmed.

"Barely fed enough to survive," Dominique read the coded text aloud.

She stopped when she registered what she'd said and folded the paper in half to stow it away.

Madam Carlier and Nathalie looked wide-eyed at her.

"You cannot stop now."

"You must tell us all he really says."

Regretting that she'd started at all, Dominique gingerly unfolded the paper. "Are you sure? It might not be nice."

"Nothing about this war is nice, Dominique, but we need to know." Madam Carlier wrung her hands in her lap. "How can we help those in need if we don't know?"

"No energy to work," Dominique read. "Breakfast watery gruel. Bread full of straw and rotten beans. Lunch watery soup. Lunch diluted further is dinner. Struggling to make required twelve baskets a day."

The next lines on the page weren't coded, they were written in plain ink as if the Germans wanted to use the note for their own publicity.

"Louise Thuliez and Phillippe Baucq arrested in Brussels." Dominique gasped. "Louise Thuliez, she's the teacher that supervised our examination."

The one I gave Alphonse's note to.

"A teacher," Madam Carlier exclaimed. "Whatever have they arrested a teacher for? A woman as well. I suppose she was teaching French and not German, saying the occupied north was still French, not part of the German empire as they claim."

Dominique remained tight lipped while she scanned for more encoded text. Nothing. All the questions racing about her head weren't going to be answered by Monsieur Carlier. While it was wonderful to know he was still alive, the short note left Madam

Carlier more distraught than she had been and set Dominique's nerves on edge.

No doubt the Germans would search the home of Louise Thuliez looking for evidence. What if they found the note from Alphonse? Had he signed it? Would the Germans be knocking on his door next? Knock! The enemy didn't knock; they barged in and arrested without reason or justification.

"Are you alright, Dominique?" Nathalie asked. "You've gone as white as a ghost."

"Is there something else you haven't read out to us?" Madam Carlier took the letter and scanned it for herself.

"Non, there is nothing else. I'm just worried for Monsieur Carlier." It wasn't a lie. It just wasn't the entire truth.

"Well, there is no point sitting around here worrying, we must take action." Madam Carlier stood and stowed the letter in the pocket of her skirt. "I'll go and see Monsieur Croix. He's taken over Achille's role with the Relief Board. He can contact them and continue the fight to get my husband released."

"I might head to the hospital." Dominique was unsure she could stand, she felt lightheaded, an army of butterflies fluttering about her stomach. "I am feeling a little unwell."

"Oui, check in with your pere, child." Madam Carlier patted Dominique's shoulder.

**

It wasn't her father, Dominique sought out when she reached the hospital but Alphonse. She had to wait while he helped move a patient from the theatre post-surgery and get him settled in a bed, a frame holding the bed linen off his amputated leg.

Alphonse rubbed the back of his neck as he came towards Dominique, a frown furrowing his forehead.

"He might be German, but I can't help but feel for him." Alphonse slapped his thigh. "I know what it's like to have one leg shorter than the other. His amputation is way worse than anything I've had to cope with." Alphonse shook his head and tried to look happy for Dominique. "What brings you here, little sister-in-law?"

"I'm not little, I'm almost as tall as you," Dominique blurted out her protest before she saw Alphonse wink. He was teasing her, trying to garner a reaction and she'd fallen straight into his trap. "*Grrr!* I'm here to tell you something important, not to be teased."

"What is it, Dominique? I promise to listen quietly, but you must be quick, I have work to do."

Dominique pulled Alphonse away from the patients and lowered her voice.

"Louise Thuliez has been arrested. Phillippe Baucq too."

It was Alphonse's turn to look ashen, although it wasn't as noticeable on his weathered skin.

"What if the Germans search her home? What if they find your note? What if they come and arrest you? What if they interrogate you and find out about me? We'll end up in a German prisoner of war camp like Mayor Carlier and Doctor Flament."

"Calm down, Dominique. Breathe." Alphonse placed his hand on her forearm and squeezed. "You're getting ahead of yourself.

Notes always get destroyed once the message is read and remembered."

"But what if she didn't? What if she had so many things to remember, she kept your note?"

"Even if she didn't burn it, there still won't be a note with my name on it. I wasn't silly enough to put my name to paper. We all have code names. There will be no way to trace it to me."

"Someone must know your code names though. What if they give in? What if they cannot handle the interrogation and save themselves by telling the Boche what they want to know?"

"We will cross that bridge, if and when it needs to be crossed."

Dominique was no longer a carefree child. She'd been wanting to be treated like an adult and now that she was, she longed for the simplicity of childhood. Long hot summer days which, before the war, would have been spent swimming in the Etang du Pont Rouge or lazing in the shade of the oaks in Foret de Mormal now passed sweltering in the hospital laundry.

Perhaps it would have been better if she'd conceded to her mother's wishes and been sent away to live with family in Paris. She may have been able to convince Eugenie to nurse out of harm's way. At least she would be able to write to her sister. Le Quesnoy was cut off from free France. It was the not knowing that was the worst.

Every noise had Dominique on edge. Were the boots marching on the street cobbles soldiers coming to arrest her? When a soldier removed his rifle from his shoulder, was he going to aim it at her and shoot? Her chest tightened whenever she heard commands yelled in German. Even at home, when Wolfgang eyed her, she wondered if he knew what she'd done. Did she wear guilt like a white flag of surrender? When he cleared his throat at the table, her body tensed, waiting for the accusation of treachery to be flung at her.

Each day she scanned the noticeboard and sought out Monsieur Potier, the mailman, desperate for news by notice or letters from Gabriel or his father. Her sanity seemed to depend on how the case of Louise Thuliez was proceeding.

In September, an Abbot from nearby Cambrai was arrested. Two fugitive French soldiers were captured a short distance from Le Quesnoy. They carried papers which implicated the Abbot.

Did the injured soldiers and *brigands des rouge* escapees have papers on them that would point a finger, or a rifle, at Dominique? Were they in free territory, home, or had they been recaptured?

In October, the Abbot was sent to Dusseldorft prisoner of war camp for six months. Shortly after his sentencing a military tribunal was set up in Brussels for the trial of Louise Thuliez and Philippe Baucq. By this time, several others had been implicated including the Countess of Belleville and Edith Cavill, a nurse. Women, who from all walks of life, believed in the value of human life above all else.

Unlike Mayor Carlier they at least got to defend themselves. Their trial lasted several weeks. The eventual news of their death sentences left Dominique conflicted. Aghast that people could be executed for helping those in need; relieved that the trial was over and she, Alphonse, Clemence, Alice and Sister Jeanne still walked free. She couldn't stop pacing, she needed to do something, talk to someone who would understand. She hurried to the hospital, a sinking feeling in her stomach, a tightness in her chest.

"Would you help again if you were needed?" Alphonse asked when she relayed the news.

"Oui, most definitely," Dominique voiced her answer without thinking, "... but I think I'd be a lot more cautious."

"You are kind and brave, Dominique. You have given hope to many who would have otherwise suffered or worse still, died."

Dominique swallowed. "I haven't done anything that you wouldn't do, Alphonse."

"We should be proud, not boastful, but silently satisfied with our efforts."

Dominique felt a weight lift from her shoulders. "Merci, Alphonse, I knew you would understand."

The weight was further eased when news came through on October 12, that Louise Thuliez's death sentence was commuted to forced labour for life. It only happened because of the outcry following the execution of Edith Cavill and Phillippe Baucq.

Chapter 24

December 1915

Le Quesnoy's second Christmas under occupation was blanketed with snow. The ponds surrounding the town froze over. In the past, children would have skated on the frozen water, pulling sleds and laughing as they raced one another but skates were a thing of the past, nothing made of metal remained within the fortified walls of the town. Laughter too, had almost vanished. There was little to be happy about, the innocence of childhood stolen by a war few of them understood.

The pond's icy crust had more serious ramifications. The precious supply of fish, a staple for many of the townsfolk, became difficult to harvest. Some of the older men managed to pierce holes in the ice. They sat for hours in the icy temperatures; their lines dropped through the hole but the only thing they caught was a cold. One elderly gentleman became seriously ill. His health, already suffering from his meagre diet, deteriorated.

"Pneumonia, old man Delatour, has pneumonia," Henri told his family as they gathered in the sitting room in front of the only fire, their ration of wood could keep burning. "He's at the hospital. At least there he'll be a little warmer and out of the damp."

"Monsieur Carlier is in the hospital too." Dominique stared into the flickering flames and hugged her shawl tighter around her shoulders.

"Has he returned from the prisoner of war camp?" Lucie asked.

"Non, Madam Carlier received a letter from him. The food there is worse than ours. Not enough goodness to sustain him. He lost weight and didn't have the energy to make his daily quota of baskets."

"What happened?" Lucie looked aghast and put her hands over Victor's ears. "Did they beat him?"

"Non, they reduced his food ration even further as a punishment." Unable to understand the German reasoning, Dominique shook her head in disbelief. "Now, he's in hospital."

"Hasn't Madam Carlier engaged a lawyer to get his sentence overturned?"

"Oui, Pere, but he is German." Dominique spoke with a cynicism well beyond her years.

"He should be working for his client, regardless of race," Henri glanced at the sitting room door, checking that Hans and Wolfgang were out of earshot. "Perhaps he is afraid of the ramifications from his own people if he is successful."

Lost in the trance of the flames, Dominique nodded her agreement. She struggled to lift her melancholy. This war that held them captive, cut off from the rest of the world, was meant to be over within six weeks and now, more than sixty weeks later their second Christmas without family and loved ones around, without the food and treats they enjoyed, fun and laughter and joyous celebrations missing, it was all the more difficult to have hope for the future.

Her thoughts wandered to Gabriel. She'd been writing him a letter and wanted to send him wishes for Christmas. She couldn't decide on an apt word, unable to imagine Christmas in a prisoner of war camp would be 'happy' or 'joyful'. Maybe if they managed to sneak in some alcohol, it might have a chance of being 'merry' but that was most unlikely. Perhaps they should be 'grateful' they had endured camp life long enough to reach Christmas. As her family rose to go to bed she settled on 'sending you best wishes at Christmas, hoping you will be back with us soon.'

Dominique hugged her mother and father, even her twin brothers. In the uncertainty of the occupation, it became a nightly routine. Noone gave voice to the possibility that war may take them away from one another but neither did they want to miss the silent, just-in-case farewell.

The sounds of fighting were as distant as the memory of French and British soldiers protecting the town but often in the wee hours of the morning shots would be fired into the air and an alarm sounded. It was a signal for the townsfolk to assemble in the square. There never seemed to be a purpose to the summons, just a demonstration of power.

Soldiers would walk along the rows of citizens conducting a head count. If anyone failed to arrive, armed men would be sent to their house to drag them from their beds. It didn't matter if they were bedridden with illness, the German Kommandantur demanded their presence.

A sixth sense told Dominique the alarms would be sounded in the morning.

She was snuggled under her blankets, cosy and warm, dreaming of Gabriel when the shrill noise pierced her slumber just as the first light was breaking through the clouds.

"*Grrr!* Sacrebleu!" She cursed; certain Gabriel was about to kiss her. She wanted to know how it would feel, to inhale his scent long since evaporated from her memory. It may have only been a dream, but it felt so real.

Reluctantly, she pushed the covers off, sat up and swung her legs over the side of the bed. Her toes touching the cold floorboards banished any remnants of her dream. She dressed quickly, layering her clothes for warmth. It was cold inside the house, so it was likely to be freezing outside. She pulled the curtains back and peeked through the shutters, half expecting snow. The ground was white, but it looked icy rather than a fluffy blanket of fresh snow.

"Put your hats and gloves on boys," Lucie was fussing over Louis and Victor in the entranceway when Dominique went downstairs. "You too, Dominique."

"Oui, Maman." Dominique knew it was easier to agree. "What do you think they want us for this time, Pere?"

"We'll have to wait and see." Henri wrapped his scarf around his neck until it sat high under his chin.

Hans and Wolfgang arrived in the hall, in full uniform and with rucksacks in their hands.

"You're leaving us, so soon." Lucie's words may have hinted at despondency, but she was anything but melancholy at the soldier's departure. She flicked a hand in front of her nose as if their leaving was ridding the house of a bad smell.

Wolfgang merely grunted and pushed between them to open the door. A blast of cold air blew in. Wolfgang sniggered as he stepped outside, leaving the door wide open like a departing punishment.

"Going home." Hans ruffled Louis's hair. "To my boys. Danke for your home."

Why couldn't all the Germans be like Hans? There wouldn't be a war if they were.

The Favier family finished donning coats, hats and gloves to brace themselves against the winter chill and left the house. Madam Carlier and Nathalie joined them for the walk down Rue Brancion to the square.

"I wonder who they will insist we house now." Lucie rested her hand in the crook of Henri's elbow. "Better the devil you know than the one you don't."

"Oui, mon cherie, oui." Henri patted his wife's hand.

They rounded the corner into the square to see the devil they knew was not standing in his usual spot on the makeshift podium with a view over the square.

"Where's Vierordt?" Dominique asked.

They had to stand in line and be counted before the new Kommandantur made his appearance. Major Von Manteuffel, as he was introduced, was half the age of his predecessors. Where

Lubbert had been chubby in face and body and Vierordt thin and wizened, Von Manteuffel looked to be in his prime. Le Quesnoy had seemed like a posting for officers who no longer had the fitness for the front lines, however Von Manteuffel filled out his uniform with definition, muscle and a physique more than capable of fighting a battle.

Why was he posted here? Dominique narrowed her eyes to study the man. Did he have an injury that wasn't immediately apparent? Was he here to prove himself and gain promotion through the ranks?

What do you want?

"Frohe Weihnachten." His first words to the crowd were accompanied by a smile.

Or was it a smirk, an attempt to lull the townsfolk into a false sense of security. Dominique kept her own smile at bay while she scanned the crowd, watching others' reactions.

"Merry Christmas, Major Von Manteuffel," came the response from several who'd learned more German than Dominique.

"Did he really just wish us Merry Christmas, Pere?"

"Oui, it appears he did."

"I bet he's about to announce some punishment as if standing out in the cold isn't enough." Dominique couldn't believe his wishes to be genuine.

"Ma fille," Henri sighed. "This war has made you cynical before your time. You must try to see goodness in everyone, even in difficult times."

Dominique tilted her head, contemplating her father's words, studying Von Manteuffel, considering her confused emotions. Would she have judged this man differently if he'd come into her life before the war? *Possibly.* If she ignored the colour of his uniform, he looked like any other man. With his blue eyes and blonde hair, he would have stood out from the locals. She may have even considered him handsome. Her toes curled up inside her boots, not from the cold but disgust. How could she ever think a German was handsome? Alice did. She fell in love with one and look where that got her.

"Two things for Christmas." Major Von Manteuffel pointed to the ground in front of the stage where a canvas sack and several cartons sat.

"He's giving us a gift?" Dominique frowned.

"Sssh, ma fille. Listen and you may be surprised."

"I hope it's a nice surprise," Dominique muttered under her breath.

Henri raised an eyebrow at his daughter and shook his head.

"Letters from Der Weihnachtsmann for the children," Von Manteuffel announced.

Children who couldn't contain their excitement rushed forward. Louis was gone before Lucie could rein him in and Victor, like his faithful puppy, quickly followed. A soldier took the sack, and the children eagerly followed him to the steps of the church where he began reading names and handing out envelopes.

"They'll be fine, Lucie," Henri attempted to calm his wife.

"Biscuits for the townsfolk," Von Manteuffel continued. "A ration for everyone. Stay in your rows and my men will distribute."

"Look, Maman, look." Louis waved his arms, a ripped envelope in one hand, a card clasped in the other. "It's from Father Christmas."

"What does he say, Louis?" Lucie tried to take the card, but Louis was too excited to give up his mail.

"He says sorry." Victor arrived with his identical card. "He cannot visit like he did before."

"Oh, non," Louis groaned. "No presents from Father Christmas. That's not fair. I've been good all year. You're lying, Victor. You want to keep my presents for yourself."

"I am not lying." Victor stepped forward and puffed out his chest. "I've been good too and I'm not getting any presents either."

Louis pushed Victor. He lost his footing and slid into the path of the soldier handing out their ration of biscuits.

"Louis and Victor!" Henri didn't have to raise his deep voice; it carried an authority that wasn't reliant on volume for effectiveness. "Stand in line, now."

The boys stopped immediately, stepped back into line and looked sheepishly at the ground.

Their contrition was short-lived though. As soon as the soldier handed each of the boys a biscuit, their faces lit up and any guilt was banished.

"Mmm, yummy," Louis spoke with his mouth half full. "Can I have another one, soldier?"

Dominique sucked in a breath. She waited for the soldier's reaction. Would he be kind on Christmas and offer a child another biscuit or would he punish him for his insolence?

"Eat nicely, Louis," Lucie intervened. "We don't know when we will get anymore."

If the soldier detected the sarcasm in Lucie's voice, he didn't react. Neither did he respond to Louis before moving along the row to Dominique.

She felt her chest tighten as he drew close. Instinct took her back to the soldier in the street; the man who wanted more than her sandwich. She snatched the biscuit offered to her, afraid to make eye contact with the soldier, hoping he would move on quickly.

She exhaled long and slow as she watched his polished leather boots turn and move away.

"Just be happy with what you have."

Henri spoke to Louis, but the message hit home with Dominique also. She stowed the biscuit in her pocket for later. She had no appetite now.

"Can we go?" Louis fidgeted, scuffing the ground with his boots.

"You may return to your homes," Major Von Manteuffel announced as if he had heard Louis's plea. "Get out of this weather."

The crowd dispersed and the Favier and Carlier families with them.

"He seems a lot nicer than Major Vierordt." Henri waited until they turned back into Rue Brancion before voicing his opinion.

"I hope so," Madam Carlier said. "Perhaps I can petition him to get Achille freed."

"It is certainly worth a try," Henri replied.

Hans and Wolfgang were replaced by two soldiers fresh from battle who been granted leave, not to return to their homes, but to come to Le Quesnoy for rest.

"Hubert Schmidt," the first of the new guests introduced himself. "Merci for your home."

His French wasn't perfect, but it allowed for a conversation of sorts. There was a tiredness to his demeanour; his shoulders sagged as if he had no energy to maintain a soldier's upright posture. His eyes appeared red like he'd been crying but Dominique doubted that was the case.

"This is Ludwig Hoffman," he nodded to his associate.

Ludwig stared down at his empty hands. Hubert nudged him with his elbow to prompt a greeting. Ludwig's trembling chin lifted; his wet dull eyes stared into the distance as if his mind was still at the Somme. He opened his mouth to speak but no words came out. He sniffed and wiped his nose with the back of his shaking hand.

"He'll be alright after a rest," Hubert offered on Ludwig's behalf. "Our rooms?"

"Oui. Of course. Dominique," Henri was firm in his request. "Show the soldiers to their rooms."

"This way," Dominique pointed to the stairs and then led them away.

She assumed this pair would be much the same as Hans and Wolfgang so wanted to maintain her distance but if there was any information to be garnered from the soldiers then she'd better not get offside with them from the beginning.

Hubert made sure Ludwig was settled in his bedroom. He put his rucksack on the chair by the window.

"You can unpack that later. Just have a rest now, Ludwig." Hubert pulled back the covers on the bed.

"Are you a medic?" Dominique stared wide-eyed at Hubert, unable to reconcile the German soldier label with the caring, gentle man before her.

"Non, he is my friend." Hubert removed Ludwig's boots. "We have been in every battle together. We have each other's back. I cannot abandon him when he most needs me."

Where Ludwig's thoughts were locked inside, Hubert seemed to want to speak so Dominique continued with her questions.

"How many battles have you been in?"

"Too many." Hubert sighed. "Do you not receive news of the fighting in your town?"

"Non, we are cut off."

"Aah, you are fortunate."

Dominique had never considered their predicament to be fortunate.

"But we have family and friends beyond the walls of this town, and we hear nothing from nor of them. Not knowing can sometimes be worse."

"Perhaps ..." Hubert slowly nodded as if he was contemplating his reply. "Let's leave Ludwig to rest and I will tell you what I can."

Ludwig was staring at the ceiling when Hubert pulled the door to.

"He sleeps with his eyes open," he explained. "The images aren't good when we close them."

Dominique was about to ask what those images were, but she saw Hubert grimace and decided perhaps she was fortunate to have not seen the carnage at the battle front.

Downstairs, they settled in the sitting room with a cup of coffee delivered by Marie.

"Where is your pere?" Hubert asked. "Perhaps I am better talking to him. I do not want to terrify a young lady."

Hubert called her a *young lady.* Dominique softened a little, grateful he hadn't labelled her a child.

"He's gone back to work," she replied. "He's a doctor at the hospital. He's having to work long hours after Doctor Flament was arrested and sent away to a prisoner of war camp."

"What was the Doctor arrested for?"

"Doing his job."

"That doesn't sound like an offence." Hubert frowned. "There must be more to it than that."

"Some of his patients may have been French and British," Dominique admitted.

"Aah, I see."

"But they sentenced him to death." Dominique sat on the edge of her chair. "It's hardly fair to be executed for doing your job."

"I can't imagine Major Von Manteuffel ordering that." Hubert sipped at his coffee.

"It wasn't him. It was Vierordt." Dominique almost spat his name. "Major Von Manteuffel has only just arrived. Do you know him?"

"I have served with him at the front. He is a good, fair man."

"I hope so. The Quercitains are tired and suffering."

"We all are ... we ... all ... are." Hubert sighed.

Chapter 25

November 1916

"Dominique! Dominique!"

"I'm coming." Dominique hurried to the front door. "Don't bang the door down."

"Quick! I have good news." Nathalie bounced from foot to foot with her excitement.

"What is it?" Dominique pulled her friend into the shelter of the entrance. "Come in out of the cold and tell me what has you so excited."

"It's Pere." Nathalie's face lit up.

Whenever Monsieur Carlier's name was mentioned over the past year it never came with good news. After two months in a camp hospital, his health improved but instead of being released, he was moved to another prisoner of war camp, supposedly with better conditions.

Puzzled by Nathalie's delight, Dominique frowned.

"Don't look so worried." Nathalie squeezed Dominique's hand. "He's been in Belgium at Grandmere's since June but has found his way to Paris. We're going to join him."

Dominique still couldn't turn her frown into a smile. It was good news for Nathalie, her mother and father but it meant she would have to farewell her best friend. They'd known one other since they'd sat nervously together on their first day at school, holding hands under the desk. Summer picnics, winter snowball fights, secrets shared, nothing would ever be the same. Dominique blinked away her burgeoning tears. She should be happy for Nathalie, not selfishly thinking only of herself.

"We are leaving at the end of the week," Nathalie continued oblivious to Dominique's turmoil. "Mere has secured permission for us to go to Paris. We're going on the train. It'll be so wonderful to see Pere again and re-unite our family."

Re-unite your family!

"Does that mean Gabriel is being released too?" Dominique gasped.

Gabriel was her only connection with the outside world. He was hers. He was her hope. Her light at the end of the tunnel.

Please don't take him away from me.

"Non." Nathalie's smile disappeared. "He is still in the prisoner of war camp."

"Je suis désolé." Guilt for destroying Nathalie's joy made Dominique apologise. "It is good that your pere will be freed. I am being selfish. I am sad. I will miss you."

"I will miss you too." Nathalie hugged Dominique.

"What about Jean-Phillippe? I thought you'd never leave your beau."

"He understands, and I get to see Paris too. I can try to contact Eugenie if you like."

"There is no point."

"What?" It was Nathalie's turn to frown. "Why do you say that?"

"You won't be able to write to me. Remember, no letters from free France are allowed." Dominique stared at the floor. "You won't be able to describe Paris to me or tell me how Eugenie is."

"I will. I will find a way, Dominique. You have kept my spirits up. I will do the same for you. That's what friends are for. We support one another to keep hope alive."

They stood in the entrance, holding hands as if it would be the last opportunity for them to do so. Dominique let the tears she'd been holding at bay fall. It felt good to let go, the release was instantaneous, as if she'd been carrying a load for far too long.

"I know!" Nathalie stepped away, energised and buoyant. "I'll write to Gabriel, and he can relay the news to you, and you can do the same back again. It might take a while but at least we'll still be in touch."

"Oui." Dominique wiped her eyes and blew her nose. "That will work. Je suis désolé for crying."

"You never have to apologize for that, Dominique. I have cried on you plenty of times." Nathalie leaned over and rested her head on Dominique's shoulder. "Remember the very first time when we were running away from Francois's bakery with the stolen pain au chocolate, and I tripped on the cobbles? You helped me then and you've helped me every time I've needed since. That's what friends are for."

"Oui. That's what friends are for, and we will always be friends."

"Even when we are living miles apart with a war being fought in between."

"I feel like we have become nothing but a hotel for the Germans over the past year," Lucie complained. "They seem to come and go every three weeks."

Dominique shared her mother's annoyance only to the extent that they had to have the enemy in their home at all. Otherwise, she'd changed her stance. She now saw the German soldiers that came to Le Quesnoy to rest as a valuable source of information. She was more determined than ever to do everything in her power to see the war finished. There was an emptiness in her heart that needed to be filled and that could only be done when she knew her sister Eugenie was safe; Nathalie was able to return to Le Quesnoy and most importantly the love she had for Gabriel was able to be more than just words on paper. She wanted to be with him, hear his voice, feel his touch, piece their fragmented lives together.

"I'll look after the ones arriving today if you like." Dominique glanced out the window to see if the new soldiers to be accommodated had arrived.

The German soldiers became the key to the world outside the fortified walls. The news they provided gave her hope that there would be an end to the fighting. The soldiers always came in twos. Dominique learned to be patient, to observe the men before she chose which one would be of most use to her. Sometimes neither were, the men maintained an aloofness as if they were superior and the Favier family mere minions at their beck and call. Time seemed to stand still on these occasions. Lucie's indignation simmered ready to burst with insults that would likely get her punished. To protect his wife, Henri insisted Dominique and Marie look after their 'guests' and suggested Lucie might like to read quietly in her bedroom.

As Lucie took the final sip of her coffee, the familiar stomping of boots on the cobbles could be heard, followed by a thumping on the front door.

"I have a headache." Lucie sighed, put her cup on the table and brushed her hand across her forehead.

"I think I'll go and have a lie down."

"Oui, Maman. I'll get the door."

They headed in opposite directions. Lucie took the staircase beside the kitchen to avoid being seen and Dominique went to the front door. She paused, her hand on the door handle while she gathered her strength.

"You can do this," she whispered to herself. "They may have a different coloured uniform, but they are just men on the inside."

She straightened her spine and opened the door, hoping this time the men would be at least kind, if not helpful and maybe even friendly. She was ready to pass judgement immediately based on their demeanour, their expressions, their greeting but was thrown off guard when it was Hubert she saw.

"Hubert?"

"Ja, it is me, Dominique." Hubert's broad smile showed his perfect white teeth. "Back again."

"I didn't expect to see you again." Stunned, Dominique stood, eyes wide, mouth agape.

"Are you going to let us in?" Hubert half turned to reveal the man standing behind him.

"Ludwig?"

"Nein." Hubert looked at the ground and shook his head. "Ludwig didn't make it."

A shiver ran down Dominique's spine. Ludwig was dead. That there were German losses too suddenly hit home. She wanted to reach out, embrace Hubert and erase the sadness he obviously carried.

But he is still the enemy.

She cleared her throat and stepped back to let the men inside. "Come in, out of the cold."

It was as much comfort as she could offer.

"Danke." Hubert looked at the staircase. "The same rooms as last time?"

"Oui."

"Ludolf and I will go and drop our bags up." Hubert ushered his comrade towards the stairs. "A cup of coffee in the sitting room would be nice."

Dominique took the hint and went to the kitchen.

"Hubert is back." Dominique filled the kettle and replaced it on the stovetop.

"And Ludwig too?" Marie's question echoed around the empty potato bin she was bent over. "I'd better put two more potatoes in the pot."

"Non, Ludwig is dead." Dominique watched Marie submerge the unpeeled potatoes in a pot of water. "Are you not going to peel them?"

"It's been suggested we don't. Given the shortage, we can't waste anything." Marie wiped her hands on her apron.

"Well, I'd rather eat them as potatoes than the horrible black bread Francois has to make using potatoes instead of flour." Dominique screwed her face up and poked her tongue out as if the taste was in her mouth.

"Kreigsbrot." Marie uttered the bread's German name with equal distaste. "Vierordt forcing Monsieur Dehove to close his wheat mill was terrible. Thank goodness he left." Marie shook her head. "What happened to Ludwig?"

"I don't know but I'm going to find out." Dominique spooned just enough of the precious coffee grains to give a taste.

There was no milk to add. It was a commodity that had long since disappeared from their diets. Farmers either had no people to help them harvest crops or no fertile land to grow the crops to be harvested to feed their animals. The Germans requisitioned the best of the cattle to supply their needs, leaving only the skinny and unproductive animals for the Quercitains. Sustaining livestock through the winter was near impossible. The milk supply dried up and the out of condition cows were left infertile.

Dominique carried a tray through to the sitting room where Hubert and Ludolf were settled into her parents' armchairs both enjoying cigarettes, sending plumes of smoke towards the ceiling.

The odour reminded her of Wolfgang and set her nerves on edge. Hubert hadn't smoked last time he'd stayed.

"You've taken up smoking, Hubert." Dominique tried to keep any hint of disgust from her voice as she sat as far away from them as possible.

"Ja, since Ludwig ..." Hubert drew on his cigarette as if he needed its calming nicotine fix to continue.

"What happened to Ludwig? How did he die?" Dominique glanced at Ludolf to gauge his reaction to her questioning.

Was he a soldier that wished to maintain the barrier between occupier and occupied? She couldn't catch his eye. He looked all around the room and then down into the depths of his coffee, everywhere but at Dominique.

"He was shot." Hubert's eyes glassed over.

"Je suis désolé a French bullet took your friend's life."

"But ... nein ... it ...." Hubert looked across at Ludolf as if he needed reassuring it was alright to talk.

Ludolf kept his head lowered, staring into the cup like there was a solution to the world's problems hidden in the coffee dregs.

"Nein, not French fire. German." Hubert drew heavily on the cigarette and waited for the smoke to pour from his nostrils before he continued. "He was shot for desertion. For not following the orders to advance."

"The German army shot one of their own!" Dominique gasped. She knew they were heartless but to take the life of a young man for not following orders when he was incapable of doing so.

"Your army does it too!" Ludolf almost spat his defensive retort. "So do the British."

Dominique flinched. She wanted to tell Ludolf to keep staring into his cup, but she didn't.

"In fact," Ludolf sounded indignant. "The British officer in charge, a fellow by the name of Haig, effectively ordered the slaughter of thousands of allied troops by sending them into no-man's land where they were sitting ducks."

Dominique couldn't deny what he'd claimed, she had no knowledge, instead, her curiosity led her deeper.

"Where is no-man's land?" It wasn't somewhere she'd heard of.

"It is the space between." Ludolf's voice became monotone. He stared into the distance as if he was being transported to no-man's land. "Where there is nowhere to hide, no trees, no trenches, nothing but dead earth littered with dead men and their dead faithful horses."

"And the gas," Hubert added. "Don't forget the deadly clouds of gas."

Dominique didn't let her distaste for the images they were painting, dampen her curiosity.

"The space between what?" she asked.

"The area that neither side has been able to claim as their own," Hubert added. "It is not a particular place, Dominique, it keeps moving as the battle commanders play out their moves. Like pieces on a chess board, we are ordered to move in a particular direction, to take out the opposition. The aim being to claim a checkmate, but no-one has been able to do that yet. We are but pawns in a very long and tiring game."

Hubert seemed a shadow of the man Dominique had met a year ago. He and Ludolf continued to talk as if to finally speak of the atrocities would unleash the memories and set them free. They seemed oblivious to her presence. Hopeful for some information that she could share with Gabriel she sat quietly and listened.

"All for what?" Ludolf sighed.

"Six miles. Sixty thousand wounded or killed for just six bloody miles."

"I can still hear the drone of aeroplanes overhead." Ludolf rubbed his ear. "It's like a constant buzz in my ear."

"Better than the screams of the fallen." Hubert squeezed his eyes shut.

"Our mates."

"German, French, British ... dying men all sound the same."

"Why did they order them to march straight towards us? Surely, they knew their fate."

"Blind faith in the cause." Hubert lowered his voice to a murmur. "Like I used to have."

"We had no choice." Ludolf shook his head. "We were just following orders to fire."

"They should have sent their tanks in first," Hubert suggested. "Perhaps more would have survived."

"Hah, nein, their tanks were unreliable, they would have broken down."

Dominique swallowed the lump in her throat. She'd heard enough. She never would have been privy to such a conversation before the war. She wished she hadn't been party to it now. It was best to change the subject. She coughed to clear her throat; loud enough she hoped, to break into their trance.

"Well, at least you get to have another holiday in Le Quesnoy."

The men stopped, slowly turned and looked at her blankly. Only the clock's ticking could be heard. Dominique blinked with the same rhythm. Had they not heard her? Did they think her rude for interrupting? What should she say next?

"It is ... umm ... it's good that you get another holiday, is it not?"

"If only it was a holiday." A small chuckle, laced with sarcasm, escaped Hubert. "Sipping fine champagne on the riviera would be wonderful. No more time in trenches and concrete bunkers in the Somme waiting for the British troops."

"Or the Italians, now they have changed sides and declared war on Germany," Ludolf added with an equal dose of sarcasm.

Silence engulfed the room. Hubert seemed to disappear into his thoughts again, gazing at nothing but seeing everything. His cigarette had nearly burnt down to his stained fingers by the time he shook his head and brought himself back to the present.

"There has been so much carnage and for what?" He shrugged as he stubbed his cigarette out in the ashtray, signalling the end of the conversation too. "We have been everywhere a young lady like you will never have to go." Hubert stood. "Is that your brothers' laughter I can hear?"

"Oui, I think they are playing hide and seek in the garden."

"Aah, the innocence of childhood." Hubert sighed. "I think I'll join them, see if I can absorb some of their happy energy."

"I'll come too." Ludolf downed the last of his coffee and passed his cup to Dominique. "You look like you need some laughter as well, will you join us?"

"Non, merci, I have to go to work at the hospital laundry."

Hubert teamed up with Louis, Ludolf joined with Victor as the opposition for a game of cricket with balls crafted from the icy snow. Clapping, cheering and laughter rang out through the garden each time the bat connected with the ball and sent a shower of snow skyward.

Envious, Dominique watched through the window.

If only. She wanted to join them. The desire to play was like a smouldering ember the war had nearly extinguished. A spark that she herself had tried hard to dampen in the guise of being treated like an adult. *Why?* Why would anyone want to lose the child inside themselves? The view of the world that came without prejudices and judgements. The ability to see delight in anything and everything.

Movement caught her eye. She looked up to see her mother watching the game from her bedroom. She was smiling. It seemed like an eternity since Dominique had seen her mere smile. She was beautiful when she did, as if she glowed from the inside.

Dominique's smile was involuntary; it mirrored her mother's. The tiny ember ignited, a speck of warmth in her chest expanded, grew in intensity and heat. She hugged herself, embracing the moment, holding it safe. *If only.* She drew strength from the power within her.

It was with a renewed sense of hope that she stepped out onto the cobbled street, knowing she would get through and all would be alright when the war finally ended.

Chapter 26

March 1917

It wasn't Von Manteuffel's doing but under his watch correspondence between the occupied and free France was finally able to flow. They weren't letters as such, but cards specifically provided for the purpose, with only twenty words permitted on each and nothing of a military nature. The cards had to pass through the Frankfurt Red Cross and the Ministry of the Interior in Paris, so a month or more passed before they reached their destination.

When the cards first became available, Dominique grabbed a handful of them and disappeared to her bedroom. She wrote to Eugenie first; the person who'd been missing from her life the longest.

My dear sister. How I miss you so. I hope wherever you are, you are safe and well. Please write to let us know you are alright. All my love, Domi ...

"Sacrebleu!" Dominique couldn't squeeze the last letters of her name onto the card. She counted the words – eleven too many. She read the message again, decided which words she could leave out and still say what she wanted. She grabbed another card and began again.

Dearest Eugenie. Missing you. Hope you are safe and well. We are
...

How are we? Dominique paused to ponder; her pen pushed into her bottom lip. Happy? Louis and Victor maybe but only because they could still use their imagination to disappear into make-believe worlds. Safe? At least more so now the volatile Vierordt had gone and Von Manteuffel is in charge. Dominique no longer watched over her shoulder when she walked the cobbled streets to the laundry fearing she was about to be arrested. Hopeful? They had to remain so for the alternative looked very bleak.

... hoping to see you soon. Love Dominique.

She counted the words again. One short. What word could she add? She didn't want to waste the opportunity.

Eternellement.

Next, she wrote to Alice. She felt guilty for judging her. She'd seen time and time again that many of the German soldiers were merely men made to put on a uniform and follow orders like the French or the British. They weren't all cruel, filled with hatred and willing to do anything for power, as their commanding officers seemed to be.

Not having Gabriel close, gave Dominique an inkling of the sacrifice Alice had made in leaving Le Quesnoy and her German beau behind. Her half-sister may have been a stickler for the rules, but Dominique conceded she came from a place of caring.

Dearest Alice. Missing you. Write of your new life. Let us know you are safe and well. Love Dominique.

"Twenty words! How ridiculous! How can we get news from free France in so few words."

Dominique picked up another card.

"Nathalie, what can I say to you my dear friend?" She murmured to herself. "I miss you. I am envious of you; in Paris while I am stuck in Le Quesnoy. I worry about you. What if the war has reached Paris as well? I am sad for you, away from your beau Jean-Phillippe and with your brother still held captive. I am hopeful for you, being able to continue your studies while I work in the laundry for the Germans."

Dominique quickly scribbled the note before her thoughts darkened.

Nathalie, my best friend. Tell me all. Life isn't the same without you. Keep hope alive. Love Dominique.

What was seen as a generous concession to occupied France, left Dominique frustrated. Twenty words was barely enough for any message. She left her bedroom and stomped down the stairs.

"I'm going to send my cards," she called out.

Before I tear them up as pointless.

"Dominique," Lucie called from the sitting room. "Come here, please."

"I was just going out." Dominique stopped at the door and leaned on the doorframe, keeping a distance between herself and whatever activity her mother wanted her to partake in.

"Don't slouch. A lady should always maintain her good posture." Lucie sat taller in her seat as if to demonstrate. "I don't think you should go out today."

Dominique frowned. "Why not?"

"I'm not sure it is safe."

"What has happened to make it any different than yesterday?"

"There have been more arrests ..." Lucie faltered.

"Who have they arrested now, someone we know? What for?" Dominique's face reddened, her insides churned.

"Jean-Babtiste Tardy," Lucie murmured.

"The school principal." Dominique's eyes widened. "What could he have possibly done to warrant being arrested?"

"Two priests," Lucie continued. "And Madam Bazaille."

"Madam Bazaille!" Dominique's hand balled into fists. "She is just a shop keeper with little left to trade. Have they said what the charges are? Is there going to be a trial?"

"Non, your pere says they've already gone."

"Gone where?" Dominique's voice rose a pitch.

"Holzminden. Your pere says there was a whole train load of them, chosen from notable families all over the north."

"Just as well we're not a notable family," sarcasm laced Dominique's reply as she thumped her fists into her hips and stood her legs astride with determination. "I must go to work in the laundry, Maman. I will be alright. They won't do anything to me, or they'll have no-one to wash their dirty laundry."

Dominique's stance was deliberate. She inhaled long and slow to calm herself. It wouldn't be safe to leave the house in such a riled state. Beneath her skirt her knees trembled but she didn't want to worry her mother.

"Oh, Dominique." Lucie's eyes glassed over. "What has this war done to you, made you take on responsibilities no young woman should have to, showed you scenes your eyes should have been spared."

Young woman.

A warmth kindled in Dominique's heart. Her mere no longer thought of her as a child.

"It's alright, Maman. That's war. We all must make sacrifices."

"You have made many more than I have." Lucie stood and came to embrace Dominique. "I don't know what I would have done if it wasn't for your pere and you."

Dominique wouldn't give into the emotion churning her insides. Pride mixed with sadness. Dread jumbled with hope. She blinked away her tears. "Hopefully it will be over soon."

"We have been hoping for too long now."

"I've written a card to Eugenie." Breaking away from the hug, Dominique pulled the cards from her pocket. "I'd better take it to the Red Cross office. The sooner I drop it off, the sooner it will be delivered, and we can hear back from her."

"Oui! Oui!" Lucie raised her steepled fingers to her lips as if adding a prayer to Eugenie's message.

"You are so considerate. Always thinking of others."

"Au revoir, Maman." Dominique pecked her mother's cheeks and left while she could.

The streets of Le Quesnoy were quiet. The only people about were also heading to work. Most of the Quercitains had no energy nor enthusiasm for anything more than essential tasks. She saw Francois busy in his bakery and decided to stop in.

"Bonjour, Francois."

"Bonjour, Dominique." Francois looked weary, even his baker's hat flopped to one side like it too lacked verve. "Je suis désolé. If only I could give you a warm croissant. No treats. Nothing but this Kreigsbrot. This is not bread. This is just filling and even then, there isn't enough to fill the stomachs of those in need."

"It is not your fault, Francois." Dominique pinched the few breadcrumbs that littered the baker's workbench. "You are doing your best with what you have. Everyone appreciates your efforts."

"Oui, but ..."

Worried Francois was going to get either angry or maudlin, Dominique interrupted him. She needed to preserve what little positivity she had.

"I've got to go. I've got cards to deliver to the Red Cross." She waved her cards so he could see. "Au revoir."

"I hope you've said bonjour from me," Francois called out as she left the bakery.

I could barely say bonjour from me.

Dominique kept her sarcastic thoughts to herself. "Oui! Of course."

A distant rumble caught her attention as she hurried along Rue Thiers. Her mind raced when she couldn't fathom the source. Was this the sound of the army tanks Hubert had talked about? Was Le Quesnoy about to be invaded by tanks? Whose tanks were they? The enemy or the allies finally coming to rescue them?

She spun around and listened, north, east, south and west. Which direction was the noise coming from? It wasn't until she reached the road to the train station that she realised the sound came from the Gare du Quesnoy. Not a tank but a train. Dominique chuckled at herself for getting carried away, again. Her mirth was momentary. What if the Germans had arrested more Quercitains and the train was here to take them away?

Or perhaps it was a repeat of the last train that arrived. Dominique swallowed the lump threatening to choke her. That train was filled with innocent women, deported from Lille, forced to leave their homes and their families to work in the countryside.

Unable to continue to the laundry without knowing why a train was arriving today and who was on it, or going to be boarding it, Dominique turned at the corner and quickened her pace. By the time she neared the station, the train was pulling up to the platform, its engine billowed steam, its brakes screeched with the effort to pull up so many carriages.

She stood behind the fence, partially hidden by the garden. She gasped when the carriages came into view. There was no room to fit any more people onto the train. Distraught faces peered through the windows. Passengers sitting, standing, children carried by frantic parents; all jammed in.

The train station crawled with armed German soldiers. Dominique remained hidden, unsure of the fate of the passengers, not wanting to join them. As the steam cleared, the doors of two of the carriages opened, and the passengers spilled onto the platform like zombies emerging from the fog. Some clung to bundles of clothing, others hugged themselves. Tears streamed down the dirty faces of children. The elderly hung their heads low, slumped their shoulders and shuffled along as if reluctant to reach their destination.

Soldiers jostled them into lines and funnelled them through the station and out onto the road beside Dominique. She was taken back to the day when the Belgians arrived except these people hadn't made the journey of their own accord. She listened. Those who dared to talk, spoke in French. Where were they from and where were they going? There was only one way to find out. Dominique sidled alongside the group as if she was part of them.

"Bonjour," she greeted a young woman holding the hand of her little girl. "I'm a Quercitain. Where are you from?"

Brown eyes filled with fear eyed Dominique warily. The woman glanced at the soldiers escorting them, then looked down at her daughter as she clutched her hand tighter and pulled her closer.

"You can trust me." Dominique knew she was being assessed. "I'll help you if I can."

The noise of the train leaving prevented any further conversation. It hissed and whistled as it left the station taking the rest of the passengers farther along the tracks.

"Saint-Quentin," the woman murmured, her eyes continuing to flit nervously.

Saint-Quentin was a town to the south of Le Quesnoy Dominique had never visited but she knew it to be much larger than her hometown.

"Why did you have to leave?" she asked. "And so many of you."

The woman's eyes went wide, her already ashen face paled further.

"German retreat." Her whispered reply was barely audible.

"German retreat?" Dominique sucked in a breath.

Had she heard what she thought? Could it be true? Could what they'd been waiting, hoping, praying for, finally be happening? If she hadn't been trying to conceal herself, she would have jumped on the spot.

But a German retreat didn't explain why the train was transporting French civilians elsewhere.

"If they've left, why didn't you stay?"

"Destroyed." The woman blinked releasing a single tear to trickle down each cheek. "Burnt everything. Nowhere to live."

It was a repeat of the start of the war but in the opposite direction. As the Germans invaded, they destroyed the homes of the Belgians forcing them to leave and now the German retreat meant the destruction of French towns. Would Le Quesnoy be next?

Dominique's pulse quickened. She had to let people know. The town leaders if they hadn't already heard. Her parents in case they wanted to somehow protect their property. Alphonse, so he could prepare for another escape if these refugees needed to do so. Gabriel, to let him know the German retreat was finally starting, to give him hope he would soon be freed.

"Je suis désolé." Dominique patted the woman's arm. "I must go now but I will find you and help you in whatever way I can. You must hold onto hope."

"Oui." The woman nodded half-heartedly. "Hope."

Dominique broke away from the group and hurried to the laundry.

The large pile of dirty bed linen, which usually felt like an insurmountable mountain of work, was now a welcome distraction, a task in which she could lose herself. She gathered an armful and plunged them into the cold water, waiting for the bubbles of air to finish their escape. She stirred the sheets with a long wooden pole, losing herself in the rhythm, digesting all that she'd seen and heard.

By the time Dominique had decided to confide in Alphonse first, her arms ached, and she had to prise her fingers from the end of the pole. She changed her hold and her stance and used the pole to haul the sheets, one at a time, from the water. She used the edge of the elongated tub to wring as much water as she could manage from each sheet before hanging it over the line that ran the length of the laundry.

Normally, she would have rinsed them again like the German officer who'd assigned her and Nathalie to the laundry had demanded. Today, she shrugged her shoulders and moved onto the next one.

"You'll never know," she murmured as if she was talking directly to the enemy. "I'm not doing anything to make whatever time you have left here pleasant."

When the last of the sheets was dripping from the line, Dominique let the water go. She watched, almost mesmerised by the swirling water disappearing down the drain.

"If only it was so easy to wash away the enemy too."

Dominique found Alphonse upstairs in the ward. He was stripping a bed, creating more work for her but she didn't chastise him for doing his job.

"Alphonse, Alphonse," she hurried to his side eyeing up the German patients in the surrounding beds. "Come quick, into the courtyard. I've something I need to tell you."

Alphonse brought the dirty linen with him.

"What is it, Dominique? I haven't seen you this excited in ages."

"Saint-Quentin has been destroyed by the Germans."

"Saint-Quentin!" Alphonse's eyes went wide. "They're usually destroying something but that's a bit closer to home."

"The lady said they're retreating and not leaving anything behind to help the allies."

Alphonse put the sheets on the bench beside him and sat down to digest the news.

"Who is this lady? How does she know? Is she reliable? Can we trust her? It might be a trap, Dominique. You must be careful. What if she has been planted by the Germans to catch people? You could be arrested if you say too much to her."

Dominique gulped. She hadn't considered that possibility. She tried to replay her conversation with the woman in her head. Had she said anything that could incriminate her? Non! Alphonse was just being too suspicious, his opinions of others jaded by the war.

"There was a whole trainload of them. Two of the carriages were offloaded here. The rest continued onward. She was a young mother with two children and no I didn't say anything to get me into trouble. I just offered to help her if I could."

Alphonse nodded slowly as if the additional information offered some reassurance.

"Retreating? Does that mean they are coming this way next?"

"I don't know but I think we need to be prepared."

"Oui, I agree. Do you have supplies stowed in your cellar? If not, it would be best to do so. If they try to destroy Le Quesnoy, we should be safe hiding in the cellar."

"You and Clemence should come too." Dominique knew their cottage didn't have any underground hiding place.

"Oui, we can." Alphonse rubbed his chin. "If worst comes to worst, we can all escape through the tunnel under the ramparts."

"Hopefully it won't come to that."

"Hopefully." Alphonse sighed and picked up the bundle of sheets. "I'd better get back to work. There are too many eyes and ears in this place. It is impossible to know whom to trust."

Chapter 27

September 1917

Much to everyone's dismay, the Germans didn't retreat from Le Quesnoy. The refugees from Saint-Quentin were accommodated wherever possible forcing the town's meagre food supplies to be spread even more sparsely. With the supply of potatoes exhausted, rice became the staple of the Quercitains' diet. Very rarely they dined on beans cooked in lard. What would have been considered the food of the poor, became a special treat for the townsfolk. They began and finished their days with a cup of coffee or cocoa, grateful that if they were frugal with their wood supplies, it would at least be hot.

"We have to go to work again today," Louis groaned, tugging on the too short sleeve of his shirt. "I'm tired of working."

"Look at you," Lucie ruffled her son's hair. "Even with the little food we have to eat, you still manage to outgrow your clothes."

"Another delivery has arrived from the American Relief Committee." Dominique had seen the notice posted on the town hall wall. "Perhaps we can see if they have some clothes that would fit Louis and Victor."

"Oui," Lucie agreed. "You can take them."

Dominique nodded, but she knew the task was delegated to her so her mere wouldn't be seen accepting charity. It was beyond Dominique's comprehension why her mere still needed to keep up appearances when nearly everyone depended on contributions from abroad for survival.

"Come on you two. Grab your sandwiches. We'd better get going."

Louis and Victor did as Dominique asked but without enthusiasm or energy.

"I'll have to find you shoes as well if you keep dragging your feet." Dominique heard herself growl.

I sound just like Mere. The thought didn't sit well.

They reached the square where the children who should have been in class learning were gathered in front of their teacher. Seeing their friends, Louis and Victor found a sudden spurt of excited energy and ran over to them.

"Au revoir, have a good day," Dominique murmured to herself, knowing her brothers had already forgotten her.

"Save your energy, children." The teacher hushed the group. "We've got a big day ahead. We're off to the Foret de Mormal again."

The children were lined up and marched off as if they too were a little army. Louis walked like he was a German soldier, arms straight, legs extended and robotic with each stride. Others joined in, laughing as they mimicked the enemy.

"Children." The teacher's warning was half hearted. It looked as if he wanted to taunt the Germans too.

"Halt!" A soldier raised his hand to stop the group at the edge of the square. He removed his rifle from his shoulder and held it out as a barrier. With his threatening stance he towered over the children, glaring at the teacher.

Dominique gasped and clutched her hands to her chest. Surely, he wouldn't open fire on a group of children.

Louis's face paled but his eyes darted around the square as if he was looking for an escape route.

"Don't do anything stupid, Louis."

Dominique's warning was uttered too quiet to be heard by her brother, but he didn't get the opportunity to run. The soldier checked the teacher's permit to leave the town and sent them on their way.

Dominique's day at the laundry came to an end no later than usual but it felt like she'd spent twenty-four hours bent over the tub instead of eight. She opened the door, blinked into the daylight as she straightened her aching back, stretched her arms skyward and yawned. The sound of children's voices reminded her to retrieve the bag of shirts and shorts she hoped would fit Louis and Victor.

As she stepped out into the street, the voices got louder and more rhythmic, not conversation but song. She recognised France's national anthem and joined in as the bedraggled group of children came around the corner. Louis and Victor were at the front, walking proudly, singing at the top of their lungs.

Allons enfants de la patrie,Le jour de gloire est arrivé!Contre nous de la tyrannieLétendard sanglant est levé!

Létendard sanglant est levé!Entendez-vous dans les campagnes,Mugir ces féroces soldats?Ils viennent jusque dans nos brasÉgorger nos fils, nos compagnes!

The weight of the day lifted from Dominique's shoulders as she joined the makeshift choir for the second verse. They moved through the streets, their song drawing the townsfolk from their homes. Some stood on their doorsteps, hands on chest. Others opened their windows, some to listen, others to sing but all to show their patriotism. Those going quietly about their business paused in silence, a long-lost smile curving the edges of their mouths, a tear trickling from the corners of their eyes.

The group reached the square and the final verse in a valiant crescendo. Back where their day had begun, the German flag still hung from the flagpole, armed soldiers stood sentry and the shopkeepers with any wares still to trade closed their doors according to German time, but the children's singing had re-invigorated the pride and passion of the townsfolk and imparted a glimmer of hope.

Dominique collected Louis and Victor.

"Just as well I got you some more clothes. Look at you. Filthy from top to toe."

"I got caught on the brambles." Victor pulled on the shredded hem of his shirt.

"And I've got a hole in my bottom." Louis laughed, turned and bent over to reveal the tear in his shorts.

Dominique couldn't help but share in his mirth. Her giggle began like a butterfly fluttering in her belly, like it had to emerge from the safety of a chrysalis. She liked the sound, the warmth that flowed through her, the lightness that accompanied it.

"You'd better not show Mere that at the dinner table," Victor warned. "She'll have Pere kicking you from here to kingdom come."

"Kingdom come must be better than the brambles in Foret de Mormal." Louis's laughter was gone in a flash.

That the war could dampen her little brother's mood made Dominique want to wrap her arms around him. She needed his carefree spirit and laughter to buoy her own psyche. He would never stand for a hug, not on the streets where someone might see. She could tickle him, knowing his wriggling body wouldn't be able to contain laughter but the fix was temporary. Only the end of the war could make it permanent.

Everyone is a soldier to fight you.

The words of the anthem made Dominique pull her shoulders back, straighten her spine and walk tall and proud trusting that one day the war would end.

"Let's get home, get you cleaned up and changed." She pushed any lingering doubts aside. "And you can forget all about kingdom come and Foret de Mormal."

Click ... clack ... Although the grandfather clock still stood tall and straight in the corner of the sitting room, its announcement of the hour was at best feeble. *Click ... clack ...* Bereft of its requisitioned copper pendulum it was as if the Germans had stolen time itself. *Click ... clack.*

"Très bien." Lucie smiled at her husband seated at the opposite end of the table. "It is lovely to have you all home for dinner on time."

Dominique hid her sigh behind her hand, unable to comprehend why after three years of occupation her mere still clung to routines and rituals. Did it make her world feel unchanged? If only that was all it took.

"But there's nothing to eat." Victor's groan was accompanied by a loud rumble. He clutched his stomach as if it needed comforting. "I'm hungry. We had to work so hard today."

"We got to eat blackberries though." Louis licked his lips.

"And you had your sandwich," Henri added.

The boys exchanged sheepish glances. The look of brothers keeping secrets as only twins could do.

"What happened to your sandwich, Victor?" Henri asked.

"Well ... um ..." Victor fidgeted in his seat, avoiding his father's gaze.

"He gave it away," Louis blurted before he could be silenced by Victor.

"He did what?" Lucie demanded.

"Let Victor speak for himself." Henri hushed everyone. "Son, who did you give your sandwich to and why?"

"There ... was ... a soldier." Victor's bottom lip quivered.

"A German soldier?" Henri asked without accusation.

"Non." Victor's cheeks reddened. "Never. I'd spit on it first if I had to give it to a German."

"He was a prisoner. A soldier from the war," Louis came to his brother's defence. "He was being made to work like us, but he wasn't being fed."

"I see." Henri tapped the tips of his steepled fingers together.

"He was skinny, Pere. I could see his bones through his skin." Victor stared into the distance as if he was back in the forest with the soldier. "He couldn't speak French, but I knew he was hungrier than me, so I gave him my sandwich. It was only Kreigsbrot but it was better than nothing."

"That was very kind of you, son." Henri patted Victor on the shoulder.

"Here you are." Marie placed a small bowl of rice in front of Louis.

"Not rice again!" Louis pushed at the bowl.

"Eat up." Henri's command was short and abrupt, but his tone carried a caring tenderness. "Think of the hungry soldier. We must be grateful for what we have. As you have learned today, it is more than some."

"And you'll get to wash it down with a cup of cocoa." Dominique attempted to placate her brother.

"You'd better eat up too, Dominique." Henri turned his attention to his daughter. "I'll need your help this evening."

"What?" Lucie frowned. "What do you need Dominique for? I thought we'd have a nice family evening while we have no Germans staying. It's the first time in what seems like forever."

"Je suis désolé, ma cherie." The dark shadows beneath Henri's eyes, now a permanent feature, aged him beyond his years, a symbol of the fatigue that never seemed to leave. "There are two women who are in the early stages of birthing, and I cannot attend both at once. I need Dominique to help."

"Dominique?" Lucie looked wide-eyed at Henri, her voice rising. "Are there not nurses at the hospital?"

"The nurses have duties attending the Boche." Henri remained calm. "There would be repercussions if they left."

"Can the women not be taken to the hospital?"

"Non." Henri shook his head to reaffirm. "They wish to keep matters private."

"Who are these women? Do I know them?"

"I cannot say, my dear. It is patient confidentiality. You understand, of course."

Dominique listened intently. She craved the answers too. This was a conversation that previously would have been held behind closed doors. In her mind's eye, she pictured the women she passed in the streets each day. Had any looked pregnant? A swollen belly could be concealed beneath the thick folds of a skirt. Just as easily, those with child could stay indoors, never to reveal their condition to the prying and judgemental eyes of neighbours.

"How can married women even get pregnant, with their husbands away at war?" In the dim light of the room, the blush that flooded Lucie's cheeks was like a beacon. She looked at her sons, closed her mouth and pulled her lips into a thin line as if sealing them forever, unable to speak the answer to her own question.

Dominique did the opposite. She sat, mouth agape, digesting what hadn't been said. Although she and Gabriel never shared more than pecked cheeks, the friendly banter of teenagers, and looks of wanting, she knew how babies came about. A man and woman didn't have to be married but they did have to come together in a way Dominique was yet to experience.

"People do what they feel they must to survive." Henri ate the last of his rice. "It is sad, but it is true, and we may not always agree with the choices they make."

Lucie nodded slowly, not daring to speak.

Dominique hurried to finish her rice and gulp down her cup of cocoa.

"I'm ready, Pere." She stood and smoothed down her skirt.

"I suppose I should be grateful; it isn't you, Dominique."

"Non, I mean, *oui*, Maman."

Henri and Dominique walked in silence across town. Dominique had a million questions she wanted to ask but stayed quiet, wary that her father might change his mind and send her home if she was too nosey.

Henri turned down a narrow cul-de-sac. Dominique knew of the area only through warnings of somewhere not to venture alone. Henri tapped discreetly on the front door of the middle apartment in a row of double storey brick houses. The door was edged open by a child with telling eyes. Her white knuckles gripped the door, ready to slam it shut on unwelcome visitors.

"Je suis Docteur Favier. I am here to see your mere."

The girl looked from Henri to Dominique, her dark eyes assessed them, judged whether they could be trusted. Before she could decide, a painful scream echoed down the stairwell like a summons. Henri pushed past the girl and climbed the stairs two at a time.

"It'll be alright. My pere is here now."

The girl shrugged her shoulders as if Dominique's offer of support was of no consequence.

Dominique glanced up and down the street to check whether the desired privacy had been fractured by the woman's pain. Directly across the street, the movement of curtains caught her eye. Just as quickly as they were pulled open the curtains closed; someone had heard.

"Je m'appelle Dominique." She closed the door against any further intrusion. "What's your name?"

"Je m'appelle Eloise."

"Dominique," Henri called from the landing at the top of the stairs. "Fetch me some towels, something clean to swaddle the baby and some hot water."

Eloise led the way, through a small sitting room with a threadbare mat and a settee with a protruding spring and patched armrests. The flickering light of a candle cast shadows on a photograph of a man in uniform proudly displayed on a dresser.

"Is your pere away fighting?"

Eloise was a miniature version of the man, wavy dark hair, intense chocolate-brown eyes and already with a frown that furrowed her forehead.

"Oui." Eloise continued to the kitchen where a hoard of children sat at the table. She reached into a cupboard beside the fire and retrieved two towels.

One, two, three, four, five. Dominique looked from one child to the next, all girls, all smaller versions of Eloise. The youngest sat in a highchair at the far end of the table and couldn't have been more than two or three years old. Had she even met the man in the photo? She was too focused on spooning her food from bowl to mouth to acknowledge Dominique.

The others turned to inspect the visitor. Eight deep brown eyes, like a row of buttons on a jacket, looked Dominique up and down before turning their attention back to their supper. Whatever was in their bowls was more important than her. She looked over the shoulder of the closest girl and inhaled the aroma of their meal, recognisable but not something she'd recently smelt.

Meat and potatoes. Dominique sucked in a breath. How did a pregnant mother, with an absent husband, manage to feed a family of this size meat and potatoes? It wasn't right. It wasn't fair. Dominique shook her head unable to decide which part of the situation wasn't equitable. The children dining on meat and potatoes when she couldn't, was a childish envy she soon dismissed. Six young girls having to look after themselves while their mother gave birth and their father was away fighting; there were many families in Le Quesnoy who were in the same unfortunate predicament. Dominique struggled with the judgement that came with the assumption she made. The woman upstairs had sacrificed herself to feed her children and was now paying the price.

Dominique opened her mouth to criticise but stopped short. Any pride she'd felt being asked to attend the birth was dashed. Eloise was half her age but obviously had a life experience beyond her years, beyond Dominique's age as well. She couldn't criticise the desperate choices the children's mother had made.

"Here's some hot water for Maman." Eloise shuffled past the table, grabbed the kettle and passed it to Dominique. "You take this up and I'll bring the towels."

The kettle was heavy, but Dominique couldn't complain, her burden was light compared to Eloise's. The steep stairs, hollowed in the middle by centuries of feet, creaked beneath her. At the top of the landing there were two bedrooms. Another painful groan drew her to the one at the rear of the house.

She paused in the doorway to the darkened room, took a deep breath and clenched her jaw to hold it and any words of judgement in. In the flickering candlelight she made out the silhouette of her father at the foot of the bed bent over the woman.

"Quick, give me some more light." Henri must have heard them approach.

Eloise pushed past Dominique, took a candle stick from the bedside table and moved to stand beside Henri as if it was an everyday occurrence.

If she can do this, I can too. Dominique stepped to the other side of the bed.

"Here is the water, Pere."

He nodded acknowledgement but didn't speak as the woman groaned and worked with the contraction sending spasms through her body to push her newborn into Henri's waiting hands.

"It's a boy, Maman, it's a boy." Eloise jumped up and down with delight.

Dominique stood, mouth open, in awe of the perfectly formed little person. The moment was surreal. She blinked rapidly unable to comprehend what she'd witnessed. The baby's eyelids lifted, his crystal blue eyes appeared to look knowingly, taking in his new surroundings, he opened his tiny mouth and tested his voice box, announcing his arrival to the world.

"Un garcon?" The woman sought confirmation.

"Oui." Henri lay the baby on one of the towels Eloise had already spread ready and cut the umbilical cord. "A healthy boy."

He dipped a clean flannel in the water and wiped the baby's face before swaddling the newborn in the towel.

"Dominique, would you please pass the baby to his mother." Henri passed the bundle to his daughter.

Victor and Louis were the last babies she'd held and then it always seemed like a chore when her mother couldn't cope with two hungry mouths. She pressed a hand to her chest before gingerly extending her arms to take the baby.

He felt tiny, cocooned in the crook of her elbow. She inhaled his distinctive aroma as he wiggled his perfectly formed pink fingers.

Any remaining judgement was vanquished. She wanted to hold him forever. She thought of Gabriel. What if it were their baby she cradled? If only she were granted the opportunity to love and nurture a little human, to help them see all the best in the world.

Her heart skipped a beat when the baby blinked, looked up at her and cooed.

"I think he's hungry." Dominique edged her way to the head of the bed, wanting to prolong the moment. She bent and carefully handed the baby into his mother's arms.

Despite her fatigue, the woman's face lit up, her mouth curved into a smile, tears of joy fell down each cheek as she embraced her son.

"Welcome to the world, my darling boy."

It made no difference to her that the baby was blonde and blue-eyed.

"What are we going to name him, Maman?" Eloise stood beside her mother admiring her little brother.

"Lucien." The woman kissed her son's head. "He is our light, our beacon of hope."

The following morning Dominique found her father in his office, a pile of paperwork needing his attention.

"Is there anything I can help you with, Pere?"

"Non, not with this paperwork. I must register the recent births I've attended."

"Lucien's?"

"Oui." Henri rubbed his weary eyes and sighed. "There have been a few. It is always an honour to bring a new life into the world, but I worry about their futures."

"Because their fathers are German?"

"Not much gets past you, does it."

"Sorry, Pere. I know it's none of my business."

"No need to apologize." Henri put down his pen and clasped his hands. "This war has made you wise well beyond your years. Like the children with French mothers and German fathers, I'm unsure whether that is good or bad, but it is what it is."

"Do you think the war will ever end?" Dominique sat on the chair usually reserved for patients.

"Oui, we must continue to believe it will."

The thud of letters dropped through the mailbox stopped their conversation.

"Mail!" They exclaimed in unison.

Dominique ran like an excited child to retrieve the postman's delivery. She clutched the precious cards and envelopes to her chest and hurried back to Henri's office. Receiving anything by post was a rare occurrence, every word savoured even if it had taken months to arrive. Her fingers trembled as she rifled through the mail, flinging the official and boring looking envelopes to her father.

"Eugenie!" Dominique kissed the card from her sister and stowed it in a separate pile on the desk, while she scanned the rest. "Gabriel! Nathalie!"

Henri's letter opener had been taken by the Germans in one of their first raids. They paid no heed to his sentimental attachment to the ornately engraved gift from his mere. Now he had no choice but to slip his thumb under the official looking envelope's flap.

He sucked in a breath, his eyes widening as he digested the letter's contents.

"What is it, Pere, what is it?"

"Alice." Henri blinked away tears. "My dear Alice."

Dominique gulped. She'd written four cards and finally received replies from three recipients, all but Alice. Sensing the worst, she went and stood beside her father, placing a comforting hand on his shoulder.

"What's happened, Pere?"

"She's dead. My eldest daughter is dead." Henri gripped the letter, crushing the news in his hands.

How could the Germans have killed her when she loved one of their own? Where was she? She should never have died alone. Why would anyone want to kill dear Alice? All she ever wanted to do was to nurse people back to good health. Why was there no-one to do that for her? Why was she not still here with us?

Why was I not nicer to her when I had the chance?

"How? Where? Why?" Dominique's chin quivered as she sought to dispel her guilt.

"Her heart gave out," Henri answered matter-of-factly.

It was broken by this damn war.

Dominique's nails bit into her palms. It was all she could do to temper her rage.

"Paris. She died in Paris." Henri unfolded the letter and read on. "December 1915. Nearly two years ago. My daughter has been dead nearly two years, and I'm only just informed."

"Je suis désolé, Pere." Dominique wrapped her arms around Henri's shoulders.

"It is not your fault, my dear." Henri patted her hand. "She has gone to be with her mere." He shook his head as if to dispel his melancholy. "Now, find me some good news amongst your cards."

Nathalie's card was the last Dominique had found but the first she read.

"My dear friend. Hold onto hope. The line is shorter now. Stay strong. We will meet again soon. Love Nathalie." Dominique frowned and re-read the message. "The line is shorter now. What line?"

"A waiting line?" Henri offered an answer as he opened another envelope.

"Nathalie is in Paris. I don't imagine she has to wait for anything, apart from my letters."

"I don't know then."

Dominique stowed the card in her pocket. She'd take it to show Alphonse. He was skilled at deciphering codes, perhaps there was a hidden message.

She picked Eugenie's letter up next.

Dearest Sister. Overjoyed to receive your note. Still nursing, doing what I can. Getting closer to home. Talk soon, Eugenie x

Dominique gasped. "Eugenie says we'll talk soon, Pere. Is that her way of saying the war is nearly over?"

"Perhaps, but don't get your hopes up too high."

"Oh, Pere, how can we not?" Dominique bounced from foot to foot. "After three years of not hearing her voice, wouldn't that be wonderful?"

"Oui, it would." Henri's voice carried none of Dominique's excitement.

"Does that letter bring more bad news?"

"Oui," Henri sighed. "But this I can deal with. Another bill, another levy to fund the German war effort. My concern, not yours. Who is your next letter from?"

Eugenie's card was stowed beside Nathalie's, like precious cargo in Dominique's pocket and she skipped to the last word on the next card. "Gabriel!"

"Oui." Henri slowly nodded, his mouth curving into a rare smile. "I can see Gabriel is more than just your best friend's brother."

Dominique blushed. Were her feelings for Gabriel so obvious?

"Perhaps you'd better keep that note for yourself," Henri suggested. "My little girl in love. That is a sight that brings hope to my day."

Chapter 28

October 1918

Lucien toddled on his chubby legs to the front door to farewell Dominique. He was a cheerful, happy little boy and his giggle had the power to brighten any day. She often visited just to be able to tickle him and hear his laughter, especially when she needed reminding there was still hope.

"Au revoir." Dominique waved to the family gathered in their doorway to say goodbye.

"Merci beaucoup, Dominique, thank you for babysitting my children again. It is so good to be able to work at least a couple of hours when I can, to help make ends meet."

The family no longer dined on meat and potatoes, now relying heavily on distributions from the relief board. Their supply of extras disappeared soon after Lucien's birth when his father was ordered from Le Quesnoy back to the front. Dominique's offer to babysit had an ulterior motive. She got to spend time with the children, but she also hoped it helped ensure their mother didn't offer herself to another soldier.

"Au revoir," the children chimed in unison.

It wasn't until Dominique left the cul-de-sac and the noise of children's play stopped ringing in her ears that she heard a humming sound. She scanned her surroundings, trying to locate its source. It began quietly, like the town's factories had been fired back up and the machines had whirred into action.

"Not likely," Dominique scoffed. "There's no machinery left."

The noise got louder. An overhead drone drew Dominique's eyes skyward. Instinct told her to hide, and she hugged the side of the building, sheltering in the doorway of a long-abandoned shop.

The last time aeroplanes had graced their skies; the war had only just begun. Back then, the Germans were on a reconnaissance mission and recognised the fortified walls of Le Quesnoy as a haven to occupy.

"What do you want this time?"

When it sounded like the aeroplane was directly overhead, Dominique leaned out, expecting to see the familiar markings of the German army on the underside of the aircraft. The iron cross, the symbol of military prowess and power, proudly displayed by the enemy on vehicles, flags, and soldiers' chests as a reward for their bravery was missing from this plane's wings.

Instead of the uniform grey, the aeroplane was painted in a camouflage of greens and browns. A circle painted on its side, rings of black and white with a red centre was like a bullseye saying shoot me here.

"Watch out," Dominique warned, expecting a German plane to be tailing. "They won't hesitate to fire at you."

It dawned on her she could be in danger, yet again out in the streets when a war was about to be fought on their doorstep. Should she run or hide?

A second plane came into view. Dominique breathed a sigh of relief when it too was painted in camouflage colours.

Her pulse quickened. Her mouth went dry. Could it finally be happening? Were these planes those of the Allied forces coming to rescue them? Dominique abandoned all caution and ran into the street.

"We're down here," she yelled, waving her arms overhead.

The aeroplane appeared to turn. Had the pilot heard her? Was he coming back to get her? Where would he land? The town square was big but not large enough to land a plane and doing so would be suicidal, the Boche would be there in a second, armed and ready to kill.

When it was back over the centre of the town, the plane released its load.

"What are you doing?" Dominique froze. "What are you showering us with? You're meant to be saving us, not killing us."

She hurried back to the shelter of the doorway, squeezed her eyes shut, put her fingers in her ears and waited, expecting the blast of artillery, silently hoping to be spared. Seconds passed, or minutes, Dominique was unable to discern how long she stood waiting, her heart thundering in her chest.

Needing to know, one way or the other, she removed her fingers. As the drone of the aeroplane faded it was replaced with the cries of people. French voices echoing about the streets. Dominique opened her eyes to witness pieces of paper fluttering to the ground, like giant snowflakes.

"Have you brought our mail?"

Dominique rushed from her hiding place and grabbed at the papers. The first twisted and turned and escaped her grasp. She snatched at another, scrunching it tightly to her chest. She bent and picked up another that landed on the cobbles. What were they? She didn't bother to look, just wanting to gather as many as possible, in case she missed out.

Townsfolk had come from their houses and were doing the same. They looked like scavengers, a flock of seagulls pecking at scraps, a mischief of rats scurrying after dropped morsels.

At the end of the street, a German soldier lowered the rifle he'd aimed at the aeroplanes and pointed it at the people.

"Stoppen!" His order made everyone freeze like children in a game of statues.

He summoned another soldier, made him retrieve one of the notes while his eyes and rifle remained focussed on the Quercitains. They heeded the warning and retreated into their homes, taking their bounty with them.

Dominique stepped back into the shop doorway, wishing it was the front door to her home. Another note lay on the cobbles at the edge of the alcove. It was too tempting, within reach if she was careful. She knelt slowly, no sudden movement to catch the eye of the soldier and reached out, pinching the piece of paper between the tips of her fingers, pulling it back into the safety of the doorway.

She flopped back, leaning on the door to catch her breath. The concrete was cold beneath her. It sucked the adrenaline from her, replaced it with a sudden coldness that hit at her core. Once again, she had put herself in danger without a second thought for the consequences. Her stomach squirmed as they slowly dawned.

Unable to leave until the soldiers had gone, she lay the notes on the ground and tried to flatten them with trembling fingers. Endangering herself couldn't have all been for nothing. Side by side, the notes were identical; a short message written in German.

"Sacrebleu!" Dominique looked skyward as if the aeroplanes were still overhead and would hear her. "You're meant to be saving us, not writing notes to the enemy."

The German soldiers talking drew her attention to the end of the otherwise empty street. She peeked out from the doorway. The soldiers had obviously read the note and were in an animated discussion. They looked happy. Their normally serious expressions replaced with smiles.

"What does it say?" Dominique studied one of the notes. Living amongst Germans for the past four years, she'd resisted learning their language, another way she could silently protest. Now she regretted her stubbornness.

Sie sind vollstandig umsingelt.

Die feindlichen truppen befinden sich weit ostlich von ihnen.

Wenn sies ich ergeben, werden sie als ehrenhafte kriegsgefangene behandelt.

"Sie means you. I know that. It's been yelled at me enough times. You, you, you." Dominique frowned. "You what?"

She peeked back down the street, hoping the German soldiers would provide more clues as to the note's contents. They'd gone. The streets were empty. An ominous silence engulfed the town.

Doors and shutters closed, not just against the weather but as a protective barrier countering the foreboding impact of the letter drop.

Dominique swallowed the lump of dread wedged in her throat. She had to act but what could she do. She folded the notes and left the safety of the doorway, walking blindly while she pondered her options.

Her feet knew more than her thoughts. She found herself at the hospital just as Alphonse was leaving.

"Salut, Dominique. Did you see the aeroplanes, the notes they dropped?"

"Oui." Dominique pulled the pieces of paper from her pocket. "They all say the same thing, but I don't know what it is."

"Neither did I." Alphonse grinned. "But I found out."

"How? Don't tell me you've learnt German?"

"Non! Sacrebleu! Never." Alphonse looked momentarily offended. "There's a patient, a German soldier who knows a little French. I asked him."

Dominique huffed. Alphonse was wasting time, she needed to know.

"What did he say?"

"It was a demand ... non, not a demand, more an invitation for them to surrender."

"Huh! They're not likely to ever do that ..." Dominique looked askance at Alphonse who was still smiling. "Are they?"

"The patient would like to. As would the others injured and confined to bed. They want to go home. They've had enough."

"So have we." Dominique leaned back against the wall, seeking its support, something solid in all the uncertainty.

"Oui, we have endured for long enough."

"It's still hard to imagine the Boche would give up though. What's different now?" The puzzle pieces weren't fitting together, something was missing.

"The note said we are completely surrounded ..."

"By what?" Dominique interrupted, her eyebrows arching.

"Enemy troops."

"We've been living with enemy troops. Are we now surrounded by more Germans? Are they asking the Quercitains to surrender? Haven't we already done that? Allowing them to take over our town."

Alphonse placed a calming hand on Dominique's arm. "Non, mon amie, you forget, the notes were dropped by British planes and intended for the Germans. Le Quesnoy is surrounded by Allied troops."

The tiniest speck of excitement began bubbling deep inside Dominique. She stared wide-eyed at Alphonse as she digested his words, repeating them silently until she was certain they were real.

"Tell me again," she requested. "I still can't believe what you said."

"It is true, Dominique. The Allied troops are going to save us. Our hell will soon be over."

Letters of hope had fallen from the sky. Dominique had been waiting, living a subsistence existence, hoping for this moment and it had finally arrived. A tear trickled from the corner of her eye. She let it fall, welcomed the relief it brought, allowed it to wash away the doubt and despair that life would ever be normal. She seized onto the glimmer of hope that brought a warmth to her heart, vowing to hold onto it, nurture it until they were finally able to live their lives in free France.

Author's Note

Te Arawhata - New Zealand Liberation Museum opened in Le Quesnoy in October 2023 and I was fortunate to visit in September 2024. The valuable resources in the museum; displays, photos and stories capturing the history of the town in World War I formed the basis for my Liberating Le Quesnoy series.

Walking the cobbled streets of the town, exploring the tunnels beneath the ramparts, and seeing the very spot where the New Zealand soldiers used their 'Kiwi ingenuity' to scale the fortified wall with a wooden ladder and liberate the town without injury to the Quercitains, helped bring authenticity to the fictional version of events I have created.

Many of the characters are real – Achille Carlier was mayor of Le Quesnoy during the occupation, Sister Jeanne was a nurse at the hospital, and together with Alphonse Courable and Alice Favier, aided the escape of English and French soldiers who were patients at the hospital when the Germans invaded. Commander Lubbert, Major Vierordt, and Von Manteuffel were appointed Kommandanturs of Le Quesnoy during the occupation. Obviously, I cannot have known these historical people so apart from their names, occupations and the actions they have been recorded as being involved in or responsible for, all else is fictional.

Dominique is also fictional but the home in which she grew up is just as I have described with spiral staircases, a walled garden and a cellar. The beautiful mansion on Rue Brancion was mostly constructed in the 1800s and the perfect location to be home to Henri Favier, a former military surgeon who retired to Le Quesnoy in1910. My research didn't extend so far as to determine whether he actually lived there, or not.

Further insight into life during the German occupation was gleaned from *Vivre Dans le Nord 1914-1918* by Jean-Paul Briastre and *The Long Silence – The Tragedy of Occupied France in World War I* by Helen McPhail, listening to James Connolly's podcasts and watching Jude Dobson's documentaries on Le Quesnoy.

The President of the Association Le Quesnoy-Nouvelle-Zelande, Jean-Phillippe Froment lead an educational tour of the ramparts and war cemeteries of Le Quesnoy and surrounding towns, even to the very farm where the New Zealand soldiers based themselves prior to the liberation. Rows and rows of crosses marking the graves of soldiers who gave their lives in the great war were a stark reminder of their sacrifice. I endeavour to honour the loss of so many by bringing this story to you.

Once the story has been written there are so many more people involved in bringing a book to life. My thanks go out to my ever-encouraging writing tribe: Joan, Frances, Shona, Stella,

Ami and Kim whose feedback is always appreciated and taken on board. Thank you to Michelle Holman for her editing, Kura Carpenter for her creative skills in cover design and the readers who volunteered to read the early copies and provide feedback. Without a team around an author, the journey from thoughts and ideas to print would not be possible and I am forever grateful for your help.

If you have enjoyed reading *Letters of Hope*, I'd appreciate you taking the time to leave a review on whichever online platform you wish or simply emailing me at tania-roberts@xtra.co.nz or contacting me through my website www.taniarobertsauthor.com

Letters of Hope is part one of a trilogy. If you would like to be first to read chapters in the second book *Fields of Faith* and get updates on all things writerly, then please sign up for my free monthly newsletter through my website www.taniarobertsauthor.com. An excerpt from *Fields of Faith* is included for your reading pleasure.

Lest we Forget

About the Author

Tania Roberts blends her passion for history and storytelling to create evocative narratives that transport readers to the eras where the wars embroiled the world. Her novels highlight the strength and resilience of women in challenging times, drawing inspiration from her surroundings in Taranaki, New Zealand. With a background in creative writing and a career as a Chartered Accountant, Tania masterfully balances analytical skills with creative pursuits, earning accolades such as a second-place finish in the Koru Excellence Romance Writers Awards.

You can keep up to date with Tania's news and books by subscribing to her newsletter at www.taniarobertsauthor.com or following her on Facebook, Instagram and/or Pinterest as taniarobertsauthor.

Also by Tania Roberts:

Books in the Kiwi Land Girl Series

Wings of Grace https://books2read.com/u/mddVgX

Ally for Life https://books2read.com/u/bpq6Mz

Battle of Hearts – https://books2read.com/u/mqBqpe

Dance of Soldiers https://books2read.com/u/4jppej

Fields of Faith

September 1914

"Look out! The Germans are attacking again!"

Eugenie and Camille were enjoying a summer stroll in les Jardin du Champs-Elysees when the gentleman yelled his warning.

"Take cover!"

Stunned and needing to know for herself, Eugenie stood looking skyward instead of running for shelter. She heard the drone of the aeroplane's engine before she saw the distinctive iron cross of the enemy on the aeroplane's underbelly.

It was a week to the day since the Germans dropped their first bombs over central Paris. The newspapers reported little, but the stories filtered through. An elderly woman living on Rue des Vinaigriers was killed and three others were injured."

Is this the last cross, I will see?

Eugenie pressed her nails into her palms. Was it anger or fear that made her body tense and her pulse race?

This is a cross to curse, not worship!

"Come, Eugenie!"Mademoiselle Tremblay tugged at Eugenie's sleeve. "Under the oak trees! Now!"

The ever-vigilant chaperone's command was more insistent than usual, like she'd regressed into her governess persona and Eugenie and Camille were naughty children.

Eugenie hurried off the gravel path and joined Camille and Mademoiselle Tremblay under the closest oak tree. Not because she wished to obey the chaperone but because she instinctively knew now wasn't her time to die. She had too much living still to do.

The sun sparkled through the leathery lobes of the oak leaves dancing in the summer breeze. It was too pretty a scene for such an ominous threat. Eugenie caught glimpses of the aeroplane as it swooped down over the city. When it was directly overhead, she squeezed her eyes shut, and held her breath, anticipating the boom that would signal the bombs had found their target.

Seconds passed. The drone of the aeroplane's engine faded.

"They're leaving." Eugenie opened one eye, then the other. "They didn't drop a bomb."

"It was a reconnaissance flight," the chaperone observed. "They know we are here now. They will be back, or another aeroplane will arrive."

"They didn't drop a bomb." Eugenie repeated as she stepped out from under the tree. "Look! They're sending us a message instead."

Thousands of pieces of dirty white parchment rained down over central Paris. Those who had been genteelly walking in the park now snatched at the notes fluttering to the ground, Eugenie and Camille included.

Mademoiselle Tremblay stood motionless and frowned at the young women. Eugenie grabbed at the note that dared to land at her feet. She rescued another from the lower limbs of an oak tree. A note floating in the middle of the fountain looked tempting in the summer heat, but Eugenie let it be. She avoided both the scent and the thorns of the rose bush as she retrieved the note caught in its blooms. Eugenie gathered as many of the notes as she could, not bothering to read them until she had a handful.

What did the Germans want to say to the French? Had they decided against a battle? Were they surrendering already? Was it an offer of peace?

Eugenie hadn't studied German at school so most of the script was indecipherable, but two words leapt from the page.

Saint Quentin.

Each word resounded like the ricochet of a bullet. The city in the north of France was a mere thirty-five miles from Le Quesnoy, her hometown, the town where her mere and pere still lived. She pictured them, her sister Dominique and her twin brothers, Louis and Victor. She missed all of them but Louis and his rascally ways the most. She itched to ruffle his hair and feel him squirm from her embrace, the one he kept coming back for.

Memories brought a smile to her face, but it was momentary. Eugenie recalled the Belgian refugees arriving by the trainload at Gare du Nord last week, their dishevelled state and panicked looks indicated they were fleeing for their lives, not coming on a summer holiday. What were the Germans even doing in Belgian?

Now something had happened in Saint Quentin, was Le Quesnoy soon to be embroiled in the war too?

Eugenie sucked in a breath. Desperate to know, she had no choice but to seek the aid of Mademoiselle Tremblay, whom she knew spoke German. The chaperone read the note and relayed its contents, her face remained stoic as if news that the Germans had defeated Saint Quentin was of no significance.

The airdrop felt like a bomb even though it was only notes of paper. There was no surrender. This was a declaration of strength, a seized opportunity to boast of early triumph, a warning of all to come.

The message was of the greatest consequence to Eugenie. It strengthened her resolve to do all she could to help with the war effort. In that moment, she made her decision, the one she'd been contemplating since war was declared.

"We should head home, "the chaperone suggested. "Before they return with a real bomb."

"Oui." Eugenie agreed but for an entirely different reason; she needed to get home and write at once to her parents to let them know of her decision.

Back in Le Quesnoy, she'd assisted her pere, Henri, in his doctoring. He was supposed to be retired, but patients still arrived at their door at all hours or sent messengers to beckon him to make a house call and he helped whenever and wherever he could. When her mere, Lucie, didn't protest too loudly, Eugenie was at her pere's side, handing him instruments, applying bandages, delivering medicines, absorbing all the knowledge she could.

She had no inkling to be married off to some wealthy Frenchman like her mere was planning. The desire to train as a doctor, to follow in her pere's footsteps was a driving force in Eugenie's life. She'd only agreed to come to Paris because it provided the opportunity to visit the university and investigate the path for her future. Andre being based in the city while he did his training was an added advantage.

With the war now on their doorstep, a university education in medicine was no longer an option. Years of study, examinations and practical training would take far too long, keep her glued to books instead of helping those in need and that was assuming the university would even allow a woman in their midst. She knew what she had to do. She'd apply to become a nurse instead.

With the letter to her parents written, and her resolve declared, there was no turning back. Eugenie was excited to tell Andre, knowing he would share her enthusiasm.

"There is a letter for you, Eugenie."

Eugenie recognised Andre's handwriting immediately. It was as if their hearts were in sync. Whenever she thought of him, it seemed he too was thinking of her.

"Merci beaucoup." Eugenie took the envelope from Camille and hurriedly read Andre's note. "Camille! Camille! You must help me!"

Eugenie scrunched the note in her hands. She had been anticipating this moment; knowing it was inevitable. All over Paris, the city's inhabitants knew war was about to change their lives forever.

"What is it, Eugenie?" Camille's concern was motherly despite her being only one year older than her cousin. "What's wrong? You've gone as white as a ghost."

Eugenie couldn't explain the tightness in her chest, like her heart was contracting, encasing itself in a weighty but protective barrier of lead. She gingerly unfolded the note to re-read Andre's words, silently hoping, praying that she'd read them wrong the first time.

My dearest Eugenie,

The adventure finally begins! We leave tomorrow from Les Invalides. We will defeat the enemy and be back before you know.

Until then, Andre.

She wanted to share his excitement and think of the battle between countries as an adventure.

"I need to get to Les Invalides!" Eugenie's plea sounded as desperate as she felt.

"Les Invalides?" Camille arched her perfectly shaped eyebrows. "Do you know a war veteran living there? Is he ill? Is he dying?"

"Non!" Eugenie uttered the rebuttal before she thought it through. Perhaps lying about her reason forgoing would be the only way to leave the house and see Andre, alone. "I mean, oui, there is a man there I must see but he is not about to die."

"Maman will be weary about letting us go anywhere." Camille wandered to the window.

"But Les Invalides is on the other side of the Seine from where the bombs landed," Eugenie countered. "And the letters they dropped today aren't going to cause any physical injuries."

"I suppose we could ask Mademoiselle Tremblay if she would accompany us." Camille paused, her finger on her chin as if she needed to ponder matters. "Maman has an appointment at la couturière in the morning. We could go and be back before she returns from her dress fitting. I'd rather not lie to her."

"Non, we wouldn't lie to your mere."

Eugenie wanted to lie to Mademoiselle Tremblay though, find an appointment for her to unavoidably attend. How was she going to get time alone with Andre if the chaperone was there with her beady eyes that missed nothing?

After a fitful night, Eugenie woke early, a million questions, all without answers, flying about inside her head like fireworks. If only they were in celebration of a joyous occasion, news that the Germans had changed their minds, a peaceful settlement had been negotiated and everyone could go home and carry on with their lives. Instead, Eugenie fretted that she was already too late and Andre would have left for battle at first light.

She felt under her pillow and sighed with relief when her fingers found Andre's note. Touching the paper was as close as she might get to touching him. She lifted the note to inhale his aroma. There was the faintest hint of masculinity but nothing she could discern as distinctly Andre.

"Don't you leave me yet, Andre!"

Eugenie tossed the bedding aside and hurried across the parquet flooring to the wardrobe where her clothes had been stowed the night before. She dressed quickly, brushed the knots from her hair, and combed it into a bun to sit at the nape of her neck.

There was no time to worry about jewellery. Eugenie begrudged the frivolous displays of wealth; especially when her aunt insisted, she wear heirloom necklaces and earrings to draw in prospective suitors. Eugenie already knew the only man she wanted to marry. Andre had declared his love, and supported her desire to become a doctor. She just needed him to come home safe from the war so he could get down on bended knee and propose.

She crept from her bedroom, listening for movement that would indicate the rest of the house was awake. She breathed a sigh of relief when all she could hear were muted murmurings from the kitchen at the rear of the house's ground floor.

Camille and her parents must still be sound asleep. Eugenie tiptoed past their closed bedroom doors and peered over the banister to the entry hall before making her way downstairs. She took the main staircase, avoiding the one at the rear of the house, primarily used by the staff.

Eugenie slipped quietly out the front door. Unaccompanied. Unchaperoned. Alone on the streets of Paris. She sucked in a breath and pulled her shoulders back. She had to look as if nothing was amiss.

It was better this way. Camille couldn't be held responsible for Eugenie's actions, likely to be perceived as reckless by her aunt and uncle. Eugenie would just have to deal with their wrath when she returned.

She walked quickly to the end of the street, glancing back several times to check the drapes in the upstairs windows remained closed. She planned to summon a taxi as soon as she turned the corner and was out of sight of her guardians. Travelling by taxi would hopefully enable her to do everything she needed and return without being detected.

Her pulse quickened; she had to reason with the adrenaline coursing through her veins, stimy the run that her legs itched to break into.

"Just walk like a lady," she murmured to herself. "Don't draw attention to yourself and all will be fine."

She stopped at the corner, unsure which way to turn. At this early hour, few people were out on the streets: a flower vendor pushing her wagon of colourful blooms, a horse and cart with wooden crates of vegetables destined for the market. Where was a tacot when she needed it?

Eugenie looked down at her shoes. She should have put on the practical boots she'd brought from home. Would the dainty heal on the boots her aunt insisted she have, even survive a walk? If she turned left, would the road take her closer to the Seine or further away? Why hadn't she paid more attention on their outings?

The Eiffel Tower's steeple refocused her attention. It peaked out beyond the trees and buildings, rising into the sky like a beacon. No wonder General Gallieni, the recently appointed military governor of Paris, had insisted machine guns and a cannon be placed at the tower's feet. If Eugenie could see it from here, then Gustaf Eiffel's feat of engineering would surely be one of the German targets.

She remembered the Eiffel Tower was on the same side of the Seine as Les Invalides. Logically, if she headed in that direction, she must eventually find a bridge to cross the river and reach her destination. Eugenie set off, hoping it wouldn't take forever.

Memories of happy picnics in the Foret de Mormal, swimming in the ponds surrounding Le Quesnoy and dances at the town hall, all with Andre ever present, at first as a childhood friend, later as the boy who first kissed her cheek and most recently as the man who had stolen her heart, added a lightness to Eugenie's steps.

The first tacot passed her without her realising. It wasn't until the second and third drove by that she snapped back into reality.

"Voiture de location!" She stood at the kerb and waved her arms.

Another two drove past, all headed in the same direction, towards the Eiffel Tower, before one of the distinctive Renault cars pulled over.

"Bonjour." It wasn't the 'done' thing for a young lady but she climbed onto the seat next to the driver so he couldn't leave without her.

"Bonjour, mademoiselle. Where are you going?"

The driver looked and sounded old enough to be her pere, but Eugenie was too close now to give up.

"I need to get to Les Invalides. Can you take me?"

The driver eyed her up and down. "Oui, that's where I was headed anyway but you'd better get in the cab. A young lady shouldn't be seen out unchaperoned."

Eugenie climbed into the back seat, opening the window so she could continue to talk to the driver.

"Merci beaucoup," she thanked him. "I'm not unchaperoned now, I'm in your care. Why are you going to Les Invalides?"

"General's request," he replied, pulling back out on to the road. "We're transporting the troops. Getting paid to drive them to Nanteuil-le-Haudouin."

"Nanteuil-le-Haudouin? Where is that? Why are they going by tacot and not the train?"

"Don't know why, but I'm not going to argue about getting paid for a thirty-mile return fare." The driver shrugged his shoulders. "If that's where they have to go to beat those damn Germans then I'm happy to do my bit and get them there."

"Oui," Eugenie agreed. "Have they left yet?"

"Oui, some have." The driver gently stroked the top of the petrol tank sitting, like the arched back of purring cat, across the vehicle in front of his knees. "These girls have a top speed of sixteen miles an hour. We'll be driving all through the night to get all the troops to the front."

Eugenie sucked in a breath. What if she was already too late?

"Are you going to farewell someone special?" the driver asked with a knowing smile.

"Oui." Eugenie returned his smile but didn't elaborate and they drove in silence for the rest of the trip.